ADVANCE

EXODUS: BOOK ONE

Praise for Gun Brooke's Fiction

Fierce Overture

"Gun Brooke creates memorable characters, and Noelle and Helena are no exception. Each woman is "more than meets the eye" as each exhibits depth, fears, and longings. And the sexual tension between them is real, hot, and raw."—*Just About Write*

Coffee Sonata

"In *Coffee Sonata*, the lives of these four women become intertwined. In forming friendships and love, closets and disabilities are discussed, along with differences in age and backgrounds. Love and friendship are areas filled with complexity and nuances. Brooke takes her time to savor the complexities while her main characters savor their excellent cups of coffee. If you enjoy a good love story, a great setting, and wonderful characters, look for Coffee Sonata at your favorite gay and lesbian bookstore."—*Family & Friends Magazine*

Sheridan's Fate

"Sheridan's fire and Lark's warm embers are enough to make this book sizzle. Brooke, however, has gone beyond the wonderful emotional explorations of these characters to tell the story of those who, for various reasons, become differently-abled. Whether it is a bullet, an illness, or a problem at birth, many women and men find themselves in Sheridan's situation. Her courage and Lark's gentleness and determination send this romance into a 'must read.'"—*Just About Write*

Course of Action
"Brooke's words capture the intensity of their growing relationship. Her prose throughout the book is breathtaking and heart-stopping. Where have you been hiding, Gun Brooke? I, for one, would like to see more romances from this author."—*Independent Gay Writer*

September Canvas
In this character-driven story, trust is earned and secrets are uncovered. Deanna and Faythe are fully fleshed out and prove to the reader each has much depth, talent, wit and problem-solving abilities. *September Canvas* is a good read with a thoroughly satisfying conclusion. —*Just About Write*

The Supreme Constellations Series

"*Protector of the Realm* has it all; sabotage, corruption, erotic love and exhilarating space fights. Gun Brooke's second novel is forceful with a winning combination of solid characters and a brilliant plot. The book exemplifies her growth as inventive storyteller and is sure to garner multiple awards in the coming year."—*Just About Write*

"Brooke is an amazing author, and has written in other genres. Never have I read a book where I started at the top of the page and don't know what will happen two paragraphs later. She keeps the excitement going, and the pages turning."—*MegaScene*

Visit us at www.boldstrokesbooks.com

By the Author

Romances

Course of Action

Coffee Sonata

Sheridan's Fate

September Canvas

Fierce Overture

Speed Demons

The Blush Factor

Supreme Constellations series

Protector of the Realm

Rebel's Quest

Warrior's Valor

Pirate's Fortune

Novella Anthology

Change Horizons

Exodus Series

Advance

ADVANCE
EXODUS: BOOK ONE

by

Gun Brooke

2014

ADVANCE: EXODUS BOOK ONE
© 2014 By Gun Brooke. All Rights Reserved.

ISBN 13: 978-1-62639-224-3

This Trade Paperback Original Is Published By
Bold Strokes Books, Inc.
P.O. Box 249
Valley Falls, NY 12185

First Edition: December 2014

Credits
Editor: Shelley Thrasher
Production Design: Susan Ramundo
Cover Design By Sheri (graphicartist2020@hotmail.com)
Cover Art By Gun Brooke

Acknowledgments

Thank you to Len Barot, aka Radclyffe, for her continued faith in me.

I'm as always so grateful to Shelley Thrasher, editor extraordinaire and author. Without you, my story would be sorely lacking.

Sandy Lowe, BSB's goddess admin, you are kind, fast, and always ready to help. Sheri, Stacia Seaman, Cindy Cresap, Connie Ward, Lori Anderson, and proofreaders...the list of the BSB family behind the scenes is what helps us authors look really good.

My first readers—they are awesome! Laura, TX, Eden, AZ, Sam, South Africa, and Maggie, Sweden. You help me not make a fool of myself, and the encouragement makes writing novels a less lonely profession.

On a personal note, I want to thank Elon, for believing I can do anything, including walk on water. My children, my son-in-law, my grandchildren—I love you all and I am so blessed every day for having you. My friend Joanne, the ladies in my book circle, my Facebook DWP group, my neighbor Birgitta, you all encourage me.

Last but not least...*you*, my amazing readers. Thank you for being with me for so many years and so many books. I hope you will continue to enjoy my offerings, and judging from the e-mails I get, our mutual love for reading/writing will prevail.

This year has been full of challenges, and all the people above have helped, whether they knew it or not, to make it a little easier. I hope I can provide some entertainment and escapism with this story that once again brings us into outer space.

Dedication

To Ove
My brother

CHAPTER ONE

Y ou just have to accept it, Admiral. You're a hero in the eyes of our people." President Tylio smiled broadly and raised her pewter mug in a toast.

Admiral Dael Caydoc barely stopped an annoyed huff from escaping. She didn't consider herself a hero. "This is my job, Your Excellence. Heroics are for others."

"But you and your crew are risking your life to save ours," the president's spouse, a sparse man with a long white beard, said. "Without your advance team, the rest of us would go into space completely blind."

"I appreciate your gratitude, but this is what I've worked toward during the entire latter half of my career." Dael gripped her own mug containing the strong traditional ale so popular among the Oconodian people. She hated it and had managed to fake drinking it her entire adult life.

"Oh, look, Admiral!" President Tylio turned toward the panoramic window. Outside, enormous fireworks lit up the sky above the presidential palace. A multitude of colors erupted, and the whistling sounds combined with muted thunder made it into an impressive spectacle.

"Isn't it gorgeous?" The president smiled wistfully. "I have to say I'm envious of you, Admiral."

"Envious, sir?"

"You're going on this amazing, life-altering mission, and the rest of us...will just have to wait." President Tylio sighed. "At least we'll have your interspace messages to look forward to."

"We'll do our best to keep the messages coming regularly. The buoys constructed by our best engineers will provide us with the best possible chances of communication. Their main purpose is to guide the population to a safe, habitable planet."

"Of course. Still, we're going to eagerly wait for your messages. The entire planet will." The president's spouse looked ill at ease. "With the exception of *them*."

Frowning, Dael clasped her hands behind her back. "By 'them' I take it you mean the ones displaying symptoms of the dormant mutation?"

"Yes." The president's spouse sneered. "I know I'm supposed to aim for political correctness, but I loathe those creatures. They're nothing but trouble."

"Nor can they choose to be anything but who and what they are." Dael spoke curtly. "I'm sure, given the choice, most of the changers would want to belong to our society the way they used to."

The president's spouse glowered at her. "Don't tell me you defend the horrific crimes they commit—"

"I never defend criminal activities, sir." Dael returned his gaze calmly. "Most cases that have gone before the courts have been proved to lack malice or intent."

"You are correct, Admiral." The president put her hand on her spouse's arm. "Especially when the gene becomes active in young children."

"Yes." Knowing that they wouldn't solve this issue then and there and that it wasn't her place to bring it up, Dael bowed politely. "My shuttle leaves in fifteen minutes. You've been most hospitable these two days, Your Excellence."

"We will keep you in our prayers and look forward to messages of your success. Go in peace and splendor, Admiral."

"Peace and splendor, Excellences." Dael bowed and sighed secretly in relief as she made her way to the presidential launchpad at the north end of the palace. She couldn't wait to get back to the *Espies Major*. The launch from the space dock in high orbit was scheduled to begin in ten hours. She glanced at her timepiece. With a little luck, she'd get six hours of sleep.

Dael stepped aboard the shuttle, and the security guard scanned her palm print for confirmation.

"Welcome aboard, Admiral Caydoc." He saluted smartly, his right hand in a straight line at the level of his chin.

She quickly read his nametag. "Ensign Pemmer. Are you part of the advance team on *Espies Major*?"

"Yes, sir."

"Are you bringing someone along for the ride?"

"Yes, sir. My parents and my younger brother, sir."

"Good. I look forward to meeting them when things settle down." Dael smiled, knowing full well what this kind of attention from the highest-ranking officer meant for a junior officer's self-esteem. Especially as they were about to deploy on an unprecedented mission.

"Thank you, sir." Pemmer saluted again, and she returned his acknowledgement before she stepped inside the shuttle.

Dael's seat was just behind the main pilot's. She would be the only passenger, as they were taking off from the presidential-palace grounds, but the last of several of these shuttles were leaving from all over Oconodos.

She closed her eyes briefly, admitting that the last several months of preparations, not to mention years of anticipation, had made her weary. Once they were on their way and settled into a routine, hopefully she'd be able to, if not relax exactly, then at least feel more at ease in the knowledge that the members of her crew were as finely tuned as she wanted them to be.

Dael glanced over at Ensign Pemmer, amazed at how young he looked. He had been selected at the academy after extensive tests, and after his initial acceptance, the young man had received rigorous training. For Pemmer to serve on the admiral's vessel indicated he was the best of the best.

Unlike Pemmer, Dael was bringing only one family member along. She had been forced to use some of her best persuasion techniques, as her grandmother was as stubborn as she was. Only when Dael appealed to her nania's sense of duty had Helden Caydoc, former fleet admiral, agreed to join her on the mission to save the Oconodians. Nania had been retired for more than fifteen years, but she was still as sharp and acerbic as she'd ever been. Dael knew she was her grandmother's only real weakness, though anyone would have to pry this out of the older woman, as she rarely offered praise of any kind. Nania had been installed in her quarters for two days, no doubt driving the young professionals in charge of her daily health care to the brink of losing their minds.

The change in the sounds from the atmospheric propulsion indicated they had left the mesosphere. The space dock, connected to the vast space station where the fleet of five Advance ships was moored, was now in sight. Dael leaned forward, again amazed at how she already felt she was on her way home, when she really was about to embark on a dangerous journey into unknown space.

"Docking procedure commencing," the computerized voice announced via the speaker system. "Adjust your harness."

Dael closed her eyes in relief as the clonking sound from the airlocks indicated they had arrived. Finally she could get to work and make sure the people of her home planet had a chance to survive. This had been her sole purpose ever since she became tied to the project years ago, after her promotion to admiral. She was well aware that her appointment as the commanding officer for the Advance project was a political gamble. Most career military officers were from old military families, and hers was one of the most prominent but also rather controversial. When she'd accepted the assignment, she found out who her enemies and her friends were among her peers. The civilian government seemed to trust implicitly her ability to find the way to their new home.

"Welcome back, sir," another ensign said smartly, and saluted as the airlock door opened. Her black hair and pale complexion clearly indicated that she originated from the ice-covered territory in the far north. Her blue-green uniform was impeccable, which was hardly surprising, but the color didn't fit everyone as well as it did this soldier.

"Permission to come aboard, Ensign Ioanto." The ensign's insignia identified the young woman as part of the security detail. "Got your spouse and daughter all settled in?"

"Yes, sir." Ensign Ioanto lit up. "I'm sure Mochail has his hands full keeping her in our quarters until we reach deep-space velocity."

"How old is she? Five?"

"Kaisa is a very precocious four. She fancies that she's the commanding officer at our house."

"Sounds like a promising future." Dael smiled. She was only half joking. Children like Ioanto's daughter held their future. If they were going to make it on a new planet, the children's welfare meant everything. Dael admitted to herself she was wary of bringing civilians along on a deep-space mission like this, but they simply had no other way to do it. They had no idea how long it would take to find a suitable planet, and for the crew to sign on and give it their all, they needed their loved ones.

Dael thought of Nania. She would make sure her senior staff was present and accounted for and then go to Nania's quarters and make sure she was all right. Nodding at Ioanto, Dael headed toward the one place where she felt most at home.

The bridge.

"Make way, make way!" Spinner hurried along the *Espies Major*'s main corridor, which resembled a hollow spine through the ship. She'd run into some issues when overseeing the landing of one of the assault craft, and now she was late. She'd only met the admiral in a very formal setting and knew that this wasn't how to make a good impression. Chewing on her lower lip, she did what she usually did, jogged right toward people until they moved. Some at the last minute, but they always moved. The fact that she was CAG, Commander of the Air Group, helped send people scurrying.

The bridge was located in the safest place on *Espies Major*, deep in its belly. The bulkheads created a cage around it, keeping potential enemies from weakening the last defense. Spinner hurried through the automatic double doors.

"How wonderful of you to join us, Commander Seclan." The acerbic tone of Admiral Caydoc greeted her. "If this tardiness is indicative of your performance during the upcoming years, we might just have to get used to delaying missions to suit your needs."

"I apologize, sir." She refrained from spitting out resentful words, but *really*, did this woman have to be so scornful in front of the whole damn senior staff?

Caydoc scanned her slowly, but Spinner knew that at least her uniform was impeccable. The missing button was one reason she was late. Sewing wasn't her thing. She glanced down at the hot-glued button, wondering if she'd managed to permanently glue herself into her jacket.

"Take the helm, Commander." Caydoc motioned toward the station before a set of ten vast screens. "Commence launch preparations. Everyone looking to us for salvation is ready with fireworks to send us off. Let's not disappoint them."

Passing the admiral, Spinner furtively took in the vision of the woman who had the ultimate power over the five vessels setting out to save the Oconodians. You had to get closer to Dael Caydoc to realize how striking she looked. She kept her ash-blond hair of indeterminate length in a tight, low bun, its volume suggesting it was quite long. Stark gray eyes under straight dark eyebrows followed Spinner as she took her station. Caydoc was still on her feet, though protocol stated that all bridge crew were to strap in securely during launch procedures. Of course, Caydoc had to be tough and hover over everyone. Spinner blinked and focused on the console before her rather than on the annoying woman whose gaze seemed to pierce her back.

Spinner flipped switches and punched in commands, something she could easily do while playing a game of spin jack—the card game partly to blame for her call sign—with the other hand. This wasn't her main assignment, thank the noble Creator, or she would have never agreed to go on this mission. The boss had no doubt thought it prudent for the CAG to take the *Espies Major* out of space dock before she resumed her duties heading up the air group of the lead vessel's attack-and-defend pilots.

"All stations, report in." Caydoc's voice whipped the order over the speaker system. Different voices reported back in a given pattern. Last was Spinner, who gave her "Helm is ready, sir" in her best authoritative manner.

"*Tommus, Hegal, Rondos, Mugdon*. Report back on flight status. Acknowledge." Caydoc hailed the other four vessels, and their captains confirmed they were ready to launch.

"Good. Maintain a fleet-wide communication channel." Caydoc was still on her feet. She surprised Spinner by approaching her from behind as she addressed the Advance fleet. "This is Admiral Dael Caydoc of the lead vessel *Espies Major*. The time has finally come for us to embark on the mission for which we've prepared for so long. Our mission is as easy to understand as it will be challenging to carry out. We are going into deep space, never to return, and our assignment is to find a new homeworld for our people. With us we have our closest family members and friends, and all the expertise we require to carry out our mission.

"One thing needs to be said, once and for all. Failure is not an option. We are going to deploy communication buoys that we will use as a means of communicating with Oconodos. This is a one-way communication system and the only way our people will know where to find us when it's time for them to commence Operation Exodus. A lot rests on us, as it's up to us to deliver hope to the people suffering on our home planet."

Caydoc had spoken in a clear, distinct voice until now. It softened barely as she continued. "We have no way of estimating how long it will take us to relay the news they're waiting for so desperately. It could be years, but we all know, the longer it takes, the worse the repercussions on Oconodos and its inhabitants will be."

Spinner felt Caydoc stand right behind her chair. "Time to go. Captains, order your helmsmen to follow the *Espies Major*'s CAG, thirty secs apart. Commander Seclan, take us out. Course 5-8-8-19."

Spinner swallowed past the unexpected lump in her throat. She thought of her brother and his family, especially the young twins, and her stomach constricted painfully before she had the only-too-familiar bout of anxiety under control. She hurriedly punched in the last command and the *Espies Major* hummed to life and disengaged from its moorings. Maneuvering the brand-new ship from the arms of the space dock, Spinner set the course and then motioned toward the bridge senior helmsman. He quickly took his station.

"In a hurry to leave us?" Caydoc murmured. "You'll miss the fireworks."

"I need to inspect the air group, sir. Permission to leave the bridge."

"Permission granted." Caydoc lifted a corner of her mouth. "Oconodians with telescopes will appreciate a demonstration, Commander."

Bristling, Spinner only nodded curtly. Doing flybys next to the *Espies Major* was a waste of resources. "Very well. Will twenty assault craft do, sir?"

Her eyes now dark, narrow slits, Caydoc spoke briskly. "Quite."

"Consider it done, sir." She hurried away from the bridge, not to mention the stifling presence of the admiral.

❖

Dael looked after the tall, lanky commander, who clearly couldn't stand to spend a single moment in her presence. For her to hand over the controls to the bridge helmsman so quickly, and without waiting for Dael's order, was not exactly insubordination, but it did not show respect for the command structure either. Dael knew her adherence to protocol exasperated some people. They just didn't get it. If you stuck to detail when it came to protocol and regulation, you might just get away with bending the major rules once in a while when it really mattered.

Someone like Commander Aniwyn "Spinner" Seclan, whose actions bordered on recklessness and who had a swagger to her entire personality, bent all the rules all the time, thinking very little of it. It was a miracle in itself that Spinner had reached the rank of commander. No doubt her superior talent for flying and her numerous medals for bravery had something to do with it.

The woman was not Caydoc's personal first choice for the *Espies Major*'s CAG, but she'd had to concede the fact that it was more important to have someone with Spinner's flexible skill set than someone with a perfect track record on all levels. She was just going to have to talk herself into not throttling Spinner on a daily basis.

CHAPTER TWO

Nania, please. The common area is not a means of surveillance." Dael glanced in the full-length mirror in her grandmother's bedroom. She adjusted her uniform, making sure the light-blue jacket and the black trousers were impeccable before turning to the older woman sitting on the foot of the bed, her thin arms folded over her chest. Of course, her nania had to start their very first morning aboard the *Espies Major* by causing trouble. "It's a place where the civilians and passengers can socialize and spend time."

"Am I to understand that jigsaw puzzles or basket weaving aren't mandatory?" Helden Caydoc regarded her granddaughter with disdain. "Nobody has yet to tell me what to do with my time. Honestly, Dael, you should know better."

"I just wanted you to be aware of—"

"I can still read." Her nania sneered and pointed at the computer console. "If I want to engage in any of the 335 different leisure-time activities available on the *Espies Major*, I know where to acquire information."

"You're being difficult. Why?" Tapping her boot-clad toes, Dael didn't let Nania off the hook. "Do you regret coming with me?" She lowered her voice. "The point of no return will be here in two hours."

"And are you trying to get rid of me?" Nania's harsh words didn't match her softening voice.

"Never."

"Well, then. You can't persuade me to return to Oconodos, not even if you set that sickly sweet woman on me again."

Smiling now, Dael shook her head and wrapped a strong arm around the petite, physically fragile woman by her side. "That sickly sweet woman cares for you and comes highly recommended. As do your other three caregivers."

"Yes, that's exactly what I'd do to get rid of her: give her the best recommendation and pass her on to some other unsuspecting fool."

Dael chuckled as she let go of Nania and put her hat on. "You realize you just called yourself an unsuspecting fool?"

"I did no such thing." Nania huffed and placed fisted hands on her hips. "Damn it, I did."

"We're having lunch at 1200 hours in the officers' mess, then?"

"All right. A person has to eat." Nania rose unsteadily on her toes and kissed Dael's cheek. "Smooth sailing, Admiral."

"Behave, Nania." Dael left her nania's quarters, chased out by Nania's sarcastic snort.

Stopping just outside the bridge, she was pleased to see her senior staff all present—except Spinner. Double-checking the time, Dael frowned. Was that woman *ever* on time?

"Admiral's on the bridge," a male ensign called out smartly as Dael entered.

"Report." Dael stood at the center, as was her habit, letting her gaze land upon each present crewmember.

"The escort ships will turn back toward Oconodos in one hour, sir. All stations are functioning efficiently, as are the other four Advance vessels," Commander Tresh Weniell said as he vacated the center command chair.

"Good. The support assault craft?"

"The last ten will be pulled back into our hangar bays when we're twenty minutes from magnetar drive."

"That's cutting it close. Who gave this order?"

"Commander Seclan, sir." Commander Weniell looked like he wanted to apologize for the CAG. "I voiced the same concern, but she was adamant. The assault-craft pilots are under her command."

"And she's under mine." Not hesitating, Dael pressed the sensor of the comm line attached to her left lapel. "Caydoc to Spinner." It frustrated her that the computer system was programmed to recognize call signs rather than formal names. Then again, it did save time.

A few moments later she heard Spinner's voice through static. "Spinner to Caydoc. What can I do for you, sir?"

"You can get the assault teams back to their mother ship thirty minutes before we go to magnetar drive."

"Do you not trust your CAG to make sure all the birds are in the nest in time?" Spinner asked with an obvious smirk in her voice.

Furious now, as her officer was skirting the edge of insubordination, Dael schooled her voice to not convey her annoyance. "I prefer to err on the side of caution, Commander. Thirty minutes. That's an order. Caydoc out." She closed the link, not waiting for Spinner to sign off. The nerve of the woman! No wonder she hadn't been her first choice as CAG. Dael could call to mind ten more suitable candidates for the job. A small inner voice reminded her of Spinner's track record when it came to flying and showing courage beyond the call of duty. Having read up on Spinner's past, she wasn't surprised that the woman had risen through the ranks to become one of youngest commanders in the fleet. Remembering that one section of Spinner's record had been sealed, only accessible by the head of the Security Service director, the agency in charge of the president's safety, she drummed her fingers against her belt. Spinner was an enigma, that much was obvious, but she had time enough while on this deep-space mission to figure her out.

"Admiral. You have a transmission from Oconodos."

"I'll take it in my office. Thank you." Dael strode into the area to the left of the bridge, which was sparse and held only a desk and four visitors' chairs. She didn't care for its barren appearance, but she would have plenty of opportunity to turn it into the type of room she preferred to work in. She sat at her desk and opened the screen that was folded into the desk surface. It automatically scanned her face and irises and then logged on to the ship's computer. Dael tapped the symbol for Oconodos, and Fleet Admiral Vayand's stern face came into view.

"Admiral." He greeted her curtly. "This will be our last live conversation within the foreseeable future. I know everyone has wished you a successful journey so often you were ready to throw them out the airlock, but I felt it prudent to touch base and make sure nothing has been overlooked."

Seeing right through the older man's gruff demeanor, Dael relaxed and smiled. "Thank you, sir. We have run so many tests and checked everything enough for the bridge crew to wish they could hurl me through an airlock."

Vayand's furrowed face split in a broad grin. "Good to know, Dael. Don't hesitate to use Fleet Admiral Caydoc's expertise. She may be old and frail physically, but that woman is sharper than all the current admirals put together."

"No doubt about that, sir. Don't worry. I won't have to ask. Nania will offer her opinion whether I want it or not."

Chuckling, Vayand shook his head. "She used to scare me to death when I was a mere commander. Hell, she still does."

"I hear you, sir. She'll be my secret weapon."

"Excellent." Vayand became serious, his eyes somber. "You will do a splendid job, Admiral. I know this for a fact. If anyone can pull this assignment off, it's you. Stay on course, and don't allow doubt to color your judgment. You have what it takes to do this, which is why the vote to send you was unanimous."

Dael stared at Vayand and had to force her jaw not to drop and make her look totally unprofessional. *Unanimous?* "I—I didn't know that, sir." Normally not a humble person, Dael now had to swallow hard to get rid of the constriction in her throat. "Thank you for telling me."

"You deserve to know. We all have moments of doubt when our confidence wanes. You have good people with you. The finest. How could we not send anyone but the best to lead them?"

Dael didn't know how to answer without sounding repetitive. "We'll do our best. We'll find a new home."

Vayand hummed, his brusque demeanor back. "We will send our next transmission according to the schedule. Be safe, Admiral Caydoc, and be successful. Vayand out." The Oconodos crest twirled into view as his image faded and disappeared.

Dael stood and gazed at the view screen on the wall, which showed the constellations awaiting exploration. She pressed a sensor, and the view of Oconodos, so innocently blue and green and streaked with white where clouds hid the surface, made her draw a trembling breath. She had longed for this day, for the mission to finally commence, but seeing Oconodos like this, diminishing in size with each passing minute, she realized with a jolt that she would never set foot on her homeworld again. Never return to the vast meadowland where she grew up or enjoy the house she had designed to fit her lifestyle perfectly. She wouldn't return to the mountain lodge and enjoy the winter snow covering the slopes leading down from Mount Conos. Now she was leading a fleet of ships, and only one thing was certain at this point: none of them would ever go home.

Sighing, Dael switched the viewfinder to face forward. She blinked, trying to fathom what she saw. "For the love of the Creator, what's she doing?" Whipping around, she stalked onto the bridge. "Commander, pull up the primary forward viewfinder on the main screen. Then explain to me what Commander Seclan is up to and why the hell someone hasn't informed me." She watched Commander Weniell comply and also how the two junior ensigns assisting the ops officer paled.

The view screen flickered momentarily and then they could all see. Glancing around, Dael took a certain delight in how they all gaped at the scene unfolding on the starboard side of *Espies Major*'s stern.

"She's crazy," someone whispered behind Dael, sounding shocked and awed.

Pressing her lapel sensor, Dael spoke with the velvety tone that those who had ever worked for her feared more than anything. "*Espies Major* to Spinner. What the hell are you doing?"

"Can't—can't talk right now. I'm busy, Admiral."

Pushing her shoulders back, Dael could hardly believe she'd heard her subordinate correctly. "Spinner—"

"*Sir*, you wanted the birds in the nest before we go to magnetar drive. You might have to settle for one bird less, but let me do my job. Spinner out."

"Spinner has disconnected her comm link, Admiral," one of the startled ensigns said, his voice unsteady.

"I could tell, Ensign." Moving with sure steps, Dael took the command chair. "I guess we just have to enjoy the show. Be prepared to scramble two rescue birds."

"Yes, sir." Clearly astonished, the ensign turned his eyes toward the screen.

Dael couldn't blame him for being mesmerized. In all her years in the Oconodian Fleet, she had never seen anyone attempt anything like this.

CHAPTER THREE

Spinner pulled at the flat, paddle-like lever with all her strength. If she misjudged the distance to her wingman even by a finger's width, both their craft could be irreparably damaged. Not to mention that they needed to be far enough away from her wingman's unstable magnetar engine to avoid being vaporized in the explosion.

She had closed off all the other communication channels after ordering all assault craft back to their mother ships. It wasn't too hard to imagine how furious Caydoc must be at this point, and closing the comm channels was a surefire way to fail to have the admiral hiss in her ears while she was trying to save her wingman.

"Gazer, I'm coming in on your port side. Get ready. Blow your hatch."

"I told you, sir, my eject light won't come on!" Panic was evident in Gazer's voice. "I'm done for. You should get to a safe distance."

"Shut up. I'm coming to get you, but you have to blow the hatch." Spinner knew Gazer's hatch might damage her craft if he blew it when she was too close. "Keep the harness on until I'm in position."

"Yes, sir."

Spinner watched the hatch of the craft send off dying sparks, which hurtled into space and disappeared well above her. "Good. Now look to your port side. You have to guide me the last few fingers, all right?"

"Got you, sir."

Spinner moved the rudder delicately now, playing it like a fragile instrument. Slowly, she lowered her craft next to Gazer's. "How am I doing, Gazer?"

"You're closing fast. Too fast, sir." Gazer's voice rose an octave. "You're going to ram—"

"I'm not. Count down the finger-width as I approach. Work with me. Don't make me have to go back to the *Espies Major* and tell your wife and daughter I lost my wingman on the first day."

"Right, right." Gazer began the countdown, his voice steadier by the second. "Twenty fingers."

"Good enough. I'm going to hold here while you unbuckle. Let me know when you're ready to move." She couldn't see Gazer from where she was, slightly above his pit, but she heard grunts as he climbed out of his seat.

"I'm done." Gazer gasped for air.

"Good. Now climb up the mechanic ladder on my starboard side. When you're at the top, wrap your arms around the last foothold, and no matter what happens, don't let go."

"You're going to tow me in hanging from your craft, sir?" Gazer sounded shocked.

"Yes. Or would you rather melt to nothing when your magnetar drive explodes?"

"I hear you." Clearly without any further objections, Gazer began to climb.

Spinner heard his hard-nosed boots hit her hull, the clunking sound ringing out each time he pushed his feet into the indentations meant to make it easier for mechanics and engineers to perform maintenance.

"I'm at the top now, sir." Gazer sounded even more winded, and the tremors in his voice indicated the level of his fear. Spinner realized when a seasoned man like Gazer sounded like this, the situation was about as dangerous as it could be.

"Got a good, tight grip there, Gazer?" Spinner punched in a command, using her outer sensors to judge the condition of Gazer's magnetar drive. What she saw made her stomach clench. They had secs rather than minutes to save themselves.

"Yes, sir."

"Good. Keep it. We have to go now. Do *not* let go!" She trusted Gazer to do his part as she pulled the rudder toward her and steered a sharp left. Pushing her vessel harder than she remembered ever doing, she heard Gazer yell in her headset. Willing him to not let go, Spinner gave a verbal command for the computer to open communications with the *Espies Major*'s bridge.

"I'm coming in hot with Gazer hanging on my starboard side. Have medics standing by and keep away from—" A vast, blinding light reflected from the ports of the *Espies Major*. "Gazer. Shock wave, shock wave!" Spinner's craft lurched and bucked beneath her, and as they whirled toward their mother ship, she fought to remain on course and reduce speed. She would still not be able to perform her trademark perfect landing, but she wanted desperately not to crush Gazer where he hung—she prayed he still clung to the craft—on the outside.

"Sir. I'm okay, sir." Gazer's voice, distorted by the violent tremors of the assault craft, was a miracle.

"Let's keep it that way."

"Shuttle bay one is all yours." Caydoc's calm voice came through her communication system. "Just get inside. Ensign Umbahr is going to use our inertia modifier to create a cushion of sorts."

Amazed that Caydoc wasn't screaming at her, Spinner maneuvered her controls with frantic hands. As they cleared the shuttle-bay opening, she glimpsed the airlock doors close behind her. She had no other way to stop her craft other than to slam the brakes, so she did, hoping Gazer wouldn't break his neck if he couldn't hold on anymore. As she was nearly at a halt, she saw a spacesuit clad form hurl past her view screen. Gazer hit the deck and rolled along it for a good fifteen yards before he stopped, slamming into some barrels. He didn't move.

"No, no, no." As soon as her vessel quit moving, Spinner unlocked her hatch, unbuckled, and climbed outside. Avoiding any helping hands, she removed her helmet and ran toward the still form surrounded by medical personnel. "Move. Move! I need to see him. I need to—"

"He's alive, Spinner." A tall, burly medic glanced up at her with something close to awe in his eyes. "He's alive, and that's because of your crazy act out there."

Spinner stared down at the pale Gazer, whose deep-red hair lay in sweaty ringlets around his head. He was in his mid-thirties, about her age, and no matter how much Caydoc was going to string her up and maybe even temporarily revoke her flight status, Gazer's wife and child would welcome a shocked and bruised, but very much alive husband and father back into their midst.

"Commander Seclan, report to Admiral Caydoc," an impersonal female voice said via the comm system.

Tapping her lapel now that she didn't have her helmet anymore, Spinner confirmed. "Will do. Spinner out."

She began walking to the lift that would take her to the belly of the ship. Not in a hurry, exactly, Spinner still realized that it would be a grave tactical error to keep the admiral waiting. They were going to spend the foreseeable future on the *Espies Major*, most likely years. It might be clever to show a little effort, even if she suspected Caydoc and she would argue their way through most of the time.

Dael looked up at Spinner from where she sat behind her desk. "I was going to say 'at ease,' but I can tell you're already in a rather relaxed frame of mind." She raised a deliberate eyebrow at the sight of the brilliant pilot's casual stance; Spinner's left hip jutted out and her left hand rested on it, which made her look defiant.

"Sir." Straightening, but not very quickly, Spinner saluted, but not very smartly.

Debating whether to point this out or not, Dael decided on a less obvious approach. "That was some flying, Commander Seclan."

Spinner blinked. "Um. Thank you. Sir." She rocked back and forth on the soles of her boots as she glanced around Dael's ready room.

Dael followed her glance. Normally, Oconodian ready rooms were sparsely equipped, with a cot, desk, chair, and a miniscule bathroom. On the *Espies Major* and the other four ships, the ships' designers had clearly understood how the ready room needed more comfort, as this was an unprecedented deep-space mission. Consequently, the bulkheads were lined with soundproofing dark-blue cloth. A five-seat couch sat under a lit area mimicking a view port, as the admiral's ready room was located next to the bridge in the belly of the ship. Dael wasn't much for decorative knickknacks, but she had never served on a ship without the four paintings her mother had created. She could tell the dramatic motifs had caught Spinner's attention.

"Not only meant as a compliment," Dael said dryly, returning her focus to the matter at hand. "You could have gotten both of you killed and destroyed invaluable equipment, thus endangering the mission before it has even begun."

"But I didn't." Spinner regarded her confidently.

"Had you ever attempted this maneuver, Commander?"

"No."

"And yet you found it prudent to attempt such flying in a hot situation?" Not about to let anything but her displeasure show, Dael leaned forward and laced her fingers loosely, resting against her elbows.

"If I had pulled such a stunt during training, I would've deserved a reprimand in my permanent record. That would've been showing off. Now I did it to save my wingman, who also happens to be a husband and the father of a young child." Her eyes narrowing, Spinner looked challengingly at Dael. "I would call *that* destruction of an irreplaceable, invaluable individual."

Gutsy. Foolishly spoken to a commanding officer, but gutsy nonetheless. Having gone through Spinner's service record, Dael knew this woman was prone to act on impulse without second-guessing herself. "I see." Dael stood, her hands still on her desk. "I don't think it's a secret you weren't my first choice as CAG, Commander."

"I've heard as much through the rumor mill, yes." Spinner smiled faintly, but the tension around her eyes revealed she had not taken kindly to this fact.

"That said, today's maneuver might just be the first thing to prove me wrong. Unless you get yourself, or someone else, killed." Dael had to chuckle inwardly at the obvious surprise that flickered across Spinner's face. As jaded and arrogant as the CAG often appeared, she could obviously be startled from behind her façade.

"Hmm. Thank you. I think. And I'll do my best not to get anyone killed, including myself." Rocking on her feet again, Spinner peered through her wild curls.

"We're ready to go to magnetar drive in a few minutes." Rounding the desk, Dael motioned for Spinner to join her. "I want you to take the helm until we clear our solar system."

Spinner nodded briskly. "Aye, sir."

"And as tempting as it must be, no space acrobatics with the *Espies Major*, Commander."

Now Spinner's smile spread to eyes that glittered a dark golden brown. "That I can promise, sir."

❖

The enormous helm console had seemed intimidating the first time Spinner had visited the space dock and toured the ship. Then, she would have been happy to be part of the advance team in any capacity. She had ended up serving as CAG because of one person's stubbornness and loyalty. Or, put simply, Oconodos's military secretary had owed her a favor. Spinner would never have called it in, as she'd only been doing her job when she airlifted the secretary and her husband from a stampeding crowd of mutated individuals.

With misguided, but well-meant, attempts to address the gathered people, the secretary had managed to fuel even more animosity. Soon the angry mob had circled the secretary and her husband and some other dignitaries. Their security officers had managed to hold off the crowd while Spinner landed an atmospheric helo with surgical precision. The look of utter relief on the secretary's face and the way she clutched her husband's arm so hard he grimaced in pain as Spinner set down clearly demonstrated her fear. The secretary's husband was even worse off, shouting to Spinner in full panic to take off again, to get them the hell out of there.

"We can't leave without your security detail, sir," Spinner said, trying to calm the frantic man.

"They have weapons. Let's go!" The man was ashen as he fumbled with his harness. "This is your military secretary, damn it!"

"Easy, Grish. Yelling won't help." The secretary looked somber as she leaned back against the seat.

"My orders are to get you all out." Spinner saw the six men and women barely holding off the angry crowd, keeping their weapons raised as they moved in formation toward the helo. Getting ready, Spinner let the helo ease off the ground. She banked to the left a few degrees, which made the secretary and her spouse cry out and cling to their armrests. Looking outside, Spinner grinned. Stirred by the helo's down force, gravel and dust whirled through the air toward the hostile crowd. One at a time the members of the security detail pulled themselves inside, and when the last one was aboard, Spinner pushed the controls and didn't wait for the hatch to close before they were airborne.

"Good thinking, sir," one of the security officers said. "I'll be coughing up pebbles for the next month or two, but that's a small price to pay."

"Yeah, it looked a bit crowded down there." Spinner glanced back and made sure everyone was strapped in and that her main target, the secretary, wasn't injured. "You all in one piece? If anyone needs tending to, you'll find a medical kit under the chairs where you're sitting."

"I think we're all fine." The secretary, clearly quick to recover, looked her usual strong and together self. "Thank you for your quick reaction, Commander. What you did took great skill."

"No problem, sir. It's what I do."

"Let's just say I owe you a favor." The way the secretary held on tight to her husband's hand showed she was still rattled.

And the secretary had kept her promise. When she learned of Spinner's desire to be a part of the advance team, she used her influence to make sure Spinner was offered the CAG position on the mother vessel. Spinner knew her credentials didn't sit well with Caydoc, but the admiral was outvoted. Considering that and the fact that Caydoc seemed to be a complete stickler for protocol and Spinner had risked a lot while rescuing her wingman before they were even fully on their way, she had to concede that Caydoc was being fair.

"Magnetar drive ready to engage." Spinner turned her head. "This time I'll have to insist you take your seat, Admiral." She heard muted gasps from several of the younger ensigns at her audacity.

Caydoc merely smirked and studiously took her seat and strapped herself in with the six-point harness. "Ensign, open a joint channel to our four sister ships."

The ensign was still wide-eyed but answered smartly. "Go ahead, sir."

"Admiral Caydoc to Advance Fleet. We're ready for magnetar drive. What's your status?"

One after another the four captains reported their readiness to go.

"Excellent. As you know, it will take us a few minutes to calibrate sensors when we go to magnetar. We will start at magnetar two and, when we finish the calibrations, progress to magnetar six until we've cleared the solar system completely. After that, if all systems are functioning and performing well, we will increase to magnetar ten and stay there until we launch the first space buoy."

The captains signed off after acknowledging the admiral's orders.

"Very well, open a shipwide channel, Ensign." Caydoc drummed her fingers against the armrests, looking eager. "All hands, all passengers, this is Admiral Caydoc. Locate the closest safe seat and use the harness provided there. We are engaging the magnetar drive shortly. You will hear the countdown in your speaker system. I know you have all trained for this, but this first time I want to remind everyone to make sure our smallest passengers are taken care of first. May the angels of Oconodos spread their wings and shelter us. Caydoc out. "

Spinner checked her harness and kept her hand hovering over the command console, exhilaration and a rare case of nerves battling inside her. The responsibility was enormous and had to weigh heavily on Caydoc, but it was undeniably also the ultimate adventure.

Several minutes later, Caydoc spoke the words that sent them hurling into space faster than any other Oconodian had ever traveled.

"Commander Seclan, commence."

CHAPTER FOUR

Dael deliberately let her hands rest loosely on her lap as the *Espies Major* seemed to take a deep breath before she unleashed the powers of the magnetar drive. Faint tremors traveled through the bulkheads and up through the decks, and Dael knew every single individual on the ship felt the enormous power that tossed them headlong into their journey of reconnaissance.

"Magnetar drive steady and we maintain our course," Spinner said.

"Excellent. Our sister ships?"

"All four have gone to magnetar drive," Ensign Umbahr reported. "We are well within communication range."

"Good. Once you've received reports from your counterparts aboard the rest of the fleet, give me the short version."

"Aye, sir."

Dael stood, knowing she was probably being silly and overprotective, but Nania *was* old and frail. What if the jump had an unforeseen effect on the elderly? "Commander Weniell, you have the bridge. I'll be in habitat level one."

"Aye, sir." Weniell stepped up to the command chair with an eager look. As he sat down, which, strictly speaking, was bad form as his superior was still on the bridge, he seemed to relish being in the seat of power.

"Oh, by the way," Dael said, and turned to the helm, "Commander Seclan, go ascertain the condition of your wingman. What is his call sign?"

"Gazer, sir. Thank you." Spinner looked quite stunned at this sudden request.

They could have ascertained Gazer's condition via the comm channel to the infirmary, but Dael also realized Spinner was itching to make sure he was all right.

Stepping off the bridge, Dael strode through her vessel, sending her subordinates close to the bulkhead along the corridor. Dael could tell how her presence made her crewmembers square their shoulders, and she thought she detected jerking movements in some of their hands, an instinctive urge to salute. Nobody saluted aboard the ship unless responding to a specific order or being disciplined by a superior officer.

Finally at her nania's quarters, she found her grandmother in great shape and quite annoyed.

"Honestly, Dael, you would think I've never been aboard a space ship before, the way you're hovering." Helden pursed her lips.

"I was worried as you've never been subjected to magnetar drive forces before." Refusing to feel guilty for being protective of Helden, Dael sat down on the love seat next to her nania's mobility chair. "You look fine though."

"Why, thank you. It's comforting to know that this demon drive of yours hasn't altered my good looks." Helden tilted her head. "I did listen to the gossip radio before we had to strap in. Who's this fabulous pilot everybody is buzzing about?" Her dark eyes glittered with keen interest.

"Gossip radio?" Dael frowned. "Oh. You mean the civilian joint comm channel."

"Yes, yes. So?" Helden waved a frail, blue-veined hand impatiently. "The pilot?"

"I can only surmise that nothing will be confidential within this fleet." Dael sighed. "One of my pilots—the CAG, in fact—pulled an insane stunt to save her wingman. Actually it was brilliant, but I can't have the highest-ranking pilot set such a precedent."

"What the hell are you talking about? She saved her wingman with a daring piece of flying. Surely you can't fault her for that?" Helden snickered, and Dael knew her grandmother was testing her and goading her at the same time.

"I can, and I did. She was brave, but she also risked her vessel, not to mention her own life, which is a valuable asset as she's a brilliant pilot."

"Which is why she could pull off such a maneuver. I understood from the gossip radio that I might look forward to the video broadcast of the event." Helden virtually rubbed her hands together at the idea.

"Not if I can put a stop to it." Dael's mood darkened.

Helden held up her hand and shook her head warningly. "Darling, don't start the first day like this. You need something to set this mission off—something that bonds people and makes them regard you not only as their intimidating leader, but also as a very real one."

"What do you mean, real one?" Standing up, Dael paced back and forth a few times. "I find a little intimidation goes a long way."

"Yes. Back on Oconodos, where your crew would return to their family and go on with their lives at the end of the day. Here, they need another type of commander. Someone stern and tough enough for them to trust and depend upon, but also...someone with compassion and a sense of humor."

"I can't believe you. You, who scare the living daylights out of bulky admirals twice your size with a mere glance, advocate compassion and humor?" Dael huffed and turned to stare at the view screen showing the distant star systems.

"Dael. Listen. You asked me along for this mission, and I came for two reasons. The first is obvious. I'm a selfish old woman who saw a chance to live out my days with my beloved granddaughter. But I also figured I could be of value one last time. You carry a great burden, Dael. You need someone who knows what that means."

Turning slowly, Dael looked at her nania and saw the woman she remembered from when she was a young girl. Not very tall, but with an amazing force shining through her eyes, sparkling intellect, and something more, something—yes, humor. "You're right. Of course you are." Dael chuckled and covered her eyes briefly with one hand.

"Of course. Will you let us watch the video transmission of the CAG's daring rescue? It'll be good for morale."

"Oh, you fraud." Dael shook her head. "You want to watch it because you were just such a daredevil once."

"Not sure what you mean. I'm on my way to weave some baskets or whatever, so I suggest you return to your bridge." Helden glared at her caregiver, a young woman. "Let's go. And no, I don't need to be driven. I can manage the chair myself."

"Don't let her shake you off." Dael smiled at the woman. "I've had to chase her more than once."

"Yes, Admiral. I brought a mobility pad for that very reason. It attaches in the back for me to stand on. That way, the fleet admiral can drive *me* to the common room."

Helden's features softened. "That I don't mind."

Dael realized the caregiver and her grandmother had everything under control. Before she left, she kissed Helden's cheek and confirmed they were still on for lunch.

Walking at a much slower pace back to the bridge, Dael thought about her nania's words of caution. She had been so busy preparing for the goal of this mission the last few years, not even once questioning her role. Perhaps Nania was right? Being a regular admiral, functioning as she'd done on Oconodos and on the shorter missions in well-known space, might not cut it. To her crew, on all five ships, she was more than their commanding officer. How the hell could she find the right tone to assume the role of…of *leader*, as well?

The infirmary was almost empty, unless you counted the crowd surrounding the bed. As Spinner approached, she recognized Gazer's wife, a chubby, freckled blonde who couldn't be described as anything but cute. She seemed surgically attached to her husband's left arm. His right arm was tightly wound around a little boy—Spinner knew he'd just turned four—who in turn seemed rather pleased with all the attention. The rest of the pilots that weren't on duty at the moment flocked around them, smiling broadly and, no doubt, teasing Gazer until he was ready to airlock them.

"CAG!" One of the female pilots jumped up from the foot of Gazer's gurney. "What a brilliant move!" She gazed adoringly at her, clearly in awe. Her bright voice made the others take note of Spinner's presence and saluted her.

"As you were." Spinner frowned and returned the salute hastily. "Gazer, you look too happy and fit to be slouching around like this." She stood at the foot of his gurney now, hands on her hips.

"Commander!" Gazer's wife untangled from his arm and rushed toward Spinner. To her dismay, the young woman hugged her closely. "Oh, I can never thank you enough. You put your life on the line, and that type of flying was so *daring* and like nothing I've ever seen, and I'm sure nobody else has ever pulled off anything like it, and—"

"Sweetie, please. Give the CAG some breathing room. She's not used to your abundance of words." Gazer grinned at Spinner over his wife's head. "CAG, this is my wife. And this guy is my son."

To Spinner's relief, Gazer's feisty wife let go of her and returned to her husband's side. "Nice to meet you, ma'am," Spinner said and nodded politely toward the young woman.

She shifted her gaze to the little boy, knowing full well every single one of her pilots was watching her curiously. The child had his father's flaming red hair and his mother's freckles. His upturned nose made him very cute. He was about the same age as Liny when she began to change. Spinner swallowed and meticulously schooled her features. She had known that plenty of children all ages would be aboard the five vessels. Normally she avoided interacting with them, but here she couldn't. "Hello, there." Stretching her tense lips into what she hoped was a kind smile, Spinner saw the little boy nod shyly back.

"You my daddy's CAG? His wingman?" The boy asked.

"I sure am."

"Then I like you."

Spinner heard shuffling feet and muted chuckles around her. Glaring at her pilots, she silenced them instantly. Turning back to the child, she suddenly found it a little easier to smile. "Thank you. Take care of your dad now."

"Yes, sir," the boy answered, and pressed his little hand to his chin in a funny left-handed salute.

Spinner squeezed Gazer's foot. "Now that I see you're alert and talking, I'll let you enjoy your entourage. Let me know when you're cleared for duty."

"Aye, CAG." Gazer met her gaze firmly. "And thank you, sir. It's not enough, but thank you."

"You can thank me by getting a clean bill of health and regaining your flight status." Spinner said good-bye to Gazer's family and then left the infirmary with a sigh of relief. She disliked hospitals of any kind. She hated being caught off guard by old emotions that had been laid to rest a long time ago, or so she thought. The idea of getting through the unimaginable hurt once again made her stomach tremble. She refused. She damn well refused to be turned into that open-sore fragile person she'd been so many years ago.

Hurrying toward her office, a room she hadn't quite had time to claim as her workspace, she decided to work off the anguish. Nothing like boring administrative CAG duties to clog her mind.

CHAPTER FIVE

Dael had grudgingly allowed Spinner's stunt to be aired on the ship-wide broadcasting system. It was ridiculous how much this clearly meant to her crew, but perhaps they saw it as indicative of how the adventure, their *mission*, would unfold. She gave in to the temptation to review Spinner's rescue one more time and was amazed at the skill required to line up two assault craft like that and not kill Gazer in the process. One slip and Spinner's wingman would have been crushed and sucked out of his space suit.

The lunch with Helden in the mess hall had attracted some attention. A lot of crewmembers knew very well who Helden Caydoc was, and more than one respectful, close-to-adoring look had been sent their way.

"You have a fan club," Dael said as she cut her grandmother's vegetables.

"I know," her nania replied calmly. "I feel like a star."

Snorting, Dael shook her head. "And so you should. You're the highest-ranking officer they've ever met, most of them. The fact that you're something of a legend helps too."

"Legend." Snorting in a ladylike manner, Helden regarded her plate with a disdainful expression. "A legend who has to be spoon-fed."

"Ah, come on, Nania. I cut up your vegetables. Nobody would dare try to feed you." Dael dreaded that day—if it ever came. Someone was bound to lose a finger.

"So, if I'm a legend and your Spinner is an action star, I'd say you're off to a good start on your mission."

"What do you mean?" Dael poured some more water for both of them.

"People need heroes." Looking thoughtful, Helden chewed on a piece of balavia root. "They need role models and something to aspire to. You know that."

"Yes, and when it comes to you, I have no problem with it. Regarding Spinner—I'm not so sure." She really wasn't. As far as courage, skill, and ingenuity, Spinner was amazing, no doubt about it. Dael could well see how Spinner would inspire the junior officers and crewmen, but as to risk assessment and following regulations, the woman was a menace.

"You admire her though." Helden smiled. "Don't even try to deny it, Dael. She exasperates you, but from where I'm sitting, she reminds me of someone you loved. Someone who possessed the same energy and guts."

"I don't know what you're going on about." Dael shoved her fork into a rather dull-looking piece of synthetic golo meat. In fact, she knew exactly who her nania referring to.

"So I imagined your rapt attention every time I told you the stories about your father's daredevil assignments? How he bent the rules, defied every protocol, and saved the day?" Helden tilted her head and regarded her with affection. "I don't think so."

"Commander Seclan has none of my father's traits or qualities." Aghast and not a little affronted, Dael let go of her utensils and instead grabbed her napkin. "Father was…special. One of a kind."

"As I would imagine this Spinner of yours is."

Glancing up at her nania, Dael knew her eyes must be what she'd heard others refer to as icy white. That seemed to happen when she was furious. "Let's just establish this once and for all." She enunciated each word clearly. "Spinner is not 'mine' in any other aspect than the fact she's my subordinate. We have no personal relations or similarities. None."

"Oh, my. You've got that look your father used to give me when he insisted that I was meddling." Nania looked unaffected, but something cautious in her features mellowed Dael's temper.

"I shouldn't have spoken to you like that, Nania."

"And I shouldn't have teased you. You have enough on your plate as it is." Helden gestured emphatically with her one good hand. "Don't even think of changing. I'm going to trust you to keep me levelheaded, with my feet firmly on the deck plates." Suddenly it was easy to smile again. "You are an unbearable tease though."

"A trait I've honed for decades." Helden looked pleased. "I found it unexpectedly useful when I headed up dangerous missions or had to suffer through endless negotiations."

"I'm almost afraid to ask." Shaking her head, Dael returned her focus to what was left of her meal and then waved Helden's caregiver over. Her nania looked fatigued now, even if the old woman would never confess to being tired. "Assist the admiral with the rest of her meal. I'm due back on the bridge."

"Yes, sir." The young woman nodded respectfully and took a seat next to Helden.

Dael kissed her nania's cheek and left the officers' mess hall. As she strode back through the corridors, she thought of Helden's observation. Could she be right? Was part of Dael's annoyance with Spinner because of the memory of her father? It was a farfetched theory and too quasi-psychological for her taste.

She would handle Spinner like any other subordinate and keep the chain of command as intact and indisputable as always. It was how she conducted herself as a senior officer and always had. Anything else would be unprofessional.

❖

Aniwyn Seclan
Commander and CAG
Day 2
Advance mission
Personal log

I can't go anywhere without crewmembers stopping me. Whether it is in the corridors, the mess hall, or even the damn gym, people want to chat about Gazer's daring rescue. I try to suggest they go talk to him, but apparently it's my rescue effort that interests them. For the love of the Celestial Lords, it was Gazer who hung on the outside of the assault craft. I was just steering it back to the Espies Major. *He's the gutsy one—I'm just the one who keeps ticking off the admiral.*

Oh yes, Admiral Caydoc. She has a way of looking at me along that perfect nose of hers, as if I were some slimy bug residing in her salad. The way she purses her lips and squints makes me feel she's thinking of how to demote me without breaking the rules. She's all about the rules; well, except for wearing the fucking harness on the bridge. Perhaps she has extra gravity soles on her boots. I just can't imagine seeing her blond perfectness fall on her ass and be at all human like the rest of us.

I wonder why she allowed the video recording of the rescue to air on the newscast. Was it to put me on the spot and make me look like a reckless idiot? Or does she think the crew needs some sort of hero? She sure picked the wrong one. I'm the CAG. I work hard for the pilots and that's it. If anyone knew the truth about me, they'd realize how hilariously stupid it is to refer to me as a role model or hero. If I were, if that was in my persona whatsoever, Paddic would still be alive.

I'm not going to let her get to me. I'm not even sure why this is an issue to begin with. I've met superior officers sterner and more hard-nosed than Caydoc, and it's never bothered me. The best course of action is to just do the job. Focus on performing my duties and never, ever let it get personal.

End recording

Spinner rested her hands on her knees for a moment and then pushed against them as she stood. Why had she conceded to herself that she was in danger of letting this get personal? Yes, the admiral was overwhelmingly striking, but she wasn't more beautiful than many of the women who'd crossed Spinner's path in the past. Was it even personal in that manner? Annoyed at how quickly her vow not to let this get to her was crumbling, within a couple of minutes, for heaven's sake, she refused to even consider any other reason for this frustration.

Checking the time, Spinner realized she had to run back to the bridge—again—to avoid missing the all-important launch of the first space buoy. These relays with multiple backup systems were crucial to the Advance fleet and what was going to save the Oconodians and let them follow when the time was right.

Fastening her uniform jacket, Spinner thought of the brilliance behind the space buoys: General Korrian Heigel, the engineer who built the Advance ships as well as designed the Exodus fleet. She was a legend not only to the military, but also to most of the Oconodians, and even if she was officially retired, she was still active when it came to the Exodus project. Spinner doubted they'd be able to find a new homeworld fast enough for Korrian and her wife to be able to join the Exodus fleet when that day came. It was probably too far in the future.

She hurried through the corridors, and one way her newfound fame worked splendidly was that most people respectfully stepped out of her way.

The bridge buzzed with enough excitement for Spinner to sneak in without Caydoc nailing her for being almost late. She took her station, once again exasperated that she felt like a silly schoolgirl who actually cared about not being scolded by the teacher. Muttering to herself, she logged in and made sure her station was operational and ready.

"All right, people. This is it. The first of the buoys that will keep us connected to Oconodos." Caydoc suddenly stood in the middle, commanding everyone's attention. "I cannot stress enough how vital each and every deployment of this piece of technology is. Without it, we cannot communicate, and our people cannot follow in our path. We have rehearsed this in simulations and in the field, many times. Look sharp. Do your job just like you trained. Let's go."

Caydoc strode one lap around the bridge before she once again stood in the center, of course not sitting down. "Ops. Report."

"Buoy One is ready and active, sir."

"Excellent. Engineering?"

"Ready to launch, sir," a female voice said via the communication system. "We have tested the wavelength relays, signal emitters, and the force fields. Everything is functioning perfectly."

"That's what I like to hear." Caydoc paused and studied the ceiling for a few moments. "Deploy Buoy One."

"Aye, sir." The engineering chief spoke smartly, and a faint hum sounded as the buoy shot through the chute and into open space. The engineer guided it to a few klicks on their port side. "It's in place, sir. When you activate its sensors from the bridge, a singularity will pull the buoy through to hyperspace."

Spinner stood closer to her console. This was where her expertise might be needed. If for some reason the singularity didn't pull the buoy into hyperspace, she would have to steer it from her workstation and guide it. They needed to have the buoy well tucked into hyperspace, a sub-layer of space where the white noise wouldn't hinder communication.

"All right." Caydoc turned to the bridge-crew engineers. "Time to open that singularity."

The young man and woman looked pale and focused as their hands flew across the computer console. After a few moments, the woman turned to Caydoc, her jaws clenching. "The singularity is open as much as possible, but the buoy isn't moving, sir."

"Commander Seclan?"

"On it, sir." Spinner had already spotted the issue. She hoped she could rectify it, or they'd waste a buoy on the second day. She punched in commands that made it possible for her to control the buoy. Slowly and carefully, using only her index fingertip, she maneuvered the miniscule stick. Immediately the buoy shifted and began to emerge. "On the largest view screen," Spinner ordered. "I need a better view of what I'm doing."

The image of the slowly disappearing piece of technology filled the largest screen. Tapping the stick, or rather caressing it, Spinner coaxed the buoy into hyperspace until it was no longer visible.

"Run a diagnostic," Caydoc said.

"Aye, sir." The ops tapped in commands and then smiled broadly. "Buoy One is emitting the encrypted beacon signal and all systems are operating perfectly."

Suddenly they heard cheering over the comm system, which Spinner guessed included happy howls from their sister ships as well. Caydoc actually smiled. Not a broad, open smile, but a definitely pleased, even triumphant, smirk. "Let's run a test message to Oconodos. This is our first milestone, everybody. The first of a multitude of buoys, placed with the same care and diligence. Good job."

For Caydoc to praise her crew was close to unheard of. It wasn't as if she never did, but it was rare and indicated how relieved the admiral was. Spinner hid a smile of her own. It was rather telling that even such an accomplished officer as Caydoc could be afraid of making a mistake.

CHAPTER SIX

Dael Caydoc
Admiral
Day 38
Advance mission
Personal log

Our mission thus far has been uneventful. Or, I should say, at least as far as the mission itself is concerned. When it comes to the crew and the civilians, the honeymoon is clearly waning, and the counselors have had their hands full trying to deal with the fallout.

Dael rubbed her temple. She was due on the bridge in half an hour, but she needed to stick to her routine or she might end up on the counselor's couch herself.

We were prepared for this, thanks to the extensive research and seminars held by Dr. Meija Solimar. Without her, no doubt people would be throwing themselves out the airlocks by now. But I didn't expect to see so many of the crew affected. Regardless of their training and preparations, it finally seemed to dawn on many of them that they would most likely never again see so many of their friends and family. Counselor Dyan talked about a cascade effect. One person cracks, which sets off someone in their presence and

*so forth. The difference between the civilians and the crew
was mainly in the way their reaction manifested itself. The
civilians tore into their family member who was part of the
crew, and the crew members collided with their colleagues.*

*To my surprise, Nania rose to the occasion. She, who
up till now has been so disdainful about what she calls "the
basket-weaving gatherings," has been invaluable. It's as if
everyone can relate to her. Civilians see her as one of them
and are impressed at how she handles herself at her age.
The crew views her as the legendary retired fleet admiral,
of course. I worry she might exhaust herself, but she has
utter contempt for any attempt on my part to try to make
her slow down.*

*Another person who is handling herself flawlessly is
Spinner. The CAG gets herself into plenty of situations,
especially when it comes to gambling, so I'm told. She is
most dependable in her professional role, but her larger-
than-life attitude when off duty is causing problems at
times. Her subordinates idolize her and no doubt would
walk through plasma fire for her. Her superior officers are
exasperated at best and disgusted some of the time. She's
not all that keen on the command structure, to put it mildly.
No doubt, I'll—*

"What the hell?" Dael's head snapped up as the alarm klaxons
blared throughout the ship.

"Admiral Caydoc to the bridge. All senior staff to the bridge. All
hands to duty stations. Collision alert! Collision alert!"

The ship's automated computer voice repeated the message three
times, but by then, Dael was already on her feet and out the door. The
corridor was flooded with people heeding the alert.

"Make a hole," Dael called out as she ran. Collision alert? What
the hell was going on? The ship's sensors were designed to steer them
clear of any space debris big enough to penetrate their shields. Their
star charts were constantly updated by celestial cartography, who
bragged they could actually see the past as well as predict the future.
They sure didn't predict this, whatever it was in their way.

Rounding the corridor leading onto the bridge, Dael immediately scanned the screens. "Report."

"Admiral, the alert went off without any warning." Ensign Umbahr spoke fast. "I'm trying to decipher the readings, but the computer has nothing to compare this to."

"Send Code Talo-Bessa-4-4-4 to the sister ships."

"Aye, sir."

"Commander Seclan." Dael turned to Spinner, who was at the helm. "Drop out of magnetar drive on my mark and go to march speed once the fleet confirms." The code would relay the urgency in the emergency stop. It was like slamming on the brakes while driving on the main road on Oconodos.

"Yes, sir." Umbahr punched in commands and pulled levers. "We have confirmation from all four, Admiral."

"Very well. Ship-wide message. All hands brace for impact. Civilians, move to a secure seat or station. Twenty secs to magnetar-drive instantaneous cessation. Mark." Dael strapped herself into the command chair and took a deep breath.

The *Espies Major* bucked beneath Dael's feet, who could envision it now rolling faster around its axis. The gravitational plating made it impossible for anyone aboard to feel it, but from the outside, it would be a spectacular sight. It was a brilliant way to have the ship rid itself of superfluous energy without tearing the hull off its bulkhead, as long as you didn't look out the view screens. Every rookie cadet made that mistake, but usually only once. The view of spinning star fields around them would make anyone nauseous for hours.

"March speed six, Admiral," Spinner said calmly.

"And here are the other four," Commander Weniell added as he sat down in his chair. "The convoy is intact, sir."

"Good. Now, what the hell is waiting for us that sent the alerts going crazy?"

Umbahr's subordinates scurried as they disentangled themselves from their harnesses and began pulling readings from the computer. Dael paid close attention to them from a distance and knew exactly when they came upon the reason. Umbahr's slack facial expression was a sure giveaway.

"Admiral, our sensors show a debris field or, I should say, an asteroid belt, twenty minutes from here, counting in magnetar speed two. If we hadn't dropped out of magnetar drive, we would've run into it, with horrible consequences."

Dael knew Umbahr wasn't exaggerating. The magnetar drive was relying on the external sensors to avoid such big obstacles. The celestial-cartography department constantly updated the result of their sensor sweeps, but somehow this routine had faltered.

"Give me the head of CC." Dael was up stalking across the bridge now, as was her habit when facing a problem.

"CC on audio. Lt. Freance for you," Umbahr said.

"Sir." Lt. Freance seemed flustered. "That one was *not* there before. We scanned only twenty minutes ago. I'm transmitting our sensor sweeps to the bridge as we speak."

"Have you run a diagnostic?" Dael frowned. Something was off.

"We have. Several, actually, both as a routine and just now. Sensors are working at peak performance. All systems from our end are a go."

Dael had opened her mouth to ask another question when Spinner interrupted her. "We have incoming!"

The *Espies Major* rolled, sending Dael flying across the bridge. She grabbed the railing on the other side and hung on. Gazing at the screens showing readings from the space around them, she saw the sparkling trails of weapons' fire zigzag across the black universe.

"Enforce shields. All ships, enforce shields. Defensive formation. Launch attack craft!" She had no idea why they were suddenly under attack or by whom, but that wasn't important right now.

"Lt. Hiblion, take the helm." Spinner stood as her subordinate took over and moved across the bridge as if the unsteady deck didn't affect her balance at all. "Admiral, I'm needed with my pilots."

"Agreed." Dael turned around the bridge, trying to determine where the attackers were coming from. "Who are these people?"

"The ships are all smaller attack craft, sir." Umbahr's hands flew across the computer console. "I'm detecting thirteen shadows on the short-range sensors. The debris field is disturbing the imagery."

"Tactical, Lt. Schpay?" Dael whipped around, looking at the tall woman behind her.

"Sir, my sensors have the same problem, but I can see fifteen shadows. They're..." She leaned forward as if she couldn't believe her eyes. "We're thirty minutes from the Gemosis homeworld at this speed. These are Gemosian raiders!"

What? "Hail the lead raider." Keeping her calm, Dael pressed the tip of her tongue against the sharp edge of her front teeth. She never showed any signs of being nervous, but her mouth tended to become dry. The sting from her teeth against her tongue produced saliva.

"Hailing," Umbahr said. "No response."

"Admiral," Freance said over the communication link. "We have scanned the debris field. It's—it's the Gemosians' third moon!" Her voice displayed how incredible this information was. "Something, or someone, has blasted the third moon to pieces."

Dael strode over to Umbahr. "Pull up the latest imagery from long-range scanners." She tapped her fingernails on the panel.

Umbahr moved the screen toward her.

As she scanned the result, the reality of the situation began to sink in. "The Gemosis homeworld is suffering floodings and disastrous earthquakes."

"With their third moon in pieces, no wonder," Dael muttered.

"Shields at eighty percent," Schpay said urgently.

"Enough of this nonsense. Target the closest raider's weapons' array." Dael folded her arms. "*Espies Major* bridge to Spinner. Surround them, but hold your fire unless they go after you directly."

"Spinner to *Espies Major*, I read you. Their flight patterns are erratic and their aim isn't all that accurate. I'd say they're panicking and scrambling in all directions."

What the hell was going on? Dael scanned the readings on one of the smaller screens. "Any sign of a third party? Of any attackers?"

"None on sensors. They might possess cloaking force fields, but the only ones with that technology are the Revolings, and they're not likely to be this far from home." Umbahr shook his head. "I'm running in-depth scans of the debris field."

"Good."

"We've taken out their weapons' array, sir. The lead vessel is dead in the water."

Dael turned to the main screen. "Zoom in. Try hailing them again."

Umbahr punched in commands. "We have audio."

Dael waited a few beats and then spoke curtly. "This is Admiral Dael Caydoc, commanding officer of the Oconodian Advance convoy. Why are you firing on us?"

Some static broke up the audio feed, but a high-pitched female voice replied, "Something—*someone*—destroyed Tegia. I...-tenant Feio...not you?"

Squinting, Dael tried to decipher the choppy message. "Lieutenant Feio? We did not fire on your moon, nor do we have reason or even the capability to cause this much destruction. Surely your world has heard of Oconodos's Exodus plan?"

"Oconodos? Oh, hell, you're Oconodians." It seemed to dawn on the lieutenant that they weren't the enemy.

Dael's thoughts raced. The Gemosians must be completely panicked, striking at anything or anyone within their space. Tegia was the name of their moon, she remembered now. Who knew what the loss of its gravity would mean for the Gemosian homeworld in the long run.

"I've given the order to my squadron to cease firing on your convoy," Lt. Feio said, her voice still trembling but sounding calmer now.

"Why don't you accompany us to high orbit around your homeworld? We might be able to help." Dael caught the surprised look on her XO's face, which didn't impress her. It should've been Weniell's gut reaction too. Dael continued. "As you might know, we're on a deep-space mission to find a world for our people to emigrate to, which means we're prepared to deal with a great many things we encounter."

"Let us take up formation at your stern, Admiral." Feio's voice sounded much stronger. "If we don't, we might encounter others just as trigger-happy as we were."

"Affirmative. *Espies Major* out." Dael strode across the bridge to Umbahr's console. "Pull up everything we have on Gemosis and—"

"Already on it, sir." Umbahr gave his trademark crooked smile. "Not sure how detailed it needs to be, but it will give a base for comparison to what they have to deal with now."

"Good." Retaking her seat, Dael hailed Spinner again. "I take it you heard my conversation with Lt. Feio. Place your crew in between our new friends and make sure any approaching vessel can see them clearly. We don't want them to think we're the culprits."

"That would be unfortunate, yes. Assuming formation. Ten assault craft to each of the sister ships to help keep the peace."

"Good." Spinner amazed Dael by reading her mind yet again. How could this annoying woman who was her exact opposite still manage to do that when it really mattered? "Stay focused. For all we know, they might have more lethal weapons directed at potential enemies than Lt. Feio's squadron."

"Will do. Spinner out."

Dael sat motionless for a few moments as the *Espies Major* led the convoy toward Gemosis. The debris field wasn't hard to navigate at this speed; their shields repelled smaller parts, but it was amazing how all the former parts of Tegia had formed a previously nonexistent ring around Gemosis. Standing up, Dael handed the bridge over to Weniell after sending him a scrutinizing glance. Something told her she needed to keep an eye on him, which she hadn't expected. She strode toward her ready room. At the present, she had more important things to attend to.

Chapter Seven

Approaching low orbit above the northern Gemosian hemisphere." Spinner pulled the lever and made sure the trajectory was clear of traffic. The airspace, including the lower atmosphere, was filled with Gemosian ships of all sizes and purposes. Perhaps the volatile repercussions planet-side had made people take to the skies.

"Tell us what you see. Sensors are still unreliable when it comes to the planet. Ensign Umbahr is trying to filter out the disturbance from the magma, but we need an initial report."

"I'll try to go lower on my second pass. Hang on." Focused on her mission, Spinner allowed the planet's gravity to pull her farther in. To her dismay, the ever-increasing smoke from volcanic activity was now making it impossible to get a good view. "Spinner to *Espies Major*. Admiral, I need to take this bird farther down to see anything. The ashes won't disrupt my engine and—"

"No. I can't allow such a risk." Caydoc sounded quite miffed.

"But, sir, if we're going to be of any help to the Gemosian people, then we need to know what's going on. If Umbahr had problems scanning before, all this damn ash won't make it any easier."

"And you crashing into an area flooding with magma is better?"

Spinner grinned broadly. "Cut me some slack, sir. I'm not the crashing type. I won't risk my bird. I love her too much."

Caydoc was quiet for a moment. "All right. Get beneath the ashes, but if our communication channel is affected too, I want you right back in low orbit. And no landing without my permission."

"Yes, sir." Saluting in solitude, Spinner turned the controls to fully manual and grabbed the lever again. This was the true way to fly. The planet's atmosphere sent sparks around her craft. They would have made a pretty sight if this hadn't been such a dangerous undertaking. Normally, entering the atmosphere was routine, but being surrounded by ashes containing too many unknown variables made the whole process precarious. She was glad her wingman was heading up her crew at a higher orbit, as she needed to focus fully on her own vessel and couldn't take on the responsibility of guiding someone else into the atmosphere.

"Talk to us, Commander," Caydoc's voice demanded over the communication link. "Do you read?"

"I hear you loud and clear." Spinner pushed the lever forward and felt tremors reverberate throughout her craft. "So far, limited visibility due to impenetrable ash. Sending you readings of the samples." She had made sure her outer sensors kept investigating the makeup of the ashes. If any of the particles would corrode or damage her bird in any way, she would hightail it out of there, orders or no orders. She loved daring missions, but needlessly damaging her vessel wasn't part of her M.O.

"We've got them. Stand by."

Spinner broke through the ash cloud and lowered her vessel toward the planet's surface. She switched to the viewfinder under the belly of the craft and pulled the image up on her secondary screen. Volcanoes spewed lava down all sides; what remained of densely populated areas were either on fire or covered in blackening magma. The ocean seemed to have receded, but just as Spinner was about to report her findings, the water returned in one enormous, crushing wave after another. She pressed the communication sensor on her lapel. "Spinner to *Espies Major*. Do you read?"

"Reasonably well," Caydoc said, static making her voice a bit muddled. "Report."

"It's hellacious, sir. The northwest area is gone. If anyone made it to the shores, they're caught in tsunamis taller than Oconodian highrises. I see some islands farther north where there might be survivors. They look covered in ice, or glaciers, and the waves haven't reached that far."

"The reports coming in from Gemosian vessels corroborate your findings, Commander."

"We have to check out the islands for survivors, Admiral." Spinner turned her bird north.

"You are clear to do a high-altitude flyby. We will report your findings to the Gemosian authorities."

"But their resources must be stretched thin, bordering on breaking. We have the resources, sir. Deploy some of the freighters—"

"Do your flyby, Commander, and then report back." Caydoc's voice was steadfast and didn't leave room for debate.

"Yes, *sir*." Spinner's jaw hurt from clenching it around unspoken objections as she increased her speed toward the island.

The island was surrounded by an armada of boats and ships, some of them tilting precariously. Circling the island and some of the neighboring ones, she saw panicked people actually trying to swim to the boats. Some spotted her and waved fervently with clothes. Shifting her bird into a hover state closer to the ground, Spinner blinked at the sight of mothers holding up their small children, their mouths open in soundless cries. She punched her communicator sensor hard. "Spinner to Caydoc," she barked, not wanting the entire bridge to overhear. "Sir, I'm at hover height above the archipelago. They're going to drown if we don't do anything. Women, small children. They're desperate!"

"Commander, return to *Espies Major*." Caydoc's voice was low, noncommittal.

"*Sir*, don't you understand? We can't let these people just die. If we help them, they have a chance once the planet settles down."

"I hear you. Your order stands. Return to—"

"Admiral, *please*," Spinner said, raising her voice. She knew she was out of line and that the command structure dictated she should obey orders, especially the repeated ones. This was what she'd been taught all her military life, but she couldn't take her eyes off the frantic Gemosians below. "We have to do something. I can't leave them like this."

Spinner heard steps as if the admiral was walking rapidly. "Spinner, listen to me. Do not argue. Return to *Espies Major* instantly, and I promise you I will do everything in my power to rescue as many as I can."

"I don't see why I should return. I can set down, place markers for the freighter. We can deploy some of the rescue rafts—"

"Return to the E.M., Commander," Caydoc said, her voice pure steel. "Do not make me repeat myself. Your flight status might depend upon it."

Furious and frustrated, Spinner muttered, "Yes, *sir.* Spinner out." How could Caydoc be so callous? Sure, she'd promised to try to save people—people who might just die because it'd take too fucking long. She was here now, ready to start the rescue operation, but, no, Caydoc was so by the book, she wouldn't see the best course of action.

Spinner shifted the levers and began to ascend. She would not disobey such an order. A grounded CAG…well, there was no such thing. Being demoted and stripped of her rank only a month into the mission was out of the question. Glancing down at the islands, she vowed to come back with help as soon as possible.

As her craft rose yet another hundred meters, what had so far been only light tremors now became violent shaking. Not intimidated by a little turbulence, Spinner ran a quick check of the instruments as she fought the controls. Her bird acted as if someone was shaking it and trying to push it upside down.

"Computer! Check propulsion system."

"Checking," the slightly metallic female voice of the computer responded. "Propulsion drive compromised by foreign agent. Thirty-two secs to shutdown."

"What the hell?" Glancing at her screens, as well as out the windscreen, Spinner saw that her bird was closer to the ground than she'd been during her flyby. "Caydoc's going to have my ass for this." Spinner engaged the larger, manual flight stick. No matter how much this would anger her superior officer, she was going down.

"Spinner's in trouble, sir." Lt. Schpay sounded urgent.

"Now what?" Having just reentered the bridge, Dael walked over to Schpay's station. "Don't tell me, she's going to start her own rescue mission."

"Don't think so, sir. She started her ascent to return when her propulsion system went dead."

"Dead?" Concerned now, Dael rounded the console and studied the readings. Yanking her communicator to her lips, she spoke fast. "Caydoc to Spinner, do you read?"

"...burning through...toward..." The broken words didn't make much sense. Something seemed to be burning, and now Spinner's audio channel didn't even transmit any static.

"Caydoc to engineering."

"Chief Dioga here," a gruff male voice answered.

"We have a vessel down on the planet. An assault craft. Something went wrong with it at the last minute. Lt. Schpay will send you the final readings we have. I want to know if it's safe to send in freighters or if this will happen to any of our vessels going beneath the atmosphere."

"I'll get back to you."

"Thank you." Hurrying, Caydoc strode to the center of the bridge. "Listen up. Ensign Umbahr, communicate our information to our sister ships as soon as you learn something new. We can't have them sending down vessels before we know they won't sustain the same damage. Lt. Schpay, I want a tactical report every twenty minutes. We still don't know what made their moon explode, and I will not have such potential weaponry sprung on us. Commander Weniell, you have the bridge. I'll be in my ready room." She nodded briskly and strode off the bridge. Inside her ready room, she inhaled and exhaled twice before she sat down at her desk. She picked up the in-ship civilian communicator and paged her nania.

"Please tell me you want me to come help out on the bridge." Helden's dry voice made Dael smile despite the dire circumstances.

"The thought had occurred to me, Fleet Admiral. Actually, I don't want you to move from the secure area, but I need your expertise."

"Things are looking up," Helden said, seriousness permeating her chuckle. "I knew you didn't bring me for mere decorative purposes. What's up? I mean, apart from the fact that this moon in pieces."

Trust her nania to skip to the nucleus of the matter. "We have a craft down and out of communication on Gemosis. Northern hemisphere, somewhere in an archipelago."

"Spinner?" Helden sounded cautious.

Pinching the bridge of her nose, Dael closed her eyes briefly. "How did you guess?"

"Since this woman wears her heart out in the open and started off this mission by risking her life to save her wingman, it seemed logical." Helden cleared her voice. "She's your best pilot, all categories. If anyone can set down a bird in one piece, it's her."

"Yes, of course. Her propulsion system is history, and I suspect it's because of the ash."

"Our vessels are protected against such things." Helden spoke slowly. "Though the Gemosian magma might have a completely alien makeup. Hmm." Dael could hear how Helden rapped the nails of her good fingers against something. "Let me talk to your engineer. I have a few thoughts I would like to discuss with him. Is he opposed to an old woman meddling?"

"Not if it's you. You're a legend, remember? And besides, he'll damn well talk with anyone I tell him to."

"That's my girl. Have him call me."

After relaying the message to Chief Dioga, Dael pulled up the latest data regarding Spinner's position and the information she'd provided. Why was it as soon as something out of the ordinary happened, Spinner seemed to be at the forefront? It had started with the wingman rescue and gone from there to minor things like fighting with a few of her peers over a game of spin jack. And now this.

As the CAG, Spinner was brilliant and her pilots adored her. If they lost her this early in the mission, it might directly affect the squadron's performance and morale. Completely disregarding the faint pang inside at the thought of Spinner having a fatal crash—after all, Dael cared about all her subordinates—she tapped the computer screen as she reached a slightly unorthodox decision. Once Dioga and Helden had had their say, she fully intended to head the rescue mission herself—both regarding the Gemosians and Spinner.

CHAPTER EIGHT

Spinner was beyond sore. Ready to have a piece of whoever was to blame for her current condition, she jerked fully awake. She was shocked at first that she couldn't see out of her left eye. She raised a trembling hand and realized her visor was broken and blood ran down along her face. Lots of it.

As she carefully removed her helmet, her memory flooded back, accompanied by a banging that wouldn't let up. Was it just in her head, from the injury, or was someone actually banging on her door? *Door?* She turned her head and sighed in frustration. She was in her assault craft. Someone was hammering against the hull, or perhaps the hatch.

"Yeah, yeah, I'm coming," she called out, immediately regretting it as her own words pierced her head and made it pound even worse. "Holy Creator, I'm so dead. Caydoc's going to eviscerate me. Twice."

Her bird seemed strangely undamaged from the inside. The hatch sensor wasn't working, so the power had to be out still. She had a memory of fire in the propulsion system. It must have spread to the electrical circuits. After having the sense to arm herself with a sidearm from the arms locker, Spinner grabbed the manual lever and pulled to open the hatch. Whimpering at how this movement sent what felt like a jagged-edged plate through her skull, she managed to get it open enough for whoever was outside to assist.

With her hand on the handle of her gun, Spinner sank to her knees. Shit, her head hurt.

"It's a woman," a male voice said. The translation feature on her communicator fastened above her right collarbone still worked, for which Spinner was grateful. They might just have assumed she was the enemy otherwise. They still might, though.

"I'm Commander Aniwyn Seclan of the Oconodian Fleet. Our convoy is just passing your system while on the Exodus mission. We're trying to help." She tried to get up, but only when the man assisted her by holding on to her arm did she manage it.

"I'm Calagan Do Voy." He was younger than Spinner first thought, looking frazzled but in good health. "A convoy from Oconodos is in orbit?" He looked hopeful. "Can they get us out of here? We have five thousand men, women, and children stranded on the island. Several of our ships—"

"Are not seaworthy, I know. I saw from the air. Where did I touch down?"

"Touch down? More like crashed." Calagan guided Spinner outside where a vast crowd was surrounding her craft. "As you can tell, you lucked out. A few more meters and you'd be at the bottom of the ocean."

Spinner stared at the scene before her. She'd managed to crash right on the precipice of one of the larger islands, and beneath them, the ocean still roared as it tried to find its new pattern due to the loss of the smallest moon.

She tapped her communicator. "Spinner to *Espies Major*. Do you read?" She heard only static, interrupted by random, stuttered words. "Spinner to Caydoc, come in." Frustrated, Spinner tried to take in the situation. "Listen, Mr. Do Voy—"

"Calagan, please." He smiled faintly. "Let's get you sorted." He motioned to her bleeding scalp. "Then we can figure out what to do next and how to call your people."

"All right." It was a good plan. She wouldn't be much use like this. "I need to get my EM-kit from the craft."

"EM-kit? Oh, emergency kit. I see." Calagan turned but was interrupted.

"Let me get it." A woman next to Calagan spoke quickly. "Just tell me where it is."

"Beneath the pilot seat. A green box with a white triangle on the lid." Grateful not to have to crawl back into the cramped space of her beloved bird, Spinner drew a deep breath to try to alleviate the nausea. She was probably concussed, and without her helmet she'd no doubt be dead.

The woman returned with the box. "I'm Darmiya, Calagan's sister. Why don't you sit over there?" She pointed at some old, weathered logs, and the crowd shifted to give them space as Darmiya tended to Spinner's wound. "You need stitches, but I've taped the gap along your hairline as securely as I can." Darmiya looked apologetically at her. "You might have a scar."

"I honestly could care less. Just one more for the collection." She grinned despite the pain. "And stitches? We don't sew our wounded, not anymore. You used the tape correctly. It's fine."

Darmiya blushed faintly and put a dressing on the strips of tape. "Just a shame to scar such a handsome face."

"Quit that flirting," Calagan said, and pushed at his sister, albeit gently. "You're hopeless."

"I would call it hopeful. This woman can be our salvation, don't you see?" Darmiya frowned at him, clearly annoyed. "I'm not flirting, just being friendly. When her people come looking for her and her craft, they'll help us in the process."

"How do you know this, Darmiya?" another woman in the crowd asked. "How do you know that the Oconodians won't just abandon us like they do the changed ones on their own homeworld? That's what her mission is about. Finding a new place to settle down and thus leave every problem behind. Does that sound like caring people to you?" She spat the words and glared at Spinner with obvious hostility.

"She's wrong," Spinner said quietly. Every voice pierced her head and made her want to throw up. "Now, please give me one of those injections marked with a red label that says Stabilizer IV."

Darmiya looked through the EM-kit. "This it?" She held up an auto-syringe.

"Yes, I'll do it myself." She'd be damned if she allowed anyone from another world to actually inject her. Spinner grabbed the syringe with unsteady fingers and pressed it against the pulse point on her neck. She jerked as the substance hissed, passing the skin barrier and entering her bloodstream.

Waiting impatiently for the effect, she almost whimpered in relief when the headache began to subside. This was a temporary measure and she could have only one more dose during the next twenty-four hours, but it was necessary. She stood and stretched her back before turning to Darmiya and Calagan. "I'm going to get a few things from my craft, and then we have to move toward those anchored ships. Are they far from here?"

"Not very. We have no way of reaching them, though." Calagan looked troubled as Spinner pressed herself through the half-open hatch.

"That's not true." Darmiya spoke determinedly. "Some of the passengers came to the island in small rescue rafts. We could use them if we need to reach them."

"They'll overturn and we'll all drown." Calagan sounded angry now. "It's an insane attempt."

Spinner was busy grabbing her backpack, which was stored in the back, behind her seat. It contained a survival kit with emergency rations and other things a pilot might need when tossed into an unexpected situation planetside. She took more ammunition from the weapons locker and then secured it. No need for the locals to get their hands on Oconodian guns. Outside, she tucked the rest of the EM-kit in her bag and slung it over her back. As she tugged on the straps, she calmly gazed at the surrounding crowd. Their expressions ran from hopeful and benevolent to disdainful and suspicious. Wonderful.

"We need to get to any means of transmission with an amplifier. If I can signal the *Espies Major* or any of her sister ships in the convoy, we have at least a chance of rescuing people." She didn't imply that they could save everyone, as they obviously realized it might be an impossible undertaking.

"Let's go, then." Calagan motioned for the closest people to move, and they made their way through what looked like an ocean of people. Young, old, and the very young and extremely old. How did the very old manage to survive the initial disaster? Impressed with their tenacity, Spinner thought of Caydoc's nania. Helden possessed such strength. It seemed the older woman had taken a personal interest in Spinner and the fascination was mutual. Sometimes it could feel quite surreal, especially when Helden referred to her granddaughter, the admiral, as angelic and cute when she was a little girl.

Looking up at the empty sky, Spinner wondered what mayhem she'd caused aboard the *Espies Major* this time. The rule was to never leave anyone behind if it was at all doable, but this time it was more than that. Darmiya was right. They would come looking for her craft, then pick up on her homing signal, and that's when they'd find all the refugees. Oh, yeah. Caydoc would supply Spinner with her own personal airlock to use on a continuous basis.

❖

"Chief Dioga to Bridge."

"Caydoc here. Report."

"Thanks to your esteemed grandmother, sir, we now have a working theory. The magma and ashes on Gemosis are not like ours back home." He cleared his throat, perhaps for using the word home about Oconodos. "On Gemosis, the magma contains an erodent, a substance that gnaws through our metal alloys."

"Hell. What's your solution? How can we use the rescue freighters?" Caydoc shoved her hands through her hair.

"The fleet admiral thought of a way. It's experimental, and we need to send down a test probe—"

"Dioga. Get to the point. We don't have much time."

"Understood, sir. The fleet admiral suggested that we spray a silicon-based substance into the circuit ducts and all over the exposed propulsion system. She said it would be like applying lip salve." He sounded amused, and Dael couldn't blame him. Trust her nania to make such a comparison.

"Then outfit a probe instantly and send it to the planet, preferably a densely ash-filled part."

"Aye, sir."

Thank you, Nania. Dael gazed around the bridge. "You all heard. Prepare to find a location to send it to. Commander Weniell, you have the bridge. I'm planning to join the first rescue team once we have the go-ahead."

"Sir?" Weniell stood, a scowl marring his forehead. "As your XO, I can't permit—"

"It's not your place to permit me to do anything." Ice in her voice and no doubt icicles shooting from her eyes, Dael merely brushed him aside.

"Perhaps, but it's my duty as your first officer to express my opinion and make you think twice before doing anything rash." His face turned redder; he was clearly angry now.

"I never do anything rash, Weniell. My actions are always thought out, more than once. I need to assess the situation and head up this rescue operation. I'm sure our government and the people who designed these ships didn't quite anticipate us running into this mess so close to home, but I'll be damned if I'll allow neighbors of Oconodos to suffer and perish if I can do something—anything—about it."

"And Spinner?" Weniell lowered his voice, well out of earshot from the rest of the bridge crew. "Does her involvement have something to do with this unprecedented act of an admiral leading a mission of this magnitude?"

Furious now, Dael spoke just above a whisper. "I will pretend I didn't hear that, but just to set the record straight, this whole mission is unprecedented. My role is more than just that of a military leader or an ambassador of sorts. If my crew thinks I will abandon them at will—and this early in the mission at that—it will lead to a whole new problem. The morale issues we've had the last few days will seem like nothing if the crew loses faith in its leadership. I will confer with my counterparts in the rest of our convoy. Your concern is duly noted. You have the bridge." She didn't wait to hear his response but turned to Lt. Schpay. "Put together a small recon team. Have them meet me in freighter-bay one."

"Aye, sir." Schpay regarded the two senior officers with widened eyes as he carried out his orders. "They'll be ready when you get there, Admiral."

"Please, take care while you carry out this mission. Losing our commanding officer will be equally bad for morale." Weniell smiled wryly.

Recognizing the partial approval, Dael spoke slowly. "Oh, I have no intention of getting myself killed. I'd be in so much trouble with the former fleet admiral if I did."

CHAPTER NINE

S pinner hoisted her backpack higher and ground her teeth. Despite the pain relief, her head and arm pounded like mad, and climbing the unforgiving territory of the island didn't help. The ground consisted of sand upon bedrock, and it was slippery as the sand rolled beneath her feet. The sky darkened as the day headed toward early evening. Soon it would become pitch-black and a great deal colder.

"Several tsunamis have hit, growing larger with each wave." Darmiya kept close; she could probably see Spinner wasn't doing entirely well. "If they keep coming, and growing, they'll wash everyone off the island and out to sea. Perhaps even overturn the ships."

"You're damned whatever you do," Spinner murmured. "That's why we have to get out to one of the boats so I can boost the signal enough to reach my convoy." She hoped that meant Caydoc and the four captains would blast into action. They had to. They couldn't allow these people to die.

"You sure she's not some sort of megalomaniac who's dreamed up this bunch of vast spaceships?" a man in the crowd behind them shouted. "For all we know, she could be part of whoever did this."

"You fool." Darmiya snarled at him. "Why would she risk her life by faking a crash and then subject herself to the same dangers we're facing?"

"What do I know?" the man said, shrugging.

"Exactly," Calagan said as he came running. He'd moved faster and was rejoining them after reconnoitering. "I saw several of our small boats and secured two of them. Some of them have been smashed against the cliffs, but these two looked intact."

"Great." Spinner forced herself to inject energy into her voice as well as her sluggish body. "How many can the boats hold?"

"Eight, maybe ten, depending on weight." Darmiya pointed ahead where the cliffs came into view. "See, over there?"

The salty air seemed fresher here, and the sound of the crashing waves became increasingly louder. Having spent most of her life in space, Spinner wasn't fond of the sea. Water was a treacherous element. Like space, it lacked breathable oxygen, but it also had a way to drag you down, unless you mastered it. Of course she could swim. Most people could. Still, when water closed above her head, she could feel an otherwise very distant panic lurk in the back of her mind.

Now Spinner disregarded her reluctance and stepped into the boat as men and women helped push it from the cliffs. Darmiya, Calagan, and six others jumped in as well, and as Darmiya started the engine, they all began to use the automatically extendable oars as well. Spinner assumed the current and the power of the ocean were too much for the small engine.

"Let me help," she yelled to Darmiya over the roar of the waves.

"No. You're injured, and you're the one we need to take care of. The one who knows how to get help." Darmiya tore at the large handle, sending the oar into the water and pulling hard against it. "Sit down and hold on. This is going to be bumpy."

"Wonderful." Grasping the low seat, Spinner was soon as wet from the spray of the waves, as if she had actually swum in the ocean. The sky was now black, and only the sparse light from the remaining moons and the stars that peered through the smoke and ash clouds made it possible to see anything.

"We're closing in on the first ships. Hell, this is going to be rough. The sea is crazy!" Calagan's face was contorted with the exertion of rowing. "Get ready, Commander. We might have only one chance to get you aboard."

"What do you mean? We're all going aboard."

"That's not possible." Darmiya shook her head wildly, sending the black curls around her cheeks flying. "Our best chance is to make sure you do. Don't let us down. Please!"

Spinner's gut ached. Not only from the repercussions of the crash, but also from the idea of this brave group of individuals risking their lives for their world, their people.

She saw the large ship tower above them. It felt as if they were a tiny nutshell next to this gigantic vessel—a luxury passenger cruiser that tilted precariously in their direction. "Creators of all things possible," Spinner said under her breath. "That thing isn't far from flipping over."

"And still it's one of the ships doing fairly all right," Calagan said darkly. He steered along the port side of the impressive ship, and Darmiya used a stroboscope light to get the ship's crew's attention.

Suddenly a chirpy sound was heard and metal steps ejected on several places along the ship's hull. Just the idea of climbing up made Spinner's stomach churn. Her head ached badly, and the idea of clinging to a ladder that high above this tormented ocean frankly scared her to death. Still, she'd do it. To chance saving these people, to persuade Caydoc to break whatever protocols she needed to disregard, she'd do it.

"Oh, no! Hold on, hold on!" Darmiya's voice held a whole new panic. "A new tsunami! They're coming closer together."

Spinner's head snapped around so fast, she moaned from the resulting pain. This was nothing compared to the terror filling her when she saw what the super-wave had done to the ships surrounding the island. People on the cliffs scurried away, but the ships had nowhere to go. Nor did they, in their small damn rowboat.

Spinner thought of the mission of finding a new homeworld for the Oconodians, of saving the part of a people who suffered because the other part was changing into something different. Perhaps this was an omen that other solutions to the Oconodian issue were possible. No matter what, she wouldn't be a part of either. She was going to drown here and now, on a world that wasn't hers, trying to save a people that wasn't hers either.

The downdraft happened so fast Spinner thought the wave was already upon them. It didn't make sense, and yet this tremendous force pressed down against her, made it impossible to breathe. Expecting for the swirling sea to engulf her any second, she drew a deep breath, not because she expected to live, but because the idea of inhaling water terrified her.

Instead, something else, a soft, satin-like fabric, surrounded her, pressed against her, and tugged her upward. It took her only a few moments to realize it was an Oconodian extraction tube; after that, everything turned black.

❖

Dael made her way back to where her medical crew was triaging the evacuated people from Gemosis. She stood among the startled individuals, some looking immensely relieved and some quite scared and confused. Children cried and whimpered, except a few who merely looked around with huge eyes.

She had deployed fourteen freighters from each of the ships, joining the Gemosians who had gathered outside the debris field in the rescue effort. None of the captains in the Oconodian advance team had objected, which made her experience humbling. She'd been prepared to pull rank, but as it turned out that wasn't necessary.

"Sir! Admiral? Over here." One of the nurses waved her over. Lengthening her stride, she had to force herself to not gasp at the sight of the pale woman on a gurney. Soaked by the ocean and the rain, her hair matted against her head, Spinner wasn't moving.

"What's her status?" Dael asked hoarsely.

"She's suffering from hypothermia, her blood pressure is too low, and her lower left arm is fractured."

"Any head injury? She's unconscious."

"She has a contusion above her left eye. It's been dressed, but we'll deal with it regardless, as her bandages were soaked by the rain and the ocean." The nurse stood back as two crewmen passed with yet another gurney.

"Spinner?" Dael touched the unconscious woman's shoulder. "You're safe now."

Stirring, Spinner's eyes opened into narrow slits. "Sir?" Her voice was a husky whisper.

"Can you see me? How's your eye?" Dael leaned over Spinner, trying to judge the reaction of her pupils as her stunning eyes opened further.

"Yeah. Yes. Good to see you, Admiral." Spinner rose on her elbows but fell back down with a moan. "For the love of the Creator. Ow."

"Careful. They're about to set your fracture and redress your bandages. If you're up for it after that, we can talk."

"Wait, sir. Please, just tell me…the others from the boat? The ship that's tilting so badly?"

"We're pulling out as many as we can and transporting them to Gemosian ships and their largest moon. We're working against time here, I'm afraid. This planet is becoming increasingly unstable."

Spinner closed her eyes and nodded, but not before Dael could read the profound sadness that filled them. "How can you be here? The air, I mean, the ash from the volcanoes, it clogged my propulsion system."

"Looks like bringing my nania wasn't an entirely questionable idea. As it turned out, she worked with Chief Dioga in engineering, and the two of them came up with a substance to add to our filtering systems. It wouldn't work on the assault craft, but the freighters have a more forgiving system."

"Thank the Creator. But, sir, what the hell went wrong?" she murmured. "How can a moon just explode?"

"The Gemosians have provided us with data. We'll have the answers soon. You just let the medics deal with your injuries. I'm— I'm glad you're safe." Dael suddenly felt awkward and the words came out choppy.

"Me too," Spinner said wryly. "If you run into two siblings, Calagan and Darmiya, please make a note where I can find them. They helped me and ought to be on this freighter."

"I will remember that." Dael watched with some concern as the medics put a supporting composite orthotic brace on Spinner's arm. Spinner pressed her lips together but didn't make a sound. No doubt it went against everything in her personality to show any sort of weakness.

"I'll check back with you in a little while. Just rest until then. That's an order, CAG."

"Aye, sir." Spinner looked up, and a crystal-clear teardrop dislodged from her eyelashes and ran down her temple and into her hair. "Damn it."

Afterward, Dael couldn't explain why she quickly bent down and wiped the wet trail away and then repeated the maneuver on the other side. She somehow knew Spinner's tears weren't caused by her own physical discomfort. If she read this complex woman right, she would never shed tears on her own behalf—only on someone else's.

"We're doing our best to reach as many as possible. Fortunately, Gemosis is not as populated as Oconodos."

"So many have lost their lives already, in the first wave of disasters." Spinner blinked, clearly trying to contain her emotions. "Don't let me keep you, sir. You have more important things to do than…this."

Dael knew Spinner didn't want her to witness any more perceived weakness, so she stood and made her way among the gurneys. They had so many rescued Gemosians now; some were sitting on the deck along the bulkhead. Dael nodded at them and some reached for her, looking ready to kiss her hands.

"Thank you, ma'am. May the deities of your world bless you." A man hugged a woman and a young boy closer. "They sent you our way when we needed you most."

"Just rest. You're safe now." Being called "ma'am" only happened when it came to civilians, and the man's utter adoration made her feel uncomfortable. Smiling briefly, Dael strode back to the small bridge. "Report."

"Our sister ships simply cannot find any more people alive, sir." A young ensign at the ops station looked up, his face pale. "One of the ships sank as the last tsunami hit, and they talked about deploying divers."

"I would surmise the ocean is too wild for individual divers to go down. Signal *Espies Major* and have them deploy watercraft." They had only four craft that could endure being submerged in water. All the others could tolerate dipping into an ocean briefly, but after a few minutes, they would start to corrode. The watercraft served a double duty as they also performed well in space, though not with the same maneuverability as the assault craft and space freighters.

"Already have them on standby, sir." The ensign looked relieved, closing her dark eyes briefly.

"Good initiative, Ensign"—Dael glanced at the name tag—"Lomi."

After she reached the helm, Dael turned to the officer commanding the freighter. "When you get the intel that we have rescued everyone from the surface, set a course for their biggest moon…What was it called again?"

"Alino One, sir," said Lt. Trepp.

"Exactly. Set a course for Alino One. We need to deliver the Gemosians for examination."

"And where will they go after that?" Lt. Trepp looked somber.

"Actually, Alino One has been terra-formed with great success. I'm not sure how many people can live there long-term, but they can definitely help care for the injured and displaced during the acute phase." Dael rested her hip against the console next to her. "I suppose it could provide a refuge for a while, but that's a tricky question. Just imagine how long it took our government to realize we couldn't choose any of the worlds in our own sector in the Exodus plan."

"What's your plan, sir?" the lieutenant asked carefully. "How long will our aid effort last?"

"You mean, how long do we squander our resources that were meant to keep us alive while we search for a new home to our people?"

"That's a bit harsh, but essentially, I guess that's what I was thinking, and I'm not the only one."

"I'm very sure of that." Her voice cooling a few degrees, Dael pushed her shoulders back. "As soon as we deal with the immediate danger, we will be on our way. Just understand this, Lt. Trepp. When we have a distress call, the rules of engagement are in play. Though we're weeks or months away from where we originate, the laws, rules, and protocols still apply. The day we turn our back on someone we have a decent chance to save, I will remind my crew of this—each and every time. Do I make myself clear, Lieutenant?"

"Yes, sir. Very much so. Actually, when you spell it out I feel safer." Trepp smiled warily. "I'm glad we found Spinner. *Espies*

Major wouldn't be the same without her. Nor would the spin jack tables in the mess hall."

"I daresay." Feeling marginally better as well, Dael motioned toward the back of the freighter. "I'm going to make another round before we reach Alino One. Once the Gemosians have gone ashore, we need to return to *Espies Major*. I don't foresee that we can continue our mission until tomorrow, but that's not too bad a delay."

"Yes, sir."

Nodding briefly, Dael walked along crowded corridors where people who hadn't fit into any of the quarters or other spaces aboard the freighter sat or lay down. When she carefully made her way through yet another corridor, the fifth one on deck three, she suddenly felt a careful touch on her right calf. She stopped and glanced down at a woman kneeling next to her.

"Please, ma'am…or, Admiral, isn't it?"

"It is. What can I do for you?"

"My name is Darmiya and this is my brother Calagan." The woman gestured to a pale man slumped by her side. "He's a bit out of it. He was the last one to be rescued from our boat."

Dael recognized the names immediately. "Have the medics seen him?"

"Yes, Admiral. We'll be fine, but I wanted to inquire about a woman who belongs to you. To your crew."

"I expect you're referring to Commander Seclan. She'll be all right as well. I saw her a little while ago on another deck."

"She's alive then? Oh, thank the deities for their mercy." Darmiya pressed the back of her hand over her mouth. "She wasn't doing very well, and yet she risked her life to signal for help…for our sake."

Clearly, Spinner had made her usual impact in the short time she'd been on Gemosis. "She asked for you and your brother earlier. When I see her next time—"

"Oh, could I speak to her?" Darmiya stood.

"Don't you want to tend to your brother?" Frowning at the woman's persistence, Dael took a step, signaling that she was about to leave.

"That's all right," the man, Calagan, piped up. "You go make sure the commander is fine. I'll just rest here until you get back."

"I'll show you the way." Her jaw tightening until she was afraid it might shatter if she didn't relax, Dael motioned for Darmiya to follow her.

"It's amazing how we bonded in such a short time," Darmiya said, her voice breathless. "She crashed right there among us and still managed to avoid hitting anyone. The commander must be your best pilot."

"Commander Seclan is very accomplished," Dael said, ready to just turn around and head back to the bridge.

"I suppose she has to go back with you to your space ship? That's too bad. Our doctors are very skilled. They could help her."

"We have our own physicians, thank you."

"Yes, I guess so. My brother and I had always dreamed of going to Oconodos, but when the outbreak of…Well, now isn't a good time."

"I couldn't agree more." Trying to be cordial since it wasn't the young woman's fault Spinner had wowed her, Dael asked something in return. "What do you and your brother do, Miss…?"

"Do Voy." Darmiya smiled. "We're in the same field, but from different angles. My brother is a computer engineer and I hold the same degree, but I invent software and operating systems."

"Really?" The wheels started turning faster inside Dael as they reached the part of the freighter where Spinner was still on a gurney. She was sitting up, her back against the wall, her arm in a sling. She looked much better but was still pale and bruised.

"There she is!" Darmiya scurried between the other gurneys and medics. "Commander Seclan, you're here."

Spinner turned her head, her eyes widening at the sight of Darmiya. She smiled warily as the young woman clung to her uninjured arm.

"The admiral brought me here. I just needed to see with my own eyes that you're okay."

"And I am. And you have." Spinner chuckled, only to grow serious instantly. "Your brother? How's Calagan?"

"He's a bit hypothermic, but he's already getting better. Your crew gave him a special blanket."

"Good." Spinner turned her gaze to Dael. "Thank you for taking personal care of Darmiya. Without her and Calagan, I'd be dead, or perhaps lynched. Some of the people on the island thought I was behind what happened to the moon."

"Ridiculous." Darmiya huffed. "They were acting out of fear and rage."

"Well, I owe you a favor for your part in keeping my best pilot safe." Dael quoted Darmiya and was only half joking. Spinner was no doubt the most skilled and fearless pilot on the Exodus mission. Darmiya's description of Spinner's ordeal caused her to shiver deep inside, a novel reaction she couldn't explain.

"Oh, no. You don't owe me anything, Admiral. On the contrary, if the commander and your people hadn't passed our world when you did, many more of the Gemosians would have perished." Darmiya looked so earnestly at Dael she couldn't help but like the young woman. "It's all so unfathomable and overwhelming. I can't even imagine where Calagan and I will go from here. Our research and our work have been destroyed. We have only each other." Tears fell down golden-brown cheeks.

"Let me see what I can do." Dael spoke impulsively, which was totally out of character, and she regretted it almost immediately. "Do you wish to stay and visit with Spi—Commander Seclan, or should I ask someone to escort you back to your brother?"

"Oh, I'd love to stay here and get to know the commander better. At least I'll have that as a memory if I never see any of you again."

Dael spoke firmly. "Very well. We're about to land on Alino One at their premier medical facility." She glanced at Spinner, who was leaning against the bulkhead, looking like she was about to fall over. "Rest up, Commander. Once we're back aboard *Espies Major*, you'll be taken to the infirmary."

"Fantastic," Spinner murmured. "My favorite place."

Dael disliked the infirmary as well, at least if she was the patient. She remembered the scratches she had on her abdomen and thighs, which would need attention too. Though she had used temporary sanitizing wands, she knew that wasn't enough. Disregarding the dull sting, she left Spinner and Darmiya.

    The Gemosian woman was obviously taken with Spinner, fawning over her and gazing at her with that particular glitter in her eyes that spoke of early stages of infatuation. A tiny knot just below Dael's sternum formed as the words hit home. Annoyed at such a foolish reaction, she merely walked away. How could it possibly concern her if Darmiya was attracted to Spinner? Her reaction didn't make sense, and she refused to give it a second thought.

• 81 •

CHAPTER TEN

Spinner walked from her bedroom into her small living-room area, grimacing at her stiff body's unwillingness to maneuver as smoothly as it normally did. "Enter," she said. Who was it this time? Since being discharged from the infirmary, she'd had a steady stream of visitors, mainly her pilots but also some unexpected ones. She wondered if this would be the admiral, but then mentally smacked herself on the back of her head. Why would Caydoc pay her a visit when she would return to her duties as CAG in two days? She would've gone back today if the doc hadn't threatened to ground her for ten days.

The door swooshed open, revealing a deceptively frail-looking elderly woman. Not the admiral, clearly, but one better. A fleet admiral. Retired, yes, but that didn't matter. Helden Caydoc was a legend, stroke or no stroke.

"Sir!" Standing at attention, which made her brain gyrate on the inside, Spinner met the fleet admiral's steely eyes.

"As you were, CAG," the woman said. "May I come in?"

"Oh, I'm sorry. Naturally. Come in. Not a lot of space, but—"

"Just move that chair a bit and my own will fit nicely." Fleet Admiral Caydoc turned to the young woman guiding her chair. "You may step out, Minna," she said. "I'll page you when I'm ready to leave. And no, you don't have to hover in the corridor. Go put your feet up."

Creator of Oconodos, she's going to be here awhile. Spinner maintained an amicable smile. What the hell was going on?

Minna left after making sure her employer was comfortable. She looked pointedly at Spinner, who nodded imperceptibly. If anything were amiss, she would have Minna back here faster than magnetar drive.

"Can I get you anything to drink, sir?" Spinner asked, not quite sure what else to say. You really didn't question a woman like Helden Caydoc about her reasons for visiting.

"I'm quite all right, CAG. Just sit down and relax. I know you've been out of the infirmary for only a few hours. I had my caregivers spy and also interrogated the hell out of my granddaughter."

"Really?" Sitting down on one of the two armchairs, Spinner tried to fathom why the old woman would take such measures. "What can I do for you, sir?"

"Well, you can cease, once and for all, to call me sir. I'm retired. My name is Helden. May I call you Spinner—or Aniwyn?"

Licking her dry lips, Spinner croaked, "Spinner's fine, sir—I mean Helden. I'm sorry. This will take some getting used to."

"I bet. It's enough that you have to stick to protocol with Dael. Two Admirals Caydoc is one too many, in my opinion." Helden raised her good hand. "Are you feeling better?"

"I'm fine. I'll be back on duty—"

"No. I want to know how you're feeling. You sustained a nasty crash."

"Yes. Yes, I did. But you know, when you walk away from said crash, it's not as nasty as it could've been." Spinner pulled a small cushion onto her lap and rested her left arm on it. "They cemented my fracture—it wasn't misaligned or anything—but I'm a tad sore."

"I would think so."

"I can't forgive myself for losing a valuable assault craft, though." Chewing on the inside of her cheek, Spinner looked carefully at Helden.

"You haven't heard? Dael had one of the last freighters lift it off the surface and bring it back. As she put it, we have ample time to fix it."

That was the best news so far. Spinner smiled broadly, dry lips or not. "She's resourceful and detail oriented, your granddaughter," she said brightly. Then she caught herself. "Oh, for the love of the Creator, I—"

"Isn't she?" Helden looked proud. She leaned forward very slightly. "It is one of her strengths, but it can also drive me insane. Especially when she's trying to meddle with what she thinks I can and can't do."

"That would have the same effect on me. Still, I might have tried to tough it out and heal on my own if the admiral hadn't made sure someone took me to the infirmary."

"Dislike the place, do you?" Sounding pleased, Helden snickered. "So does Dael—almost as much as I. And look at this." She gestured to her chair. "I can't fend for myself to save my life."

"But you and Chief Dioga saved a lot of other lives today," Spinner said. "I know it must be a pain to have to rely on others for even the most personal things. I do get that. Today, you showed us all that this doesn't mean life is over or that you can't contribute. Age or disability aside, I agree with those who claim you have the sharpest, shrewdest mind of the entire advance fleet."

Looking shocked at Spinner's words, Helden nodded slowly. "You speak with such immediacy and conviction, I'm inclined to believe that *you* believe this. Regardless, that's a nice sentiment."

"Sentiment?" Snorting, Spinner shook her head. "I don't do sentiment, Helden. I get in trouble a lot for not being as correct as the CAG is expected to be. I'm still baffled that I was promoted. I know why, but Admiral Caydoc had the last word, and she isn't impressed with me."

Chuckling, Helden tilted her head in a way that reminded Spinner of how Caydoc regarded her at times. "I beg to differ. She grudgingly admires your skill and courage, and one day she will know you well enough to be less bothered by your shortcomings when not in the pilot seat. And you, Spinner, will grow into the part of being an officer during this mission. Of that I have no doubt."

"Why is that?" Spinner frowned. "I mean, how can you possibly know?"

Her voice growing impossibly soft, Helden maneuvered her chair close enough to pat Spinner's knee. "Because I knew your mother, Spinner."

Spinner just stared. "What?" she whispered.

"Pamas Seclan was my aide de camp. I knew her well."

Chest constricting, closing around her lungs like an ironclad barrel, Spinner could hardly keep her temper down. Only the fact that Helden was a frail old woman kept her from shouting at her to get out. "Then you should know that her leaving me and my father when I was eight meant she couldn't have much impact on my life or my character." Spinner knew she sounded borderline rude.

"I beg to differ, Aniwyn."

The soft use of her given name made Spinner recoil. "I'm not comfortable talking about my mother. My head hurts. I need to lie down. I'm sorry to cut the visit short—"

"I'm sorry, Spinner." Helden withdrew, even backing up her chair a little. "It was ill-advised of me to bring that up—I shouldn't have, not now when you're still not feeling well."

"I honestly can't think of a time when bringing up my mother would be a good thing." Spinner fought the nausea; she really didn't want to throw up all over Caydoc's grandmother.

Helden regarded her in silence, her eyes pensive, perhaps even sorrowful. She tapped a sensor on her armrest. "Minna? Sorry to cut your break short. I need your services."

Minna answered mutedly, acknowledging she would be there in a minute. Spinner groaned inwardly; a minute right now seemed like a lifetime.

"So that you won't withdraw from me for all eternity, let me fill you in on some interesting news." Helden managed to sound entirely casual. "We have intel that the moon did not explode due to any malicious activity. The Gemosian officials—I should say the *surviving* officials—have a theory that the mining operation on Tegia used garnet oil." She looked expectantly at Spinner, who tried to process this new information and shove any harsh personal subject far back into her subconscious, where it belonged.

"Garnet oil?" She realized what Helden was in fact saying and closed her eyes in dismay. Opening them slowly, she sighed. "What in the hell possessed them?"

"I'd like to know that too. I guess they'd mined this moon for centuries, and the conventional blasting and drilling at the immense depths were becoming unprofitable and difficult. So, some genius says, why not just pour a few drops of garnet oil into one of the shafts, not realizing how those drops would spread to the inner core of the moon."

"Which consisted of?"

"From the debris scans, frozen water."

"Damn." Spinner was no geologist, but she could easily picture the disastrous chain of events when some idiot's so-called bright idea about how to make more money had killed thousands, perhaps hundreds of thousands of Gemosians.

"Damn indeed." Helden regarded her with softer eyes. "I would say that your initiative, your crash, if you will, expedited the saving of far more people. With you planetside, Dael could get the rescue operation going much faster and with much less discussion."

"Screwing up has its advantages on occasion, you mean?" Snorting joylessly, Spinner plucked at the hem of her shirt. "Well, there's a first time for everything."

"So you're still not going to take credit for anything. I'll have to try harder."

Spinner was about to argue when the door chime buzzed. "Enter," she said instead, expecting Minna. But it was Caydoc, who looked taken aback at Helden's presence in Spinner's quarters.

"Nania?" Caydoc remained just outside.

"Ah, well. I was just leaving. There's Minna now." Helden motioned behind Caydoc. "Great timing, Minna. Let's leave these two to talk among themselves."

Minna whisked Helden, who merely waved her good hand as a good-bye, past Caydoc and out into the corridor. Caydoc looked after her grandmother, seeming puzzled, before she turned back to Spinner.

"Come in. What can I do for you, sir?" Spinner stood, even if she knew protocol didn't dictate her standing at attention in her own quarters. Perhaps the latest blow to her head had finally knocked some respect for the chain of command into her. She snickered inwardly. Not likely.

"You can start by sitting down again. May I?" Caydoc gestured toward the other armchair.

"Of course. Can I get you something to drink?"

"Why don't I program some tea for us?"

"By all means. Thank you." Spinner fought the feeling of being in a completely surreal, upside-down reality.

Caydoc rose and busied herself over by the kitchenette. The automatic hot-beverage dispenser quickly provided two mugs of steaming hot tea. Spinner preferred coffee but realized tea was better right now. More stimulating drinks than that wouldn't be good for her jumbled brain.

"May I ask what you're doing here, sir?" Spinner sipped her tea and regarded Caydoc closely over the rim of the mug.

"You may. First, I wanted to check on you. The last time I saw you, you weren't looking well at all. Second, I had some news I thought you'd be interested in."

"Helden—your grandmother, I mean, told me about the red garnet."

"She did?" Caydoc's eyebrows went up. "Well, that was part of my news. The Gemosian officials are scrambling to figure out where to send their people. Alino One can't sustain all the survivors, so they've actually opened up communication with Oconodos as well as Loghia. The latter is a bit ironic, since they're the ones who invented and manufacture red garnet."

"Oh, for the love of the Creator." Spinner put her mug down. "So all are off the planet?"

Growing serious, Caydoc spoke solemnly. "The ones alive are, yes. Some could perhaps still be left behind that our sensors cannot detect, but none of our scans shows any humanoid life signs."

"I can hardly believe it. Greed and ignorance caused this?"

"Yes." Caydoc sighed and leaned back. "We've done what we can so far. I've briefed the command on Oconodos, and they will continue to use our buoys to communicate with the Gemosians. If nothing else, they can offer knowledge and advice." She straightened again, and for some reason she appeared ill at ease. "This brings me to another matter. When debriefing some of the passengers that we rescued from the archipelago where you crashed, the Gemosians came up with an unusual request. It seems that your friends, Darmiya and Calagan Do Voy, are not your average scientists. Apparently they are widely known among their people as the geniuses of their generation."

"Really?" Spinner thought of the pretty young woman who seemed slightly naïve in her way of expressing herself. In a sense she wasn't really surprised. Darmiya and Calagan had been forceful, and the rest of the Gemosians present had followed their example without objecting too much.

"Really. Now, the Gemosian officials are, as I said, desperate to find somewhere for their population to thrive. They've asked to send Darmiya and Calagan with us on our mission. They offer us their knowledge, brains, and so on, and in return, they will keep in touch with their government. If necessary, the displaced Gemosians will join operation Exodus when the time comes."

Now this was unexpected. Spinner had to smile. "Things have a way of becoming tangled, don't they?" She chuckled. "We run into totally catastrophic events and then our mission grows. Has the Oconodos government approved this addition?"

"They have. They claim the ships' designer took into consideration that we might need further accommodation. I suppose they meant if our population grew faster than expected."

"What numbers are we talking about? I mean, for the Gemosians to join the Exodus vessels?" Spinner rubbed her temple. Her head was pounding, but she wanted to know.

"One more ship, I think. One hundred thousand individuals."

"Sweet Creator." Spinner leaned sideways, closing her eyes. "And they still claim this change won't jeopardize the essential mission?"

"Not according to the command and the politicians back home. If they can dock twenty-two ships together, I suppose twenty-three isn't such a stretch. As we have to find the homeworld before they can be underway, they have time to figure it out." Caydoc stood. "I should let you rest. I just thought you'd like to know Darmiya will be assigned to the *Espies Major*. And her brother, of course."

Not entirely sure why Caydoc was so adamant to tell her this, Spinner nodded slowly. "All right. We'll try to make them feel welcome."

"We return to magnetar drive in six minutes." Caydoc hesitated, glancing down at her shoes for a moment. "May I ask why my nania was here?"

"Sure. I'd tell you if I knew. She talked about the red garnet and said she wanted to see how I was doing. I was flattered, of course, but she really doesn't know me, so—" Spinner shrugged.

"The two of you looked intense. She wasn't up to her usual snooping, was she? She's by no means senile. In fact, she's still very, very sharp. That said, she edits very little that comes out of her mouth these days."

Not sure what made her be so blunt with her commanding officer, Spinner said, "She knew my mother. I'm not entirely comfortable discussing that topic, so I may have reacted with some hostility."

"Oh, trust me, she can take that. Your mother?" Caydoc stopped talking for a moment. "I apologize. That's none of my business."

"Apology accepted. Don't worry about it. I'm a big girl now." Spinner chuckled mirthlessly. "Though some would beg to differ."

"I can tell that, between us, Nania and I have exhausted you. Rest up and report to the bridge when Doc clears you."

"Aye, sir."

After cleaning their tea mugs, Caydoc headed for the door. Halting, she turned around. "You know, Aniwyn, when we're alone like this, I would prefer that you call me Dael."

Spinner gaped. Scrambling to find her voice, she replied, "Thank you…Dael." Dael was such a stark and beautiful name, befitting the impressive woman who stood there looking so intently at her. "You can call me Aniwyn or Spinner—I respond to both." It wasn't completely the truth. Most people called her Spinner, and several people had no idea what her given name was.

"Aniwyn is a beautiful name. Otherworldly, even."

Otherworldly? Spinner started to wonder exactly who had hit their head, she or Dael. "Thank you."

"As I said, rest up." She left and the door closed behind her with a hiss.

Spinner slowly stood and headed for the sleeping area. She normally wasn't all that keen on unsolicited advice, but she was exhausted. As she curled up on her bed and struggled to pull a blanket over her with her good arm, she thought of her strange exchange with Dael. "Call me Dael," she muttered. "Great idea. What if I get used to that and then slip up on the bridge? Brilliant move." She shifted until she found the position that hurt the least. Closing her eyes, she tried to figure out why Dael had looked so weird when she was informed that the Do Voy siblings were joining their crew. Nothing made much sense. Perhaps if she slept on it, it would sort itself out in her head when she woke up.

Drifting off, Spinner relaxed into the mattress and rubbed her cheek against the soft pillow. Faint voices spoke in some half-awake dreams, repeating words she'd heard only moments ago. "Aniwyn is a beautiful name"…"knew your mother"…"otherworldly"…"she was my aide de camp"…"Call me Dael."

Spinner moaned. She didn't want to hear that again. Stirring restlessly she pressed her face into the pillow. As if the Creator heard her inner plea, dreamless sleep finally claimed her.

CHAPTER ELEVEN

Dael Caydoc
** Admiral**
Day 92
Advance mission
Personal log

The mission has been uneventful the last month and the crew seems happier, more content. Our counselor suggested part of it might be explained by the disastrous event when the Gemosians' homeworld was destroyed. Our two resident Gemosians have blended well with the crew, and they are in regular contact with the representative for their officials.

Nania is always nagging me to join the crew in recreational activities. This is rather ironic since she was considered such a stickler for protocol and regulations when she was on active duty. Now, she is joining all sorts of activities, despite her condition. I reminded her of her acerbic comments about basket weaving when we first started out on this mission, but she of course claims I'm exaggerating and putting words in her mouth. I swear to the Creator, if I didn't adore her, I'd toss her out an airlock.

The deployment of the buoys has gone well. I always dread it, for some reason. Well, I guess it's not hard to understand why. If we fail with the buoys, we can't send

*updates to Oconodos and our people can't follow us to
our new home. We have enough buoys to keep us going
for years, which I certainly hope we won't have to. I don't
expect to run into a perfect planet at every turn, but the idea
of a seemingly endless deep-space journey is not appealing.*

*Today, Spinner conducted an emergency drill with her
assault-craft pilots. It was a great success. I don't think
I've ever seen her content like this. After the Gemosian
tragedy, she bonded with the Do Voy siblings, and as far
as I know, the three have been inseparable. I would even
go so far as to say she's corrupted Calagan and Darmiya
into playing spin jack and trying some of the moonshine
brandy that keeps appearing despite the security officers'
best attempt to find the culprit who makes it. If anyone knew
I had procured two bottles to have "just in case," they'd
be completely shocked. Alcohol isn't exactly prohibited on
deep-space missions, but we're reaching the outer limits of
our own system and I cannot be too harsh on the crew. Not
if I want them to function at peak performance. This is their
life, their existence, and we all know there might be such
danger at any given time, they need to truly relax, even if
that means bending the rules. Yes, I know, if any one of my
peers on Oconodos heard me express this opinion, they'd
claim I've lost my mind. I used to run such a tight ship, and
in most cases I still do, but I've never worked under these
circumstances before, where my crew has their family and
friends onboard.*

*My direct opposite when it comes to rules and
regulations would be Spinner, of course. She seems to
operate under the assumption that rules are more like
recommendations and that she can pick and choose which
ones to follow—and which to disregard. Unless she's in her
assault craft leading her squadron, that is. She's prepared
to take risks personally, but she expects her subordinates to
follow her orders to the letter, and I hope to the Creator she
won't lose one of them. She is quite formidable as a daring
pilot, but I have seen the evidence of how vulnerable she is.*

Not sure why I feel so protective of her. Nania would claim Spinner's gotten under my skin, which is an enormous exaggeration, but she would be right in the sense that Spinner is special. Either you loathe her or you can't help but like her.

The door chime put a stop to Dael's recording session. "Enter." Darmiya strode inside, her innate energy levels permeating the very air around her. "Hello, Admiral," she said, her eyes sparkling a unique bluish purple. "I hope I'm not disturbing you while you're doing something terribly important."

Dael had to smile. As much as she tried to distance herself from the crew and the civilians, it was impossible not to respond to this woman's guileless persona. "Not at all, Ms. Do Voy."

"Oh, Admiral, how many times do I have to ask you to call me Darmiya?" She actually pouted. "I know it's not right for me to call you by your first name, you being the big boss around here, but *please*, call me Darmiya?" The young woman tilted her head, a gesture that might have looked fake and wheedling on anyone else.

"Very well, Darmiya. I will keep that in mind. So, what can I do for you? Please, take a seat."

"Oh, right. Thank you." Darmiya sat down, arranged the flowing, green skirt of her dress, and pushed the dark, curly hair back over her shoulders. "Admiral, eight days from now, we need to have a party."

Blinking, Dael tried to figure out this unusual request. "What? A party? For whom?"

"For us. For the crew. For you!" Grinning broadly, Darmiya looked utterly pretty and charming. "In eight days, you will have been on this mission for a hundred days. I think it's worth celebrating, and everyone I talked to agreed. We could even make it a tradition of sorts. Every hundred days in space is worth celebrating, don't you think?"

"A party?" Dael's brain felt sluggish as she tried to imagine throwing some sort of bash on a military vessel. A military vessel with civilian men, women, and children, she corrected herself.

"Yes, sir." Frowning now, Darmiya lost some of her glow. "Oh, no, you think it's a terrible idea."

"No, no. I didn't say that. I've just never thought about it, but I can tell you have. What would this celebratory party entail? And who have you talked to?"

"I've talked to Spinner, of course, and Gazer, Pemmer, Ioanto... Calagan, of course. The usual gang." Looking expectantly at Dael, Darmiya seemed to have gained new hope of a positive outcome. "My thought was to dock the five ships together—I know that can be done—and have a joint party. That would also have the benefit of us getting to know the other crews and their families. When we always stick to our own ships, it is so easy to divide the crewmembers up into 'us and them.' If docking isn't possible, we could at least have the view screens streaming while the parties are going on."

Impressed, Dael nodded slowly. "You've really given this a lot of thought." That shouldn't be such a surprise as Darmiya was one of the most intelligent among her people. "What kind of party?"

"At first we talked about a masquerade. I love masquerades, but we agreed that would be too elaborate. Perhaps we can do that at the two-hundred-day mark when people have had more opportunity to make costumes." Actually rubbing her palms together, Darmiya continued. "This time, using the different mess halls for eating, dancing, and games of spin jack...just socializing, would be enough, I think."

The idea of docking all ships had its pros and cons. They couldn't dock while in magnetar drive, of course, so they would lose time. Security would be an issue as they would be one huge sitting target. Darmiya had a point about the crews bonding, though. Perhaps there was a way around it?

"I'm not opposed to these ideas of yours, Darmiya, but it's short notice for planning, and I need to bring the matter up at the next meeting with the captains."

"Yes, I realize that, but you're the ultimate boss, right?" Darmiya smiled encouragingly. "And Spinner said you truly care about the crew, more than most believed to begin with." She looked so innocent saying this, but Dael's heart thudded a few painful beats.

"Quite the compliment from Commander Seclan, I'm sure," she murmured.

"Oh, she thinks the world of you. Once there was this guy who had a bit too much brandy—oh, now I'm saying too much."

"I know about the brandy, Darmiya. Go on." More curious than she let on, Dael laced her fingers and rested her hands on her desk.

"Well, this man, he complained about some extra duties and how that messed up his private life. He expressed himself pretty crudely. I actually learned some curse words in your native tongue that I didn't know. You should've heard Spinner. First, she had him stand at attention, which looked rather funny as he was dressed in baggy leisure pants and a very colorful shirt, and then she said, 'Crewman, the admiral works longer hours than any of us. If I hear you say anything remotely offensive about her, you will find your ass in the brig and then we'll see what your wife and children say about *that*.' That shut him up really fast."

Only Dael's self-control kept her from actually gaping at Darmiya's reenactment of Spinner defending her admiral. "That's—that's quite something."

"Isn't it? I would say, after that, because a lot of people were in the mess hall at the time, it seemed several people had their own take on why they admire and like you so much."

Now Dael had to stand up and turn her back to Darmiya. For some unfathomable reason, this young woman's words, so without pretense, brought the message home. She had never doubted her crew was loyal to her and the mission, but for them to actually express any type of fondness for her? This was something entirely new. Previously, she'd been admired and feared. She knew she could be intimidating and had found this façade useful many times and part of her command style. But liked? So far from Oconodos, soon enough farther from their homeworld than any of the previous vessels had been before, perhaps being liked was also a very good thing.

"Very well, Darmiya, you may go ahead and form a party committee. Name it something appropriate and make sure your committee knows this is a provisional decision for now. I will bring it up with the captains this afternoon and then let you know the details of our discussion. Good enough?"

"Oh, very good, Admiral!" Bouncing up from the chair, Darmiya looked like she was only a fraction away from hugging Dael. Fortunately she stopped herself and instead made a funny little salute with two fingers touching her temple. "Thank you, sir. Everyone will have so much fun."

"I hope so. Dismissed." Dael said the last word with a smile, to let Darmiya know they were parting on good terms. She had a feeling that, as bubbly as this woman was, she was as vulnerable as Spinner. No wonder the two of them had found each other.

As Darmiya left, Dael's last thought made her heart ache. Why would it matter to her if Darmiya and Spinner discovered each other on a personal level? Darmiya was stunning and Spinner was...well, she was enigmatically beautiful and definitely alluring to a young woman who no doubt saw Spinner as the hero she was.

Deciding to shove the pain that this whole concept brought her deep into the recesses of her mind, Dael sat down and prepared the addendum to the meeting with the captains later. No doubt they'd be taken off guard and quite shocked. Grinning now, Dael realized she looked forward to that. If nothing else, it would keep them on their toes.

❖

"She said yes?" Spinner stopped running so abruptly the treadmill nearly smacked her into the wall behind it. "You sure you didn't imagine it?"

"Not funny, Spinner." Scowling, Darmiya slapped her upper arm. "The admiral's going to bring it up with the captains of the other ships this afternoon. She told me to form a party committee."

"Good luck with that, then." Spinner rubbed her arm. "Was it necessary to hit the arm I fractured?" she muttered, trying to envision the admiral agreeing to have a fleet-wide party. "Did she say what kind of party she'd allowed?" She put her towel around her damp neck and sipped from her water bottle.

"I suggested dancing, eating, and gambling," Darmiya said, looking completely angelic.

Spluttering, Spinner managed to get water up her nose and into her lungs. "You suggested gambling?" She avoided Darmiya's attempt to slap her back, wheezing. "You're entirely certifiable. You know that?"

"I have no clue what you're talking about." Darmiya shook her head. "Oh, there's Calagan and Pemmer. Hey, boys, over here. I've got news."

The two men walked over to them, Calagan looking suspicious. "Don't tell me. You've antagonized the admiral enough to have her ditch us on the nearest planet that can remotely sustain life."

"Idiot," said his sister affectionately. "The party's on!"

Pemmer's jaw dropped, his eyes actually bugged out, and then he began to laugh nervously. "Admiral Caydoc wants a party? *The* admiral?" He sat down on one of the exercise machines and punched in the code that would enter his personal settings. As he began to push against the weights with his feet, he regarded Darmiya and Spinner with disbelief.

"See? I'm not the only one who's stunned," Spinner told Darmiya. "Look at that poor guy. You've knocked his world off its axis."

"CAG? She's not joking?" Pemmer shifted his gaze and met hers.

"No, she's the head of the party committee."

"Which you're all a part of!" Darmiya made a wide motion with her arms. "We need to invite some people from each ship to help plan so everyone feels involved. Deities above, this will be such a welcome break from the research lab. I love my work, I really do, but lately I've worried that my eyes will become square-shaped from staring at a screen all day."

"Back up, back up," Spinner said, waving her hand in a circular motion. "*We* are all part of the committee? Just like that? You can't just draft people—"

"But we hatched this idea together." Darmiya looked confused, her eyes darting between them.

"We were a tad tipsy from the brandy, sister." Calagan placed a hand on her shoulder. "I'm in, though. I think a party would be great."

Spinner was about to say she didn't have time and therefore had to bow out, when Darmiya turned her stunning eyes toward her. Groaning inwardly, Spinner knew that if she refused she would feel like she was kicking a small animal. Besides, if anyone could set up a decent spin-jack tournament, it was her. "Sure. I'm in."

Darmiya actually squealed, and as she shifted to look at Pemmer, who was sweating profusely now, she didn't even have to say anything to him either.

"Yeah, yeah. I'll help out. I'm pretty sure I can get my wife to assist as well," he said, out of breath. "What about the kids?"

Darmiya beamed. "Yes, they should have a say, definitely. Let's get some of those."

"She sounds like she's actually shopping for some children." Spinner looked at Calagan. "I thought I was beginning to know her. She's impossible to stop, isn't she?"

"You have no idea," Calagan said with a grin. "Once she has her mind set—"

"I'm here, you know. I can hear you." Darmiya clearly did her best to scowl. "We have to get this going. We only have eight days. Seven, really, as most of today's already passed. Spinner, you'll handle the spin-jack tournament. Pemmer, you're an amateur musician, aren't you? You can be in charge of the dancing. Calagan, you and I'll help create a buffet. And I'll see if I can draft some kids." Looking completely energized, which made Spinner rather envious as her schedule now was beyond full, Darmiya stood and waved before hurrying toward the door.

"Force of nature," Pemmer said weakly.

"Pain in the posterior." Calagan grinned. "And bossy."

"Isn't she?" Spinner stood. "I better hit the shower. I've got to file my report and hook up with some spin-jack aficionados on the other ships."

"See you later then." Calagan took over the treadmill Spinner had just abandoned. "I look forward to beating you. I seem to have a knack for the game."

"Dream on." Spinner grinned, suddenly energized despite everything. She hurried toward the locker room. Amazing that Dael had agreed to a fleet-wide party. She tried to picture Dael pitching the idea to the other captains. She would've loved to be present for that communication.

CHAPTER TWELVE

Dael stood at the far end of the section of the assault-craft bay where the crew had made a place for dancing. She had already circulated once between the different venues, even having a small glass of brandy. Surprised at how skilled whoever was making it was becoming, she'd savored the drink before swinging by the spin-jack rooms. There—of course—Spinner and her entourage were busy winning at their respective tables. A flat, emotionless expression had replaced Spinner's normally easy-to-read demeanor as she sat slumped in her chair, her eyes carefully scanning her opponents. Dael stopped at the table long enough to see how this frustrated the other players, especially the captain of the Mugdon, who was shoving pharmo nuts into his mouth at an increasing speed as the game progressed.

Unsurprisingly, Spinner put her cards down after placing her last one in the pile, faceup. "Spin jack," she said, matter-of-factly, a tiny smile at the corners of her mouth.

"Damn it, not again!" Captain Gossamay said, and frowned. "I should've known better."

"How's that, *sir*?" Spinner shot him a glance as she gathered the cards and her winnings. The other three players at the table stiffened visibly, as did Dael.

"You win a lot. You're the local cardsharp, or so the rumor has it. How can anyone have this much luck, that's what I want to know."

"What are you suggesting?" This time Spinner didn't even bother with the "sir" as her eyes became darkened slits.

"You tell me, Seclan." Leaning forward on his elbows, Gossamay pulled his lower lip up. "I say it's too much luck and warrants a certain…caution on our part."

"You're accusing me of cheating? Stacking the deck? In essence stealing from my shipmates—my pilots that I trust my life with, that I'd give my life *for*?" Spinner's voice was low still, but flames erupted in her eyes now.

"Nobody's accusing you of anything, Spinner. Are we, Captain Gossamay?" Dael stepped into the light around the table.

Gossamay flinched; he clearly hadn't seen her before now. "Sir," he said, and rose.

"As you were, Captain. Keep enjoying the game in all friendliness. Spinner? I'm sorry to drag you away from all this fun, but I need a moment of your time, as a member of the party committee."

"Yes, sir." Spinner tossed the deck on the table and left her markers. "Do share the chips among yourselves. I only agreed to play in this tournament to show everybody a few techniques and strategies."

Dael knew Spinner well enough to detect the hurt beneath her cool tone. As they walked out into the corridor, Dael regarded her surreptitiously. "I would surmise Captain Gossamay is a bit of a sore loser."

"A bit."

"And he didn't take too kindly to losing to a person below him in rank."

"True. And I'm a woman. He must be one of the last of the male chauvinists." Shrugging, Spinner sighed. "Where are we going, by the way?"

"Not sure. To the assault-craft bay, I think. I'm told it's quite transformed." Dael chuckled at the look of bewilderment on Spinner's face. "I really didn't need you for official business—"

"But you wanted to get me out of there before I struck a superior officer." Spinner finally relaxed, grinning now. "I owe you, Admiral."

"Dael. Remember. You're off the clock."

"Dael." Spinner shoved her hands into the pockets of her black trousers. Her blue metallic shell left her toned arms bare, and the feather-beaded necklace she wore looked exotic around her neck.

Dael had always regarded Spinner as not very feminine, but this outfit emphasized her female form in a most alluring way.

Shocked at her own thought, Dael ripped her gaze from Spinner's body. "Here we are. Who made the playlist?"

"Gazer and his wife. They're accomplished amateur musicians, which came in handy." Spinner's cheeks were colored a faint pink as they turned the corner and entered the assault-craft bay.

Ribbons and fabric hid most of the vessels, blinking lights set the mood, and the music pulsed enticingly. People filled the dance-floor area, swaying to the rhythm, faces aglow and smiling. Dael now knew that Darmiya was right. This was a very good idea. The crews were bonding, and she hadn't seen such happy smiles since they left Oconodos. All hell could break out tomorrow, they all knew this, but tonight, a party was going on and the crew was having fun.

"Do you dance, Spinner?" Dael didn't turn her head, merely spoke out loud, hoping for an answer.

"Um, dance? Sure, but nothing fancy."

"I would call this more fun than fancy. Do you want to dance?"

"I don't know—wait, you mean with you?" Spinner looked shocked.

"If not me, then go ask someone else." So awkward now, Dael felt as if someone had shoved clothes hangers into her dress. It flowed around her in pretty green waves, but Spinner's words made her long for her starched uniform instead.

"I'd love to dance with you, Admiral." Spinner bowed cordially and held out her hand.

Finally able to swallow again, Dael took it and they entered the outer perimeter of the dance floor. The fast beat of the song felt alien to Dael at first and she moved conservatively, unlike some of the very young people who spun like whirlwinds in the center of the crowd. Spinner moved lithely, no crazy moves, but flowing and way too sexily. Dael swallowed as Spinner's shell rode up, showing her midsection very briefly as Spinner danced with her arms extended above her head.

Gradually relaxing and allowing the music to fill her senses, Dael let her body move of its own volition. She couldn't take her eyes off Spinner, even if she tried, and soon they were dancing closer, nearly touching.

The music shifted, slowed to a low, pulsating beat that sent people into each other's arms. Around Dael and Spinner, the crew and the civilians held each other tight as they swayed to the music. Before Dael even had time to realize they could leave the dance floor, Spinner's right arm wrapped around her shoulders and her left hand cupped Dael's waist.

Her breath hitching, Dael couldn't do anything else but reciprocate and mirror Spinner's touch. They swayed slowly, not really taking any elaborate steps but merely rocking back and forth from side to side. A female voice Dael recognized but couldn't name started singing longingly of a lost love. The words cut deeper than Dael would ever admit, but they also made her press her forehead against Spinner's shoulder. It was a way to hide her expression, but also a way to stealthily inhale the other woman's scent and feel her warmth.

Spinner tightened her arms around Dael. The idea of holding this elegant, stunningly beautiful woman at all, let alone in a close embrace as they swayed to the music, was almost beyond belief. When Dael had asked her to dance, Spinner was sure she'd misunderstood and was about to commit the ultimate faux pas, but when the invitation had turned out to be real, she nearly lost her nerve.

Humming quietly to the famous song about lost love, Spinner inhaled the sweet citrus and flower scent of her dance partner. She knew better than to try to talk. Nothing she could say would make this moment any better—it was perfect as it was. Spinner could tell from the furtive glances around them that they were attracting a bit of attention, but she honestly didn't care. If the admiral wanted to dance, surely she was allowed to do so. It was probably not the most clever of moves to dance with a person whose reputation was as colorful as Spinner's, but she didn't bother with that notion either. This wasn't likely to happen again, and she was damn well going to enjoy it while it lasted. That's when it happened.

Dael moved closer and leaned her forehead against Spinner's shoulder, holding her closer around her waist. Spinner instantly forgot how to breathe, only to gasp for air a moment later. Dael moved her head again, now resting her left temple against Spinner, which meant her breath caressed the skin on Spinner's neck.

This reaction, this *attraction,* wasn't something she'd confessed to before, even to herself. Always so pragmatic, and definitely not romantic, Spinner had used sex as a sort of physical stress relief more than anything else. Now, with this astonishing woman in her arms, her heart was racing past all possible limits, and all she could think was how lovely it felt and how good Dael smelled.

It had to end. Of course it did. The music went back to a wild dance song, the beat drowning out any normal thought, which made both of them take a step back, Dael actually grimacing while gesturing to her ears. She pointed toward the assault-craft bay doors. Spinner automatically nodded and guided her away from the floor and out into the corridor. There, she remembered who she was holding onto and quickly lowered her hand.

"That was…nice." Dael looked slightly flustered. "I haven't danced in a long time."

"Neither have I." And Spinner knew she'd give almost any body part to do it again. With Dael.

"It was very enjoyable," Dael said, sounding even more formal than usual. "Thank you."

"You're welcome." She ought to be the one giving thanks. Spinner lowered her eyes to the deck before convincing herself to dare meet Dael's gaze again. "I enjoyed it. A lot," she whispered. "I hope this won't cause trouble for you."

Frowning now, Dael tilted her head. "Trouble? How so?"

"You saw how Captain Gossamay reacted. I tend to stir up trouble without even trying to. I wouldn't want anything to interfere with your command—"

"And you think my command of this fleet is so weak that a dance with one of my pilots could jeopardize it?" Her eyes growing colder by the second, Dael straightened her back.

"What?" Spinner's mind whirled, trying to figure out what the hell she'd done now to destroy the best moment she'd had in forever.

"No, not at all. I didn't mean that. I—I, well, I guess you just proved my point, Admiral." She hated the tone of defeat in her voice as she tried to explain herself.

"How do you figure that?"

"We both enjoyed the dance, and then I seemed to destroy it with just a few words." She made sure her lips stretched into her trademark broad grin. This way, Dael had no way of knowing just how horribly tears burned behind her eyelids at the same time.

Instead, Dael relaxed marginally. "All you did was express concern for my sake, didn't you? My reputation?"

Relieved, but still upset, Spinner could only nod.

"And I go into full 'how dare you question me' mode." Dael touched Spinner's lower arm briefly.

A small crowd, cheering and singing, walked toward them, and Spinner gently motioned for Dael to follow her behind one of the doors leading to a storage area. The light was dim, but she could still see Dael's surprised expression.

"I do worry that people may unfairly criticize you for interfering when Captain Gossamay nearly accused me of cheating. And then you even danced with me, a slow dance, at that."

"If anyone has something to say with whom I choose to dance, or my prerogative to break up something that could've escalated into a very ugly event, it'll be my extreme pleasure to set them straight." Dael's lips formed a predatory smile.

"For the love of the Creator, you sound like you'd enjoy that a little too much." Spinner smiled carefully in return. "Well, since we dodged that bullet, I'm glad you asked me to dance and I don't harbor any regrets. Any longer."

"Good." Dael kissed Spinner's cheek, her lips barely touching flesh, but still Spinner's knees trembled. The irony of her clichéd reaction didn't escape her. She found her bearings quickly enough to reciprocate with a similar caress. Dael's quick, unsteady intake of breath didn't escape her.

"I think I need to keep mingling in the different rooms for another hour. I know the party doesn't end until yet another hour after that, but I want to check on Nania. She spent two hours with the other seniors, and no doubt I'm going to get an earful of how that's too close to basket weaving."

"Basket weaving?" Spinner snorted. "Is that what she calls totally boring activities?"

"Exactly," Dael said. "Well. Thank you for the dance. Enjoy the rest of the evening, but I recommend staying away from the spin-jack tables—for tonight at least."

"Good advice." Spinner planned to head for her quarters. She needed to think, to regroup from her confusing emotions.

"Good night."

"Good night, Dael."

Dael smiled briefly and disappeared down the corridor. Spinner took a deep breath. For the first time, she wished she had a loved one with her aboard the *Espies Major*. She didn't have anyone to confide in that wasn't directly involved with Dael at one point, professionally speaking. Never much for girl-talk, she could for the first time see the benefit of having a special friend to confide in. She thought of Darmiya. Maybe one day they'd be that close, but her new friend seemed to have a bit of a crush on her. That didn't make her a good choice as a confidante.

Spinner found an unoccupied lift, which took her to deck seven where her quarters were located. Running into several partygoers, she smiled automatically and breathed a sigh of relief when she could finally close the door behind her. She went through her usual evening ablutions, more out of habit than anything else, and tumbled into bed. After pulling the covers over her head, she left a tiny gap next to her mouth and nose, for air to flow.

She needed the cocooning, a remnant of her childhood when her absent mother had left her in the hands of a father who not only disliked being left to take care of two children on his own, but who also blamed said children for her leaving in the first place. When she closed her eyes, she could hear him rant at her younger brother. She saw images of him raising his hand to hit and how she leaped between them, absorbing her brother's punishment. This punishment fell upon the two Seclan children continuously until Spinner was sixteen and legally emancipated herself from her father and took her brother with her. He tried to stop her, but she'd recorded enough evidence of the abuse for the courts to give her custody.

Spinner squeezed her eyes shut. All these scars and memories because Pamas Seclan had left them. It hadn't been Spinner or her brother's fault. The blame would always fall on her mother, for leaving, and her father, for the abuse.

Closing her eyes even tighter, Spinner used the same technique she had perfected during many years. She willed herself to sleep.

CHAPTER THIRTEEN

Dael Caydoc
Admiral
Day 134
Advance mission
Personal log

Three days ago, our long-distance sensors confirmed our hope that one of the planets in the star system we just reached has an atmosphere that can sustain human life. No animals that can prove too dangerous are registering, nor do we detect signs of any civilization. I've coordinated with the sister ships for teams to explore parts of the three major continents. As this is of immense importance, I've decided to accompany the team that will explore the southern hemisphere. The imagery we're receiving shows luxuriant foliage and clear lakes and rivers. I cannot wait to breathe new air.

Commander Seclan will head up the mission of mapping the planet from the air. Two hundred of the assault craft have been outfitted with cameras to perform this task, as we will need reliable maps if we are to recommend this world to our leaders on Oconodos.

Commander Weniell isn't happy about my going planetside, but these days he knows better than to try to stop me. It's also a matter of morale. If I hesitated to set foot on a new world, how could I ask any of my crew, or their loved ones for that matter, to do it?

End recording

Dael inhaled the sweet, wonderful air where she stood next to the freighter, which had landed on a meadow not far from a wide river. Flowers in all kinds of purple, pink, and white were sprinkled over the field. At the far north from their position, a dense forest stretched in a semicircle for several klicks.

"I think we should put up our base camp farther toward the tree line, sir." Ensign Umbahr stood at her side, his binoculars raised to eye level. "That way, we're protected if we have bad weather."

"You're expecting bad weather?" Dael looked up at the sky. Farther east, some clouds were gathering.

"According to *Espies Major*'s forecast, we might have rain, or perhaps hail. Our habitats should protect us, but being too much out in the open isn't a good idea. We have no way of knowing how strong the winds can become on this planet. Perhaps we should get you back to *Espies*—"

"No. I'm staying. Have the crew put up the habitats in the location you deem best, and tell the scientists to start collecting samples. I will join the team ready to explore the forest."

Umbahr looked like he wanted to argue against this but clearly opted to not ignite his admiral's wrath. Dael smiled inwardly. Smart move.

She joined the forest team, who were arming themselves as she approached them. The leader, Lieutenant Schpay, nodded briskly as Dael started doing the same. Tucking two sidearms into her hip holster, she opted for a crossbow and draped two full belts of darts across her chest. One held tranquilizers strong enough to sedate a fully grown golo bull, and the other, darts meant to kill on impact. The modern-day crossbow didn't have a lot in common with the ancient hunting weapon used four hundred years ago. This weapon was indeed as silent as the old-fashioned crossbow, but Dael chose it whenever possible because it could be used with a multitude of projectiles: everything from old-fashioned arrows to high-technological darts for different purposes. Dael knew some hunters used aerosol-darts able to kill several animals simultaneously without damaging the meat. You needed a special permit to use such darts as a hunter, and since that had never been an interest of hers, she had never requested one. Her sidearms were charged with a hundred rounds of metal-tipped garnets each. Her holster held two hundred rounds more.

"Don't forget to wear a helmet, sir." Schpay motioned toward a chest sitting next to the arms locker.

She wasn't fond of wearing protective gear—she found it restrictive when it came to moving fast—but knew it was insane not to. The vest contained shoulder pads that extended outward around her shoulders, covering her entire torso from the hip up. She strapped leg braces around her thighs and attached them to the rings at the bottom of the vest. Moving her arms in a wide circle, she was fairly pleased with her movability.

"I'm all set. Everyone ready?" she asked Schpay.

"Yes, sir. Ensign Toshian is taking point, you and I will pair up behind him, and we'll have six more security guards behind us. We're also bringing two zoologists. They'll document and perhaps take samples if we encounter local wildlife."

"Very well. You're in charge of this team. Lead on." Dael was happy to let her crew lead so she could mainly observe. She'd handpicked a lot of the senior staff and even some of the junior officers. They in turn had handpicked their subordinates, which meant she trusted them to do their job well also.

They crossed the field in formation, ready to engage potential dangers. It was as if the planet was trying to show its best side though. The sun warmed enough to cause rivulets of sweat to run down Dael's back under her uniform. The tight vest wasn't helping keep her cool.

As they closed in on the tree line, Dael started to wonder if they would be able to make their way inside, as the foliage looked almost like one brown-green wall. Schpay and Toshian each produced a large hatchet-looking blade and began slashing away at the smaller twigs, thus creating a passage.

If the air was sweet out on the meadow, it was thick and sugary inside the forest. Very little light filtered through, and for some reason, the planet looked less idyllic in here. Dael pressed two sensors on her helmet, one to turn on a light and the other to lower a mesh visor. Schpay and the others did the same.

"All right, people. Toshian and I will take point. We need two in the front to cover each other. Behind us, Ensigns Coymi and Daga will take up the flank on either side of the admiral." Schpay stated everyone's position with a calm voice that didn't allow for any objections or questions. Dael wasn't entirely pleased about being given the rookie position, but Schpay would have been neglectful in his duties if he didn't safeguard the highest-ranking officer's position.

"Let's move in. Sharp attention." Schpay motioned for Toshian to keep chopping away at the foliage they encountered, effectively creating a path for the team behind them.

The greenery, so lush and beautiful, both awed Dael and made her cautious as she carefully stepped inside this forest. The ground felt spongy, as if they were walking on centuries of decaying plants that could hide just about anything.

After half an hour, they reached a clearing. Here the sun reached the ground, which hardened it and made it easier to walk on. In the center a large rock formation gave them all pause. It didn't look manmade exactly, but deliberately stacked. The individual rocks were as big as Dael's fist.

"How the hell did they get there like this? And why?" Ensign Toshian rubbed his neck under his tall collar. "That's not a natural formation."

"Could it be animals?" a female ensign asked from behind Dael. "The rocks look like someone rolled them here and piled them up."

"Could be," Toshian said, but sounded hesitant. "I have to scan them for traces of DNA." He stepped closer, and Dael was just about to caution him when a small, rodent-like creature scurried out from the pile of rocks. Dael raised her crossbow, aiming it at the light-brown creature. It was about the size of Dael's lower arm and twice as wide. Its fur was matted and dirty, which Oconodian rodents usually wouldn't put up with. They groomed themselves obsessively, but this creature looked like it never bothered.

"Don't shoot it, sir," the female ensign said urgently, and moved halfway in front of Dael. "We need to collect samples of these—ow, shit!" The young woman jumped back as the rodent suddenly stood on its back paws and opened its mouth wider than what seemed possible. Large fangs seemed to shoot from its lower jaw, and something sprayed in a fine mist from its mouth.

"Did anything get on you, Tanith?" Schpay barked as they moved back in unison.

"Just above my glove. Stings like hell.

Dael wasn't going to take any chances. Having never lowered her crossbow, she fired a dart set to kill into the small animal. It fell over with a squeal, a high-pitched, chilling sound. The ground seemed to move under Dael's feet and she backed up farther.

"Fall back. I think this was a huge mistake," Dael barked, taking over command.

"Sir! Watch out!" Toshian yelled as he fired relentlessly with his garnet rifle. The rounds singed the rocks as he sprayed the pile. Despite his direct aim, a flood of rodents streamed out of the many exits, all of them emanating the same high-pitched squeals. Dael's heart pounded and felt like it moved up into her throat, making it impossible to swallow. Disregarding the threatening panic, she kept firing and heard the rest of the team do the same.

"We've got to get out of here." Toshian's voice nearly broke as he almost fell while trying to kick two rodents off his leg.

Dael knew it would be close to impossible. The dense forest was treacherous at best, and trying to move out while firing at the rodents, who moved much faster in this terrain, wouldn't work.

"Form a circle and keep firing. Tanith, you're injured. Stay inside the circle and call for backup." Dael glared at them. "Now!"

Their training kicked in and they formed a circle, all of them facing outward while shooting at the vicious creatures. Dael heard Tanith call for backup, and one of the voices answering her rather panicked plea was Spinner's.

"Tell the admiral to hold on. We're on our way. I have your coordinates, Tanith."

"Hurry, oh, please, hurry."

Concerned at the slur she detected in Tanith's voice, Dael risked turning her head to look at her. Something in the substance the small animal had sprayed on Tanith was making her ill. Her skin, where it was visible, was turning a strange yellow, and the white in her eyes was yellow as well, with redness at the rims. Her legs trembled and she was clutching her communicator.

"Hold it together, Tanith, do you hear me?" Dael was afraid Tanith would go down and be swamped by the rodents, who seemed to be quite tactical hunters. They kept circling the group of twelve humans.

"I'm running low, sir," one of the crewmen called out.

"Here." Dael dislodged two of her clips with rounds for her sidearms. "Can you reach them?"

"Yeah. I have them." The clips disappeared from her hand. "Thanks."

"Make every one of them count." She raised her crossbow again after reloading it with more lethal mini-missiles. Help would come, but at the rate these horrifically poisonous little creatures kept growing in numbers, it might not come quick enough.

"We have to fall back toward the west, sir," Schpay called out. "Seems like these damn rodents are getting reinforcements before we do. We're surrounded, but they're scarcer toward the west."

Glancing quickly in Schpay's direction, Dael verified his conclusion. "Help Toshian. I'll make a wider path among these horrid creatures." She drew both her sidearms, kept them slightly apart, and fired at the rodents as she made them scurry to the side. Some hissed at her, spraying whatever venom they possessed, but her gear and uniform were protecting her. So far.

"Just keep going, sir. We're right behind you."

"Don't let anyone fall behind, Lieutenant!" Dael watched carefully where she put her feet. If she fell among the small animals, it was all over. Toshian's reaction to having a miniscule amount of the venom made for chilling theories as to what would occur if someone were doused in the substance on a larger area or, worse, got it in their eyes or mouth.

"Sir! Watch out!" Schpay called, making Dael stop cold. Behind her, an ensign half-carrying Toshian accidentally pushed her forward. Flailing to regain her balance, Dael knew she wouldn't make it. She closed her eyes hard as she fell.

CHAPTER FOURTEEN

Assault Craft 25, this is the CAG. You have the lead position. Keep mapping and surveying the northern hemisphere using ACs 26 to 200. ACs 2 to 24, follow me to the southern hemisphere. Acknowledge."

A series of tiny lights lit up Spinner's console, showing her that everyone knew what she expected of them. She changed heading and saw on her sensors twenty-three assault crafts out of the original two hundred do the exact same maneuver.

"Spinner to *Espies Major* bridge. We're en route to the site on the southern hemisphere to assist the admiral and her team." Her ribs clenched around her lungs, making her feel out of breath. The initial request for assistance hadn't provided a lot of information. "I need continuous updates."

"Admiral Caydoc is with a team in the forest. Ensign Umbahr received an alert transmission, requesting backup. He said the voice on the other end was definitely that of Lieutenant Schpay." Commander Weniell spoke fast.

"Any information regarding the status of the admiral?"

"Apart from knowing Schpay was clearly alive and able to talk three minutes ago, we have not been able to reach them. Umbahr is moving in with a team. I need you to perform a short-range sensor sweep at these coordinates. Transmitting them now."

Spinner's computer console beeped. "Received and logged in, sir."

"Help the crew on the ground to find them, CAG."

"Will do, sir. CAG out." When the first landmass of the southern hemisphere appeared on her screen, Spinner regarded the coordinates and adjusted her course as she transmitted them to the rest of her subordinates. "These are the coordinates where the admiral and her team were last heard from. Something has gone wrong, and the team on the ground needs to know their exact location in the area. It consists of dense woods, so use the short-range sensors and fly as low as you can without planting your face in the bedrock. Acknowledge."

Yet again, the small line of lights showed everyone was alert and knew what to do.

As they raced to reach the presumed idyllic area where, for all she knew, Dael and her crew could be dead or dying, Spinner used every single method she'd perfected over the years to remain calm and focused. She couldn't afford to allow her heart to rule her actions.

She'd saved many lives, directly and indirectly, during her career. Her latest direct effort had been Gazer, who now was back flying as her wingman. Before that, she had rescued the military secretary, her husband, and her security detail. Those daring rescues had paid off because she focused and did her job, went above and beyond, as that was the only way she knew how to operate. Yet this time it was about Dael—the woman who'd chosen to dance with her in front of everyone present, who'd kissed her cheek. Granted, their paths had hardly crossed in a private setting since the party, but regardless of that…this was *Dael*.

"All right, people. The area is coming up in front of us, five klicks ahead. Wing-to-wing formation. Sensors to maximum resolution. Doppler engaged. Heat sensitivity engaged. Acknowledge."

They moved as one in a low swoop, nearly touching the treetops. Spinner let her bird keep the required distance from the ground and her wingmen while her eyes never left the sensor readings. *Damn it, Dael, I'm coming for you. I swear I am.*

Two flybys later, she still saw no signals larger than tiny blips on the sensors, and she was beginning to despair. Cold sweat dripped down her back, and she operated the controls with stiff fingertips. She had to check the internal sensors to make sure the interior temperature wasn't below freezing, which of course it wasn't.

"One more round, people," Spinner said, disregarding her ever-clenched jaws. "This time, one click farther south. Acknowledge."

Another swoop, this time actually grazing the treetops. And one par later, a massive sensor reading. Several voices called out over the communication system. "I see it, I see it. Shut up now, all of you." Spinner hit another channel sensor. "CAG to Lt. Umbahr, CAG to *Espies Major*. Transmitting coordinates that our sensors picked up. Looks like a massive blip. Too big to be just the team. I estimate that they're under attack by some sort of wildlife."

"Good job, CAG. Return to mapping and surveying—"

"Negative, sir." Spinner interrupted Weniell. "You have more than a hundred and fifty of my assault crafts doing that. I'm setting my team down and we'll be assisting Umbahr's rescue efforts."

"Spinner, do not—"

Spinner hit the sensor again, effectively silencing her commanding officer, who she couldn't be bothered with at the moment. If this landed her in the brig, so be it. "CAG to assault craft 2 to 24, land in circular formation on the meadow to the far south of the forest. Use caution, as Umbahr's team has already erected some habitats. Acknowledge."

The assault craft descended in a perfect circle and touched down onto the beautiful flower-filled meadow.

"Looks too damn pretty to be true," Spinner muttered as she unclasped her harness. Opening the arms locker, she strapped on two sidearms and a crossbow. She also took a four-barreled rifle and made sure she had enough rounds to take out a small village by herself. As she opened the hatch, she glanced quickly around to make sure no beasts were waiting to munch on her. She jumped onto the ground, landing softly on the grass, and her pilots did the same. Some of them had taken off their helmets, and she scowled at them.

"Put the cans back on, people. You don't know what's in that forest."

When twenty-four of them were suitably protected, Spinner fell into a jog toward the forest, when all she wanted was to race there as fast as possible. But she needed to conserve her strength to avoid being totally exhausted once she reached the team. Soon enough they passed the treeline. Inside the dense forest, she felt nearly blind. "Try night vision," she ordered her team. "I see a manmade path over there. I'll take point again. Gazer, you take rear. We do *not* deviate from the path, is that clear?"

Voices agreeing streamed through her headset. Spinner motioned with her hand and began making her way as she scanned the area around them with the sensors built into her helmet. Again, she wanted to run but instead strode as fast as she could.

They reached a clearing after a while. A rock formation in the center looked too constructed to be naturally occurring. The team spread out and examined the structure and the ground around it.

"Sir!" Gazer waved her over. "This registers as human blood." He pointed at the ground.

Spinner regarded the spots on the ground. They weren't large enough to warrant concern, but she still shrugged off a serious case of goose bumps. "Any chance of determining whose blood?"

"Hang on, my scanner is processing it. Usually takes a bit of—ah, it's Ensign Toshian's."

"I see."

"Wait, there's more. It' mixed with some sort of alien toxin, which has some weird qualities. I'm filing this for transmission later when we're out of this Creator-forsaken place."

"Good." Reading the footprints, Spinner estimated the direction Dael's team had taken. Then she knelt, regarding something between the familiar prints from Oconodian-issued boots. "Look at this. Tiny paws. With long needles like claws. I couldn't see any of them over there in the clearing where the ground was much harder. These must be from the enemy, the creatures responsible for the attack."

"You're right. Look at the number of them." Gazer grimaced and hoisted his crossbow.

"CAG to 2 to 24. Use extreme caution. We're dealing with some creatures that look deceptively small. We don't know if they come from the trees or the ground, so stay alert." Spinner motioned for them to follow her as she tracked the boot prints and the tiny paw prints. "Where the hell are Umbahr and his team? The *Espies Major* and we both sent the coordinates. They should've been here before us."

"I have no idea, sir." Gazer shrugged. "We just have to keep tracking Caydoc's team."

He was right. Once they found Dael and the others, they'd go after Umbahr's team. The path was becoming increasingly narrow, as if the ones in charge of cutting down branches and other small shrubbery didn't have time to perform any more than the rudimentary amount.

Spinner called out as her foot caught on something, perhaps a big root, and she went down on her knees. Gazer was at her side ready to haul her up, when she stopped him. The item crossing the path wasn't a root. Instead she was staring at a leg clad in shredded uniform fabric.

"Help me here, Gazer. It's one of ours." Spinner swallowed against her fear. It better not be Dael or she'd go homicidal on these creatures they had yet to encounter. She pushed the branches away, broke some, and knew Gazer was swinging the large knife he carried above her. Eventually they uncovered a slender body lying facedown across the path. Carefully, Spinner tore off her glove and felt for a pulse beneath the casualty's visor. The skin was cold and damp, and no pulsations betrayed life in the person.

"Dead," Spinner said. "Gazer, help me roll them." Her. It turned out to be a woman. Chalk-white face, filmed-over eyes staring into nothing, mouth half open. It wasn't Dael. It was Toshian.

"Fuck," Spinner whispered. "Whatever those vicious creatures are, they did a number on her. I hope she was dead beforehand." Toshian's uniform was shredded beyond recognition. Tiny claws had scratched at pale skin, and something, perhaps small, long teeth, had punctured the pulse points they could reach. Swallowing repeatedly, Spinner gently put Toshian down, making sure no one else would trample her. "Place a marker on her harness so we find her again later. We have to keep going."

Pressing her lips together, Spinner rose and continued along the barely visible path. Every few steps she made sure no other bodies lay strewn in their way, but as far as she could see, Toshian was the only victim.

Suddenly she thought she heard something. Stopping, she raised her hand, giving the sign for her team to stop and be quiet. Distant voices coming from farther northeast made her want to start running, but she couldn't make out what they were saying, and unless she was mistaken, she thought she detected smoke. Her flight suit was entirely closed to the surrounding environment, but faint tendrils of dark-gray smoke wisped among the greenery.

"Something's going on up there," Spinner muttered over the communication channel. "Gazer, take 10 to 24 over to the left and then move in on my signal. I'll bring 3 to 9 with me on the left flank. Weapons drawn, rifles on high, crossbows to kill."

"Aye, sir." Gazer nodded solemnly, and she could tell from the tension around his eyes that he didn't expect this one to be easy.

"Let's honor Toshian by getting all our team members back in one piece. All right?" Spinner motioned for them all to commence moving. She lowered herself, bending halfway forward to remain just below the smoke, not because she was afraid to inhale it—that wasn't possible because of her flight suit and helmet. Instead, the smoke could make visibility a challenge, and she wouldn't be able to rescue anything if she stepped right into whatever had killed Toshian.

Soon they were close enough for Spinner to get a better idea of what was going on. At the forefront of Dael's team, Lt. Schpay was swinging a large branch that was on fire, keeping what looked like oversized rats at bay. And were those fangs sticking out of the lower jaws? She shuddered. Every now and then a "rat" would come too close and seemed to spray something, and a strange thing happened. Whatever was in their glands was combustible. No wonder most of the creatures kept their distance. If their toxin made contact with the fire that Schpay and the others fire brandished, they virtually exploded.

Spinner motioned for her team to pull off branches and light them.

"CAG to Gazer. Alert your team that we need to create fire in order to help Caydoc and her people over there."

"I see it. We're collecting branches already. Can you spot Caydoc from your end?"

"Negative. She might be injured." The idea of any of the toxin ending up on Dael's skin nauseated Spinner. Determined to get to the team ahead of them quickly, she yanked a branch free and placed her sidearm against it, firing a low charge that made it erupt into flames instantly.

"Follow me. Don't let any of those damn rats near you. We don't know how much of their toxin is required to kill you."

They hurried toward Schpay and the others, swinging branches, and the closer they got, the clearer it became how worn out the men and women securing the perimeter were.

"CAG to Schpay. Keep going, and don't take your eyes off the animals. Reinforcement is here. Twenty-four of my pilots and I are approaching with more fire."

"Oh, thank the Creator." Schpay huffed as he swung his branch in a wide circle. "I have six people down. Two with toxin on their skin, one with a broken leg, one with severe bites, and two with head injuries."

"Can you give me the admiral's status?" Spinner hurried on, so close now to Schpay she could see how the small animals were now turning their heads in her and her team's direction. "CAG to team, watch yourselves. They've caught our scent now. We don't know how tactically advanced the rats are. They might circle around us."

"Count on it. That's what they did with us, before the admiral fell down the ravine."

"She what?" Spinner shivered. "What happened?"

"She…she was trying to create a safe way for us to fall back, taking point. As the creatures attacked in great numbers, neither of us had seen the ravine. She stepped out into thin air and disappeared over the edge."

"And she's alive?"

"Last I heard. One of my team climbed down. No creatures down there with them, so I would say that's our route to fall back if we could just get the chance. Ah!"

Throwing herself forward, Spinner saw Schpay go down on one knee. Perhaps he had tripped, or something could have attacked from behind. Spinner ran, wielding her burning branch. As she was only two secs away, she saw three or four of the rodents hanging from Schpay's left uniform sleeve. Not hesitating, Spinner jumped forward, stabbing at the attacking animals with her branch. Screaming with a terrible, piercing hissing sound, they let go and scurried away. Spinner tugged at Schpay just as the rest of her team approached from both flanks, screaming and chasing back the rodents. Gazer had let go of his branch and was spraying round after round into the now-fleeing animals.

"Oh, thank the Creator," Schpay said, and staggered to his feet. "We ran out of ammunition a while ago."

"Let's get down the ravine before they come back." Spinner looked around her. "We need people to deploy rope ladders. Are the wounded secured enough to go into the ravine in hammocks?"

"Yes. As long as we maintained the perimeter, I had two people administer field dressings, neck collars, and ortho-support." His eyes darkened. "I also have one deceased on the trail toward the clearing with the rock formation."

"Toshian. Yes, we saw her. We'll send a special angel-guard back for her." Spinner's heart fluttered at one of the saddest assignment a team could perform. Angel-guards meant bringing home a fallen comrade-in-arms. It usually brought entire silence to a unit until their colleague and friend was back. Spinner briefly touched his shoulder. "In the meantime, we have to rescue the living. In her honor, right, Lieutenant Schpay?"

"Yes, sir." He pushed his shoulders back and took in the scene around them. "As your team is holding the perimeter we need to evacuate our wounded. Do you have amplifiers for the communicators? I haven't been able to get much more than static when trying to reach the *Espies Major*."

"We do. I need to go down to confirm the admiral's status. Here, connect the amplifier to your system and start sending exact coordinates. One evac freighter should be able to transport all of the wounded in one run."

"Aye, sir."

"All right. Get to it and I'll lower myself down the ravine. No signs of any creatures down there?"

"Not so far," Schpay said wryly.

"Reassuring." Spinner crossed the area Schpay and his team had fought so hard to preserve, taking a few moments to reassure the wounded that help was coming. The two crewmembers in charge of keeping them comfortable and above all, alive, seemed rattled and pale but held themselves together.

"You'll all be out of here soon. We have more than twenty-five people guarding the perimeter." More would come if Ensign Umbahr's team finally showed up. Spinner was getting worried. What if they'd run into another horde of those rats?

Two of Schpay's team members stood over by the edge of the ravine, both armed with thick burning branches. "Listen up," Spinner said. "Here are some extra rounds. I don't have a lot left, but enough for you to have at least two more cartridges each."

"Thank you, sir," the crewmember on the left, a young woman, said, glancing up. She looked as frayed as the others, but also determined, with a steadfast gaze. "You can only do so much with fire sticks."

"True, but from where I stand, you all performed a miracle holding the animals off as long as you did. Now, I'm going down to check on Caydoc. I'll use my own mesh, as those roots don't look entirely reliable."

"Need any help securing it, sir?" the other crewmember, a man, asked.

"No, that's all right. Just keep vigil until the evac freighters come. They'll take the wounded first and then the rest of you. Lieutenant Schpay is calling in the coordinates and information as we speak." Spinner fastened the mesh as she spoke and then lowered herself over the edge. Her legs trembled somewhat, but not so much from fatigue as from superfluous adrenaline. She looked down and spotted two of the crew tending to another one lying motionless on the ground between them. They gazed up and waved frenetically.

"The admiral's become unresponsive, sir," said the one to the left, who sat at Dael's head. "She's breathing, if a bit shallowly, and her pulse is fast and uneven."

Spinner landed with a thud, almost falling over before she caught her balance. Glancing around them, she saw they were almost at the end of the ravine, which opened up onto the large meadow where they'd landed, an estimated four klicks away.

Kneeling next to Dael, she saw the admiral was wearing her headgear with her visor up. Spinner pressed her fingertips against Dael's pulse point on her neck. Her heart rate was indeed fast and uneven. "Sir. Admiral? Can you hear me? Open your eyes, please?" Spinner reluctantly placed two knuckles at Dael's sternum and rubbed hard. It felt heartless to induce more pain, but she needed to know Dael's level of consciousness. "Admiral Caydoc! Open your eyes." She bent closer to Dael's ear, whispering frantically. "Dael. Please!"

Slowly, dark lashes fluttered and opened into narrow slits. Below them, dark circles looked like bruises against Dael's pale skin.

"Mmm. Stop it."

"Then look at me and I will stop, sir. That's it. Help is coming. Evac freighters."

"Crew…toxic creatures…"

"I know, sir. We have the perimeter secure above. You fell down the ravine, remember? No sign of the rats down here." *Yet.*

"My head hurts." Dael shifted as if trying to sit up.

"No, no. You just lie down and relax," Spinner said, feeling utterly ridiculous at such words. Dael's glance showed she agreed. "I mean, don't move until a medical professional has evaluated your condition."

"Very well." Dael closed her eyes.

"Try to stay awake, sir." Spinner made sure no toxic creatures were looming anywhere nearby. When she couldn't detect any movement, she pulled off her right glove and did the same with Dael's and held her hand firmly. Squeezing it, she grinned as Dael's eyes opened more than before. "That's it, sir. Stay awake until the evac gets here. I'm staying with you and the ensigns here. You're safe. I have plenty of ammo, and we can light the branches that these two so cleverly gathered, should any of those rats dare approach us."

"Thank you." Dael squeezed her hand back, very weakly. "Toshian…I saw her go down in the midst of that horrible pile of rodents."

"We lost her, sir." Spinner rubbed her thumb on the back of Dael's hand, trying to console her. She knew how it felt to lose someone under your command, and Dael was in charge of all of them. This was her mission, her responsibility. "I've marked her location, and angel transport will take her home after we've evacuated all the others."

"So young."

"And yet very seasoned. She loved being a part of the Advance team."

"Do—do you?"

"Do I what?" Spinner frowned, trying to keep up. "Oh, you mean, do I love being a part of this mission? Yes. I can't think of anywhere I'd rather be. Well, apart from in this forest with those fucking rats, that is."

A smile ghosted over Dael's face. "Rats, huh? Sure could do without them in the future."

"Yeah. I guess this planet isn't much of a paradise after all."

"I'll say." Dael stopped talking, looking too exhausted and pale. She didn't close her eyes again but kept her eyes trained on Spinner, as if the sight of her wayward pilot grounded her.

"I hear the freighter." Spinner looked up. "We'll have you in the infirmary in no—"

"Sir! Look!" The female ensign stood, frantically lighting her branch. "Oh, Creator of Oconodos, we can never hold all of them off."

Spinner looked in horror at the veritable billowing field of rodents approaching from the inner depths of the ravine. She lit several branches and placed them in the ground between Dael and the onslaught of animals. The hissing sound from them sounded like triumphant laughter. Clearly their toxin had no intraspecies effect, as a faint mist hovered all around them. What happened if a person inhaled that stuff? Surely that couldn't be good. Visions of Toshian's body, torn to pieces and with burns from the toxin all over, made her grip her weapon harder with one hand and her communicator with the other. She hoped her message would still go through even though she'd given her amplifier to Lieutenant Schpay.

"CAG to evac freighter, what's your status?"

The hover pilot answered immediately and the connection was good. "Landing in a few minutes on the meadow, sir."

"Negative. Fly hover-style into the ravine. You have our coordinates. We're under attack by the indigenous creatures. We don't have time to run with stretchers. Not sure what the situation is above the ravine, but we're looking at thousands of animals here."

"I'll see if it's doable to hover into there."

"Hurry, or the admiral, two ensigns, and I will be dinner." Spinner could imagine the pilot tearing at the controls, stressed, as the life of the admiral depended on his skills.

"Time to lay down cover fire," Spinner said, and stood with her feet a shoulder-width apart, her weapon raised. She was trained to hold this position for hours, and she would as long as she had ammunition. "I need one of your to take care of the third on the left and the other the third on the right. I'll be firing into the middle and overlap with you. Use the pellets setting. Any questions?"

"No, sir," the two ensigns said.

"Fire at will." Spinner opened fire, using the setting on her weapon that sliced the projectiles into nine smaller pellets, spraying them onto the target. She figured with these small and lightning-fast animals, they'd have better luck that way.

The rodents fell in droves as they started shooting. The squealing among them sent shivers all over her skin. She didn't dare take her eyes off her target, even though she wanted to check on Dael more than anything.

"Admiral, talk to me. Are you all right? You still with us?" Spinner bellowed to make herself heard over the weapons' fire.

"Hard to get some rest in this mayhem," Dael said, sounding much closer than Spinner had thought possible. Then two hands supported themselves on her hips. "Keep firing, Spinner."

Dael was standing up? How the hell had she managed that? Was she secretly one of the changed ones or just superhuman in her own way? Spinner felt one of her sidearms being pulled free from her harness. Dael then grabbed hold of the harness and began firing on rodents that had slipped through the onslaught of projectiles.

"We're not going to hold them off for more than a few minutes." Spinner kept shooting, but she focused primarily on making sure she'd catch Dael if the other woman suddenly went down for some reason.

"Just keep shooting. Tell me when you need to reload."

"Yes, sir." Grinning wryly, as having Dael issue orders actually made her feel better, Spinner sprayed more pellets into the mass of rodents. How many were there and how could it be that they moved almost as one? Were they part of some super-rodent hive mind? Groaning at that unpleasant idea, she glanced at the display at the top of her rifle. "Unhook another cartridge, sir!"

"Here." Dael gave her the cartridge as Spinner popped out the used one, letting it fall to the ground. It only took two or three secs, but that was enough for the animals to advance far too close. "Hell!" Firing at the virtual ocean of rodents, Spinner knew they couldn't hold them back. "Dael…"

"I know, Aniwyn. Just keep shooting." Dael clung to her shoulder now, firing also, but with less accuracy than before.

A roar from above nearly deafened Spinner, and she snapped her head back. Six assault craft came from behind them, literally opening fire. Equipped with flamethrowers of the impressive sort, they plowed through the layers of approaching animals.

"Yeah!" Spinner threw her free arm around Dael to keep her from falling. "My people are here—just in time."

"I see, I see," Dael murmured, leaning heavily against Spinner. "Thank the Creator." Then she slumped sideways, dropping Spinner's sidearm as she did indeed go down.

"Dael, oh no." Leaving the ensigns to clean up the few rodents who scurried in all directions in full panic, Spinner lowered Dael carefully to the ground. Holding her gently, she watched the evac freighter hover and then land next to them. Above, another freighter hovered at the level of the forest, extending a ramp over to where the rest of the crewmembers were located.

Four medics came running with a stretcher and cautiously lifted Dael onto it. "You all right, CAG?" one of them asked as they strapped the now-unconscious admiral securely to the stretcher, effectively hooking her up to medical surveillance machines aboard the freighter at the same time.

"I'm fine." Spinner turned to the ensigns. "Let's get aboard. The admiral needs the infirmary, and you're not eager to hang around any longer, are you?"

"No, sir!" The ensigns jumped aboard, shortly followed by Spinner. As the hatch closed, she regarded the charred remnants of the horrible creatures who'd only responded true to their nature, but in such a way that no doubt a lot of the crew would have nightmares about rats for a long time. She strapped herself in for takeoff and couldn't remember when she'd been so relieved to get back into space.

CHAPTER FIFTEEN

Dael moaned and opened her eyes. She could tell she was in one of the infirmary beds. The linen was made of that scratchy mesh she detested, and the lights were hurting her eyes, making her close them again. Slowly this time, she opened her eyes again, blinking a few times before she could focus.

"Ah, Admiral. Welcome back," said the chief medical officer, whom everyone aboard the *Espies Major* lovingly called Doc. His steel-gray, abundant hair framed a weathered face, blue-green eyes, and bushy, black eyebrows. Tall and burly, he leaned over Dael. "You've been napping for about two hours. I was about to try to revive you with some perk-me-up meds, which I'm sure you somehow knew, apparently."

"How did you guess, Doc?" Dael grimaced and sat up. He knew better than to stop her.

"Oh, your dislike for medication and my profession is no secret, Admiral." He smiled. "Although, I must say, even you must agree I come in handy sometimes."

"Doc, you know me better than that. I'm eternally grateful for all the times you saved my rear as well as those of my crew. I just don't like—"

"—not being in control. Being strapped to a gurney and forced to accept medication and treatment. I know." His gaze mellowed. "You took a nasty blow to the head. I'd recommend a night here with us before you return to your quarters."

Smiling briefly, Dael shook her head, immediately wishing she hadn't. "How about a compromise?" she asked. "I go back to my quarters, but I accept whatever medication you decide I may need."

"That, if nothing, shows me how desperate you are to get out of here. Humor me and let me examine you at least once now that you're lucid, sir."

"Very well." Since that gave her enough time to get her bearings, she allowed it.

"Apart from the concussion, you're remarkably unscathed. Bruised, yes, and you'll be sore as hell for the next few days, but all in all, you survived that fall with remarkably little damage."

"And because my crew risked everything to keep me safe," Dael said shortly. "They could've left me, but they didn't."

"Just like you didn't leave Spinner to fend for herself on Gemosis, you mean?" Doc raised a bushy eyebrow. "You may think you hold the crew at an arm's length, in a manner of speaking, but they adore you."

Such words made her more uncomfortable than his examination. Standing up, she looked down at the white shirt that ended just above her knees with dismay. "I want some actual clothes. A leisure suit, size female six." The sooner she got out of this flimsy shirt, the better.

"I'll have a nurse assist you and also bring you some painkillers. I'm going to have to insist that someone from my staff go to your quarters every other hour to check on your neurological status."

"That will not be necessary—"

"Oh, but it will. It's that or I'll pull medical rank and have you confined to a bed here, and it'll go on your permanent record that you had to be removed from duty." His eyes were no longer jovial.

"Fine."

"Good." Doc nodded curtly and left her cubicle. Dael pressed the communication sensor located on the sideboard. "Caydoc to Weniell. Report."

"Sir, you're awake. Thank the Creator." Commander Weniell sounded equal parts relieved and concerned. "How are you?"

"I'm fine. I need an update on the status of the crews, our ships, and our location." She wasn't in the mood to listen to gushing emotional outbursts at this point.

"Of course, Admiral. We have extracted all ground personnel. Their reports show signs of the creatures that attacked your team present all over the southern hemisphere. Only the desert-like areas seem to be free of them, but our people could not survive there as nothing grows and the access to water is extremely limited."

"The air survey?"

"All two hundred vessels returned in one piece. They completed the mapping survey and looked at the northern hemisphere, but our geologists have deemed it cannot sustain our people. The bedrock is infused with so many alien metals that the water and the air would need extreme filtering. They said it would be the same as terraforming the environment, which would take too long and they still couldn't guarantee it would last."

"I see." She was disappointed but not surprised. Just the idea of sharing a world with those venomous rodents made her shudder. "What about Umbahr and his team?"

"They were stuck on a cliff, down to their last cartridges and ready to jump, when we airlifted them out of there."

"So, only one casualty?" Clenching her fists, Dael hugged herself.

"Yes. We retrieved Ensign Toshian's body, and after her postmortem, we'll have the ceremony for her journey to the Creator." Weniell sounded matter-of-fact, as he usually did when dealing with an emotional topic.

"Very good. I'll prepare some words from the command. I need you to talk to her family and friends, let them know they're welcome to speak at her ceremony. I'll personally visit with the family tomorrow." Right now, she'd risk fainting if she stood up for too long.

"Very good, sir."

"Are we still in high orbit with the other ships?" This was one of the things she disliked about the infirmary—no view ports and no screens that showed the stars outside.

"Yes, sir. I didn't want to give the order to resume course at magnetar drive until I had a chance to brief you."

"I consider myself briefed, Commander. As soon as everyone's aboard, do take us out and back on our original course. Time to continue our search. This time I'd love a world without lethal rats."

"I hear you, sir. I'll start the countdown protocol to magnetar drive."

"Keep me informed. I'll be in my quarters once I get out of the infirmary." With a nod, Dael accepted the clothes a nurse brought her. "Caydoc out." She turned to the nurse. "Thank you. As a matter of fact, I may need assistance with putting on the pants, as just tipping my head forward is making me dizzy." It pained her to admit it, but she couldn't disregard the truth.

"Does the doc know, sir?" The nurse—Dael checked her nametag—Lieutenant Mohey, looked concerned. "Your scan showed concussion but no intracranial bleeding. Yet," she added sternly.

"The doc is aware of how I'm doing and we have an agreement," Dael replied, bending the truth just a tad. She hadn't said anything about how dizzy she was.

"Very well. Let me help you." Lieutenant Mohey assisted Dael with her underwear, trousers, and soft boots, which made her feel self-conscious, but she tried to disregard her reaction.

"Thank you," Dael murmured as she pulled on the velvety wool shirt.

"You're welcome, sir. Here are the painkillers. The doc was adamant I watch you take them."

"No doubt he made you promise to shove them down my throat if I didn't cooperate." Dael took the tablets and downed them dry.

"Not in those exact words, but fairly close, yes." Lieutenant Mohey actually smiled, which transformed her narrow face completely. Looking mischievous, she nodded approvingly. "I can now let you go, if reluctantly, as I'm the one tasked with knocking on your door four times tonight. Unless you have someone who can stay with you? Perhaps you can stay at your grandmother's?"

"Oh, no. She has caregivers in her quarters around the clock. I'd never get any rest. I'll just have to live with the fact that you'll tiptoe inside. When you come the first time, I'll give you a temporary access code so I don't have to let you in."

Lieutenant Mohey looked astonished. "Really? That's most accommodating. Thank you."

"See you later, then." Dael nodded politely and walked out of the infirmary with a sigh of relief. Not having to smell any more disinfectant or listen to hissing ventilators was enough to make her headache lessen. As she entered her quarters a few minutes later, she leaned against the door and closed her eyes. She intended to get something to drink, then just sit in her favorite chair, one of the few items she'd brought from her house on Oconodos, and perhaps read, if her head allowed it.

"Caydoc to bridge." She knew she was normally better at delegating, but this last turn of events had made her uncertain.

"Weniell here, sir. What can I do for you?"

"Just checking in. I'm in my quarters now and fully expect you to include me in any hails if something is amiss. Just making sure you understood that." She could picture her staff wanting to protect her, but she would have none of that.

"Aye, sir. Understood."

"Very well. Smooth sailing, Commander. Caydoc out." She fetched a glass of mayana juice and sat down in her chair. A deep sigh later, she placed her glass on the table next to her and then fell back asleep.

Spinner ran along the corridor, sending people scurrying to the side in order to avoid her. "Thanks! Sorry." She waved her hand in the air, hoping the people she'd nearly trampled this time saw the apologetic gesture. Enough adrenaline pumped through her body and enough images of hissing, toxin-spraying rats ran through her mind to last her a lifetime. Which she prayed to the Creator they wouldn't. Nor the images of an injured Dael, lying vulnerable and immobile on the ground in the path of said rats.

Increasing her speed, Spinner was well aware she could run laps around the *Espies Major* until she fell down from sheer fatigue, but she wouldn't forget how seeing Dael in that position had made her feel. Why would she fret so over her commanding officer? As she'd never mixed business and pleasure before, she honestly couldn't imagine why her heart was aching the way it did right now. Or had been hurting, for quite some time, as it were.

Groaning, she turned a corner and nearly ended up in Helden Caydoc's lap. The woman merely smiled brightly as Spinner righted herself at the last moment. "I'm so sorry, sir. I didn't—"

"See where you were going?" Helden said helpfully. "I could tell. You looked like you were in a hurry."

"No, well, I suppose." Trying to catch her breath, she placed one hand against the bulkhead and steadied herself. "I think better when I run. Sort of."

"Ah. I've been to check on Dael, as she refused to stay in my quarters."

"She's not in the infirmary?" Spinner's hand slipped, making her have to take a step sideways.

"I knew she wouldn't stay there for long." Helden Caydoc frowned. "You look a bit weary. You should come for one of Minna's herbal teas. How does that sound?"

Spinner hesitated. She was dying to know how Dael was doing, and she couldn't just pop in on the admiral and ask. Thinking fast, she saw her chance at some information from a knowledgeable source. "I'd love to. But I do want to grab a shower first, if that's all right."

"Certainly. That'll give us time to get sorted when we get back." Helden Caydoc waved with her good hand as her caregiver guided the chair along the crowded corridor.

As Spinner hurried back to her quarters, her mind was reeling. She remembered vividly how Helden had asked her about her mother, torn at her carefully constructed defenses with accomplished ease. Perhaps it wasn't entirely safe to join such a woman for some tea. Regardless of that, Spinner would risk having personal questions directed her way if she could get some reassuring information regarding Dael. More than that, she needed to talk to Helden Caydoc, who cared about Dael personally. Perhaps she could even hint at her own feelings, even if part of her thought that was an even worse idea. She had such an urge to have someone to talk to about the dance, the kiss, and knew absolutely nobody else she could trust.

Somehow it took Spinner only a few minutes to reach Helden Caydoc's quarters after she'd showered and donned her clothes. Before she could second-guess her decision, she rang the door chime. Quick steps inside revealed the presence of one or more of the caregivers.

Minna smiled warmly. "Hello, Commander."

"Spinner, please."

"Spinner." Helden emerged from the adjacent room. "Come in, come in." She waved with her good hand. "You look like a different person in the leisure suit, be it military issue or not. I just got paged regarding the senior condola tournament, which I'm hoping to win, of course."

"A condola tournament?" Wasn't Helden reluctant to entertain the other senior passengers, or had she misunderstood Dael? As for playing condola, which was a board game for people with a talent for math and logic, it was probably something Helden excelled in.

"Yes, as it turned out, the other people here approaching my age have all sorts of interesting backgrounds, and it's clear they're no more interested in basket weaving or crocheting scarves than I am." Helden grinned. "So, after a short discussion, we decided to challenge each other to a condola tournament. As it turns out, Ensign Umbahr's grandmother used to play professionally, which I realize might become a challenge, but there's no dishonor in losing to such a brilliant mind." She studied Spinner closely, tilting her head in a way achingly reminiscent of Dael. "Now, enough about my extracurricular activities. I suppose you're here to inquire about Dael?"

"Um, this might be a really bad idea, and I wouldn't want to cause any sort of conflict of interest or—" Realizing her nerves were making her babble, Spinner just stood there, feeling utterly foolish.

"Why don't you sit down? The tea's brewing and we have time for a chat."

Relieved, if still jittery, Spinner sat on the two-seat couch and watched Helden adjust her chair until she was comfortable. Her affected hand was twitching, something Spinner hadn't noticed before. "Are you all right?"

Helden followed her gaze. "Oh, you mean, my hand? It does that sometimes when I've overextended myself a bit. Today was stressful until I had good news about Dael. As she's safe and reasonably sound, I don't mind a bit of spasticity. Now, let's focus on you."

Taking a deep breath, Spinner dug deep inside for courage. "When it comes to your granddaughter, I don't have anyone else to talk to."

Helden didn't say anything, only nodded.

"When you say today was stressful, that's just for starters. I pictured her dying in several different ways, and when we finally were faced with the poisonous rodents, and I was sure neither Dael nor I would survive, all I could think about was…the dance."

Helden blinked. "The dance? Excuse me? I might be getting older than I thought. I thought you said dance." She tipped her head to the side.

"I meant, the dance during the large party we had aboard the ships."

"Ah, yes. Now I understand. I didn't do much dancing myself, so that's why I didn't make the connection." Helden seemed quite relieved, which would have been humorous at any other time. She motioned for Spinner to continue.

"Yes, everybody was partying with family and friends, and don't get me wrong. I do have friends aboard the *Espies Major*, but I really felt lonely that evening as I'm one of the few who doesn't have a family member aboard."

"I can certainly understand that."

"So, today, when I thought I might never get a chance to talk to Dael ever again, yeah, that was stressful."

"And now you feel comfortable talking to me? That's flattering and quite the turnaround from when I showed up at your quarters unannounced." Helden was nothing if not direct. Her light-blue eyes were youthfully clear, and Spinner could see how her gaze could easily turn steely and commanding.

"I know. I never meant to be rude, but you caught me off guard that time." Spinner realized it was easy to be just as direct back. "And I'm still not ready to discuss my mother or my childhood. What I need, no, *must* talk about, before I implode, is that I danced with Dael."

Helden's lips formed a silent "O." "You and Dael danced, you say? That night?" Her eyes began to glitter.

"Yes. Two dances. I'm not sure that was so smart."

"If that's what you think now, I take it you felt something then." It wasn't a question, and Helden didn't seem appalled or by any means disapproving. Spinner wasn't sure why she thought Helden would be, just that she'd worried about it while walking over here.

Perhaps very few things ever got to this woman, except of course when her granddaughter was injured.

"I did. I did feel something."

"And Dael?"

"I don't know. I think she enjoyed it. The slow dance was, I mean, it *felt* intimate, but I'm bad at reading stuff like this. I felt weird. You know. Funny-weird."

Now Helden smiled, a mild and friendly smile that didn't make fun of Spinner's words or feelings. "Feeling weird while slow-dancing with my granddaughter. I take it that it was weird in a good way?"

"Mostly."

"What part wasn't?"

Spinner cleared her throat. "The one where I apologized for potentially compromising the chain of command by not being good for her reputation among the crew."

"Oh. Well, I can see where that wouldn't go down well." Helden smiled wryly. "And besides, my granddaughter thinks very highly of you. I personally can't see how anything about you would harm her command."

"She said something like that in her own caustic way."

"Ah."

"And then we somehow salvaged the evening and she kissed my cheek before she went back to mingling." The last words came out so hoarsely she had to cough to clear her voice. This was probably a huge mistake, but saying it out loud to someone, and especially someone who listened so very intently, made it real, even after all this time.

"Now, you realize, both these things are not something Dael would normally do. She's not much for dancing, even if I've always claimed it came naturally to her. She's not a very tactile person, unless it's personal. That should speak volumes too, I think." Tapping her lower lip, Helden looked pensive, as if filing all this information away for future reference.

Stunned at these revelations, Spinner's mind whirled. Her belly warmed slowly and the fluttering there stopped causing nausea. Dael didn't usually let anyone in like this—according to her grandmother. Of course, Helden wasn't privy to all aspects to Dael's life, but

Spinner still thought she had her granddaughter pegged overall. It was rather indicative that both she and Dael had withdrawn from each other after the party. Maybe not for the same exact reason, but with the same outcome. *Emotional introverts.*

"Thank you for telling me. I feel both stupid and adolescent coming to you like this, but I swear I was convincing myself today, when I thought we both would become rat-food, that I'd missed my only chance not to act like such a coward. I was so sure all along that I'd lost something that could potentially be special." Not sure she was making sense, Spinner waited for Helden's response.

"When it comes to Dael and her relationships, I don't interfere, of course. But I feel I know something about you that most don't, and though I realize you don't want to talk about Pamas, your mother, she's one of the reasons I chose to return your confidence."

There went the flutters again. Damn it. "All right. I understand. I think."

"Dael isn't easy to figure out, even for me, but she lets me get away with a lot because we're close and she's very loyal to those she cares about."

Spinner remembered how Dael had defended her at the party when someone outranking her had virtually accused her of cheating in spin jack. Spinner kicked her shoes off and pulled her legs up. It had been so unexpected, both the insinuation and the defense. She'd been so furious at the implied accusation that she'd come close to launching herself at him. That would have sent her straight to the brig. "She deflected a situation at the party where I might have struck a superior officer."

"So she stepped in and kept you from failing yourself."

"And her. Which would've been worse," Spinner murmured.

"I can see why you think so, but I have a feeling Dael would think the opposite. You would've beaten yourself up for not controlling your emotions. Something your mother struggled with as well, I might add."

Recoiling, Spinner hugged her legs close. "I know."

"Your father, what was his first name again?"

"Helden, please." Spinner blinked at the second burning sensation of the evening, ready to bolt if the tears actually started falling. After all, there were limits to this weird moment of confessionals.

"There I go again, being an old busybody. I'm sorry." Helden rolled closer. "I hope you'll put up with my moments of poor judgment, Spinner. I actually think we can become good friends, despite the age difference and my affinity for meddling."

"I can't really accuse you of meddling when I'm the one visiting with you." Spinner smiled weakly. "And I owe you for reassuring me regarding Dael. Which you did, even if I'll probably find another reason to second-guess her or myself at the first opportunity."

"Well, we can't have that festering." Helden held up her hand. "You just come knocking here any time you want. I mean that. People will no doubt tell you that I'm a right old bitch, but those I take a liking to will tell you I'm a loyal friend."

"They don't have to tell me that." Spinner stood and put her shoes on. "I better head for my quarters. It's been a long day."

"I hear you." Helden grinned. "Just don't fret alone, all right?"

"All right." Impulsively, Spinner bent and kissed Helden's cheek. "Thank you."

"Good night, Aniwyn."

"'Night."

Outside in the corridor, Spinner stood lost in thought for a moment. Still processing her talk with Helden in the back of her mind, she didn't care for the idea of going back to her empty quarters and dreaming of venom-spraying, saber-toothed rats. There was really only one place she wanted to be right now. She wanted to make sure Dael was all right, to actually see it with her own eyes.

Spinner took a fortifying breath and turned in the opposite direction. The worst thing that could happen was that Dael cut her off at the kneecaps and told her to mind her own business, right? Spinner honestly didn't care. If she irritated Dael by caring, then at least she would know Dael was well enough to become really annoyed.

CHAPTER SIXTEEN

Spinner thought her heart might just stop from sheer exhaustion before Dael answered the door. It beat so fast it actually hurt, and now she questioned her spontaneous decision to head for Dael's quarters.

"Enter." Dael's voice sounded strong, which was reassuring, but Spinner still entered with cautious steps.

"Um. Hello." Spinner found Dael sitting in a deep-red recliner next to the couch. It had to be her own chair, as it didn't match the rest of the military-issued furniture. She was dressed in an off-white leisure suit and looked smaller out of uniform, but no less formidable.

"Commander?" Dael frowned as she moved to get up from the recliner.

"No, no, don't get up." So they were back to titles again? Glancing around, Spinner took in Dael's private quarters. Large for a military vessel, they held very few personal things, mainly readers, music cubes, and that red chair. "I just wanted to make sure you were all right. Doc wasn't happy that you bailed from the infirmary." Spinner didn't quite know what to do with her hands. She refused to clasp them or do anything that revealing; instead she forced them to relax at her sides.

"Thank you for…your concern." Dael sat down again, looking relieved. She moved with care, which made Spinner think she was in more pain than she'd care to admit. "Won't you sit down? I haven't had the chance to hear your side of this disastrous recon mission."

Happy that she wasn't immediately dismissed, Spinner sat on the two-seat couch slightly angled from the recliner. Now that she was closer, she could see the bruises marring the left side of Dael's face. "You didn't even give Doc a chance to fix those, huh?"

Dael automatically touched her face. "I know. I should've. I just wanted to get out of there so they could focus on the ones who were worse off than I was." She shrugged. "To be honest, the infirmary isn't one of my favorite places."

"You don't have to explain that to me. I try to stay clear of it as much as possible."

"So, why were you there talking to Doc?" Dael tilted her head in a way that made her look younger than ever.

Her cheeks warming slightly, Spinner pushed her fingers in under her thighs. It was that or start to fidget. "I was looking for you. The medics yanked you away from me so fast and took you on the evac freighter before I could really assess your wounds. I…I was worried."

Dael put the reader away with slow, measured movements. Her eyes seemed darker as she pulled her legs up beneath her. "As you can see, I'm doing quite all right. I just spent some time with Nania, and she also gave me an earful about leaving the infirmary against the doc's orders."

"What was his main concern?" Spinner took her cue from Dael and leaned back on the couch, folding one leg under the other.

"You're rather inquisitive. I guess since you were the one to keep me safe when I was down, you're entitled to ask. Doc thinks I have a concussion, but apart from a headache and some vertigo, I don't have any of the other symptoms."

Increasingly concerned, Spinner shook her head. "But, if there is a risk of concussion, surely you shouldn't be alone during the night? I've suffered enough concussions to know how important it is for someone to check your status every three or four hours."

"Yes, the doc was going on about something like that."

"And?"

"And a nurse will come knocking a couple of times tonight."

"What if something happens just after they've been here?"

Her eyes narrow slits now, Dael started to look annoyed. "I'll be fine."

"As I see it, you're going to be here alone." Spinner knew she risked getting tossed out on her ears, but Dael had admitted she sort of owed her for keeping her out of harm's way. Perhaps she'd get away with pushing the issue.

"I could've stayed at Nania's, but she has caregivers with her day and night, tending to her. No way I could get any rest with them tiptoeing through her quarters at all hours." Dael shook her head dismissively.

"And the fleet admiral was your only option?"

Dael looked at her like she wasn't sure what Spinner meant. "Yes? She's my only relative aboard. You know this."

"Yes, but not your only *friend*." Smiling carefully now, Spinner was hoping for Dael to catch on.

"Friend? I—"

"I'd like to think we've come at least that far, sort of off the record." Spinner scooted closer. "After all we've been through, we've come to trust one another, haven't we?"

"You've put your life on the line for this ship and its crew on several occasions. For me."

"No, that's not what I mean." She knew Dael was stubborn and not one who let people in easily, but she refused to let Dael take a step, let alone several, back from where they'd come. Not when it might also risk her health. "I mean, you and I. When we're off duty, we're becoming friends. Or we were, I think, until the party."

Dael's cheekbones had lost color again, but now they turned pink. "That's just it. I'm always on duty."

"That's true to a point," Spinner said, forging on. She shifted even closer, as stealthily as possible. "But, now, tonight, Doc says you shouldn't be alone and yet you are. Would you allow me, as a friend, to spend the night here so I can check on you? I can call the infirmary and cancel the nurse."

Pushing her feet down onto the floor with a thud, Dael frowned. "You—you wish to stay here tonight? To be my medic or something? Fairly out of character, Spinner, wouldn't you say?" She folded her arms in front of her.

Spinner knew Dael was trying to keep her distance on all levels, but the words still stung. "Are you telling me you think I'm unfeeling and that I don't care?" she asked softly.

"I didn't say that!"

"You implied that I couldn't possibly be a good friend or caring enough to tend to someone who may or may not have a dangerous injury. Not very flattering." Spinner tried to sound her usual flippant self, but the tremor in her chin was all too real. The only way to cover that up would be to lower her gaze to the floor, and she wasn't prepared to take her eyes off Dael.

"For the love of the Creator, I'm sorry." Gesturing widely with one hand, Dael grimaced and then grabbed her shoulder with the other hand. "Damn."

"Please, Dael." Granted, Dael had asked Spinner to use her first name when they were off the clock, but it still felt presumptuous, even here in Dael's own quarters. "In addition to me, the rest of the convoy couldn't bear to lose you. You're our admiral, our pilot in all this, physically and emotionally. If we didn't take every precaution to keep you safe, no matter the circumstances, we'd all be worse off. Don't you see?"

"Ah, so this is you performing your duty." Pressing her lips tightly together, Dael glowered, but she seemed too fatigued to put any real emphasis behind her expression.

"You know better. I'm off the clock. I'm not as tired as you, but not far from it. Today was pretty horrible. Actually, it was disastrous and we lost a good person…We could've lost more. We could've lost you." Her throat constricting, Spinner did her best to remain calm. She couldn't imagine carrying on without Dael, without this impressive, stunning woman, who meant so much no matter how bittersweet it was to admit it. The least she could do was offer to keep Dael safe. Then at least she would have that.

"I apologize," Dael said, surprisingly. "I know you worked without rest to get us out of there. I'm not ungrateful, just a grumpy old bitch." She smiled wryly. "And you still insist on spending the night to be my nurse?"

"I don't like the infirmary, and the way they poke and prod you, any more than you do. That's why I learned as much as I could, to know when I could keep away and not endanger myself or anyone else. That's why I know about the procedures regarding potential concussions. Wake the patient up every other hour and check their alert status."

"All right." Dael nodded and seemed to melt back into the recliner. "You may regret the offer when you realize I intend to sleep in this chair. I tried lying down on the bed, but that caused my head to pound enough to make me dizzy."

"So I'll take the couch. I've slept in worse places, believe me."

"I hesitate to ask." Dael motioned with her hand across to the cabinets inside the door. "You'll find more blankets and pillows in there."

Spinner got up and crossed the room. "Can I get you another blanket? You look kind of cold."

"Yes, please." Dael sounded surprised. Was she perhaps not used to anyone paying close attention to her wellbeing?

Spinner returned with her arms full of bedding and pillows. She tucked a soft blue blanket around Dael and made sure the recliner was at a perfect angle for her. After making the couch up with some other blankets, she stood and looked uncertainly at Dael. "Better page the infirmary." She used the console on the wall next to Dael's desk. The nurse on call was reluctant at first, but when Spinner offered to put the admiral on, she relented.

"Just page us if anything's amiss, Commander. You know the importance of keeping to the protocol when it comes to head trauma."

"I certainly do."

They disconnected, and even if Spinner was sure she could perform the checkups on Dael, the idea of her deteriorating made her swallow hard. She arranged her features back to appearing calm and assertive. "That's it, then. All right if I use your bathroom?"

"You don't need to ask. Go right ahead. I finished in there just before you knocked on my door. You'll find what you need—"

"In the cabinet. I saw." Smiling briefly, Spinner strode into the bathroom. As she performed her usual ablutions, she examined her reflection. She was dressed similarly to Dael, so she'd be comfortable and ready to move at a moment's notice in case Dael became ill. *She won't. This is just a precaution.*

"Light at guide level only," Spinner ordered as she reentered the living area. This way she'd have sufficient light to see Dael, but it would be dark enough for them both to rest. She curled up on the couch after making sure her timepiece was set to wake her in two hours. "Are you comfortable?" she asked in a low voice.

"Quite." Dael sounded sleepy.

"Good. Me too." The couch was actually very comfortable. Hugging a pillow close, as was her habit, she closed her eyes. The sudden images from the extraction of Dael and her team flickered on the inside of her eyelids, and she snapped them open again.

"What's wrong now?" Dael asked, sounding a tad exasperated.

"Sorry. Nothing. Just go to sleep. I'll—I'll read a bit first, I think." Spinner reached into her pocket and pulled out a data tablet. Browsing, she chose a book she'd started two nights ago and began to read.

❖

Dael was shivering and someone was nudging her insistently. She tried to move away from them and tug at her blankets at the same time. The jungle had been so damn hot. How the hell could she be so cold now?

"Dael. Answer me. Tell me your full name, rank, and IDSEC number. Come on. Don't force me to call Doc. He'll have you transported back to the infirmary on the spot."

"Spinner?" Dael opened her eyes and squinted in the dim light of her quarters. Right. Spinner was here to check on her. Was she cold too? She didn't look cold—just very tired.

"Dael Samdalari Caydoc, admiral in the Oconodian fleet, ID number 549-DD-22." Her voice trembled, but the words came out easily enough.

"Thank the Creator. I really didn't want to infuriate you by dragging you back to the infirmary." Spinner leaned closer and felt Dael's forehead. "You're cold. Why didn't you tell me?"

"You didn't ask me that. You wanted my name, rank, and—"

"Yeah, yeah. We have to get you warm again." Spinner frowned and tapped her lower lip. "Would you be able to recline on the couch next to me? For warmth?"

Dael jerked. "On the couch...with you?"

"Yes. For warmth. Basic survival training, remember?" Spinner had the audacity to smirk. "Shared bodily warmth."

"Or we could raise the interior temperature of my quarters." Going for haughty, Dael pulled the blankets up under her chin, though she did feel rather silly while doing it. Like some ridiculous damsel in distress.

"We could do that, but the temperature is actually normal in here, so I don't think it's entirely physical. You're probably having a delayed reaction to the trauma."

"It wasn't my first time being in danger, you know." Dael sighed impatiently. She rubbed her temples, losing track of the blankets.

"Of course I know. I've read your bio. I just don't get why you won't let me help you. You fight me every step of the way." Shaking her head, Spinner simply pushed the blankets away and held out her hand. "Come here. You'll be fine, and maybe I'll finally be able to sleep some."

"You can't sleep?" Concerned now, Dael took a closer look at Spinner. She had dark circles under her eyes and her shoulders slumped some, which was far from how the normally feisty Spinner appeared.

"I know you're tough as nails, but when I close my eyes I keep seeing those damn rats racing toward you." Spinner sighed. "Please, Dael."

The vulnerability in Spinner's voice made it impossible to refuse. Sighing, Dael scooted over to the couch. "All right, Aniwyn. Let's camp out on the couch, though I need to half sit."

"Me too. No problem." Eagerly, Spinner arranged pillows and blankets so they both could lean comfortably on the deep couch. "Turn on your side just a little bit, like that, yes." Spinner shifted behind Dael, and then it was like a soft, wonderfully scented furnace snuggled up. A lanky, toned arm wrapped around Dael's midsection and held her close without pressing too hard. "Comfortable?"

"Very." Dael had no idea how, but she was. Spinner was warm against her back, and the distant stars streaking by at magnetar drive speed were such a beautiful sight through the small view port. "I think I can go back to sleep."

"I'll wake you in another two hours." Spinner sounded breathless and sleepy at the same time. This should've bothered Dael on some level, she was certain, but she wasn't sure why or how. She was simply too tired.

Spinner's arm was reassuring. Dael hoped her own presence would allow Spinner to sleep undisturbed until the alarm went off. She closed her eyes and drifted off immediately, Spinner's soft scent lingering, accompanying her into a non-threatening, peaceful dream.

CHAPTER SEVENTEEN

S pinner?" Dael tried to free herself, but the sleeping woman behind her had wrapped her arm around her very firmly. She wasn't about to confess to anyone just how reassuring it had felt to have Spinner wake her up every other hour and have her repeat her name, rank, and IDSEC number. Dael had murmured the information and offered a few more words to demonstrate that her brain wasn't in jeopardy and then promptly gone back to sleep. Virtually in Spinner's arms. That hadn't happened since her military academy days. She didn't like cuddling and certainly not sharing her sleeping space. Her concussion had to have something to do with this anomalous night.

"Aniwyn!" Dael grabbed Spinner's lower arm. Perhaps she really needed to pinch her? "I need to get up and so do you."

"Huh? Oh, hell…" Spinner stretched behind Dael, effectively pressing her entire body against hers. This seemed to wake up Spinner better than any pinching. "Dael! How are you feeling?" Spinner let go of her and sat up. Her curly hair stood in all directions in wild disarray, her eyes darkening with concern.

"I'm fine. Thank you. You performed your task perfectly." Dael knew she sounded stuck up and reserved, but waking up like this, in the arms of another woman, had unsettled her. Her legs trembled and she still didn't have her breathing under control. It wasn't the first time she'd reacted like that around Spinner, which was yet another warning sign.

"Ah. I'm glad you think so. I'm even happier you feel better. Any headache?" She frowned and examined Dael's features carefully. "You're still pale, but the shadows under your eyes are almost gone."

"Why, thank you. What a relief. Mind if I get up? We seem to be tangled in the same blanket."

"Oh, sorry. You were so cold last night, I pulled one more over us." Spinner rose and climbed right over Dael, effectively freeing her from the blankets and her own limbs. "There we go. If you use the bathroom, I can make breakfast. What would you like?"

So, Spinner wasn't just going to leave. Of course. And it would be too rude to suggest it. Dael wanted to groan out loud but stopped herself, as this would not be polite either. "Tea and some bread rolls, please."

"Juice?"

"Why not?" Dael stood and carefully maneuvered to the bathroom, grateful her legs felt steady and cooperative, unlike yesterday. The door automatically closed behind her as she entered the ensuite bathroom. She went through her regular routine and, coming out of the shower tube, she grabbed a towel and wiped off the mist gathering on the mirror. She examined her face and had to agree with Spinner. Her complexion wasn't as pale and her eyes not as hollow as last night, even if she wasn't quite herself. Styling her hair in her usual austere, low bun, she realized that wouldn't work. She wouldn't be able to take the tugging of her scalp. Sighing in annoyance, she pulled the pins out and started over. A plain, low ponytail had to suffice. Grimacing at the suddenly so very youthful person who glowered back at her, Dael turned and donned the uniform she always had waiting in a cabinet next to the shower tube.

After she stepped back into the living room area she stopped at the table where Spinner was sitting, focusing on one of her computer tablets. She had indeed made breakfast, but not just the bread roll and tea, but slices of fruit, which had to come from the garden bays, juice, and hot nirami rice pudding.

"Do you perchance have a personal caterer?" Dael sat down, her eyes still not able to take it all in. She hadn't had a breakfast like this since long before she left Oconodos.

"That's too funny." Spinner snorted and poured some tea. "I'm rather a good cook, although making pudding is hardly cooking. I hope you like it."

Dael suddenly realized she was hungry, which probably had something to do with the fact that she hadn't eaten since yesterday morning. Without saying any more, she more or less inhaled the pudding, bread roll, and juice. Slumping back, she sipped the strong tea with delight. But she stopped with her mug halfway to her lips when she noticed Spinner's stunned expression. "Something the matter?" She smiled into her mug and then sipped her tea again.

"I just wondered if you have a pet I don't know about that helped you devour your food that fast." Spinner laughed, sounding very pleased. "I guess you were hungry." She finished her own pudding at a somewhat slower pace.

"I was. Thank you."

"Well, it brought back the color in your cheeks."

Such a personal remark should normally have made the admiral show up and take over her persona, but instead Dael let Spinner's obvious delight wash over her. Here was someone who truly seemed to care about her wellbeing, who cared enough to spend the night and set the alarm every other hour and then cook her breakfast.

"Good thing it did. I'm due back on the bridge soon." Dael put down the mug. "You, on the other hand, have the morning off. You're not on duty until after lunch."

"I—what? Why?" Spinner looked completely taken aback.

"You didn't get a good night's sleep, and you need more rest after what you did yesterday before you're back on duty."

"All right, all right. I wouldn't mind a chance to go swimming or something."

"Each to their own preference. Thank you for…last night." Her cheeks warmed and she hoped her embarrassment didn't show too much.

"My pleasure." Spinner crinkled her nose and then smiled broadly.

Dael's breath caught at Spinner's audacity, but she couldn't muster any true resentment. Spinner had this larger-than-life aura and played by her own rules when it came to certain things. Then there was the fact that they had danced. That in itself meant nothing, but the way she'd felt while dancing with this woman, so wild and certainly not the type she'd ever even considered going for, was entirely unexpected.

"Well. I'll see you on the bridge this afternoon."

"I guess that's my cue to leave." Spinner rose and stood still for a moment, as if she were hesitant to leave. "Be kind to your body today, all right?" She took Dael by surprise by bending down and kissing her cheek. Two small pecks, but the fact that it happened at all made Dael's thighs press together.

"I will," she murmured huskily. "You too."

"Yes, sir." Spinner took her computer tablet and then left after a small wave.

Dael still sat in the same position, trying to bring her emotions to a place in her brain where she could decipher them, where they would make sense. She raised her fingertips to the place on her cheek where Spinner's lips still seemed to linger. She couldn't figure it out but knew this was dangerous on so many levels.

"Aniwyn," she whispered. "What the hell is going on?"

"Are you trying to set a ship-wide record?" Darmiya asked, holding on to the edge of the four-lane swimming pool. Like all water reservoirs, it consisted of recycled fluids and was located in the lower belly of the *Espies Major*, along with ten smaller pools that provided the same exercise, but against an artificial current.

"No. Not really. Why?" Spinner held on to the divider between their lanes, trying to act casual. "I just felt like—"

"Pushing yourself to the limits the day after you were part of a near-disastrous event during a mission. I don't think so. Either you're working off the post trauma, or something else happened when you left us yesterday that you haven't told me."

"Really, Darmiya, do all Gemosians have such wild imaginations?" Spinner shook her head.

"Very funny. Remember that you're talking to a hard-core scientist. I see. I take notes. I compare. I deduce."

"Oh, really. And lucky me, I get to be your test subject for today." Groaning, Spinner dipped under the water and then hauled herself up on the edge of the pool. "I'm not trying to set records and I'm not working anything off." The latter was, of course, a blatant lie.

"You are so." Darmiya joined her on the ledge. "Remember, I was there to greet you when you returned to the ship yesterday. You were frantic, cursing at the ones who wouldn't tell you how the admiral was doing and shoving the medics out of your way." Darmiya quieted. "Wait. What did I just say?"

"I was shoving people, traumatized out of my mind."

"Don't be silly. I'm serious. You were frantic about the admiral. That's it!" Darmiya lit up like she'd just won the last hand of spin jack. "You care about her."

"She's my commanding officer, the person who carries this mission on her shoulders." Wrapping a towel around her shoulders, Spinner wanted to slap her hand over Darmiya's mouth.

"Nah, that look in your eyes yesterday said something else." Darmiya lowered her voice and gazed around them as if they were on a covert mission. "Don't worry. I won't breathe a word to a soul."

"What word? There's nothing to breathe."

"Don't forget that I've gotten to know you very well since my brother and I signed on. I know, I know, I had this sort of hero-crush on you, I did. I'm totally over that. Ask my brother. I'm very fickle." Darmiya smiled broadly.

"I don't have to ask him. I think you've broken two hearts already among the bachelor ensigns."

"Wait now. Don't change the subject. This is about you and the admiral." Darmiya's voice sank to a whisper. "Does she know? Or better yet, does she feel the same?"

"You have got to be kidding me!" Spinner was angry now at Darmiya's carefree persistence. "You're totally wrong about everything, and I don't want to continue this conversation any longer. I'm due at the bridge." Furious, Spinner stood. "Just because you're my friend doesn't mean you can just carry on like my life is there to amuse you."

"Ah, come on, Spinner. You don't have to get so angry. It's just girl talk." Darmiya stood as well, looking confused. "What harm does it do to just gossip a little between us friends? Unless it's very, very serious." Darmiya's eyes grew huge. "Is it?"

"You're unbelievable." Turning to stomp out of there, Spinner stopped when she felt Darmiya's small, cold hand on her arm. "What?"

"I'm so sorry, Aniwyn." Darmiya rounded her, clutching at her towel with her free hand, the other one holding on gently to Spinner. "I can be such a nosy little idiot sometimes. I'm just so glad to have a real friend for the first time in ages that I took it too far." Darmiya looked imploringly at Spinner, her black hair in dark corkscrews around her triangular face making her look like an oceanic princess. "Please. Don't be mad. I take everything back. Everything. It's none of my business."

"If we're going to stay friends, Darmiya, you cannot put pressure on me—or anyone, I should say—like this. Things said in confidence are just that: confidences that are given freely to a trusted friend and companion."

"And I'm neither, am I?" Darmiya shrank backward, pulling her towel closer. Her lips were now bluish from being cold and wet, which made her look utterly pitiful.

Spinner harnessed her anger and reeled herself in. Darmiya was a brilliant scientist, very impulsive and on occasion a bit more naive than might be expected of someone her age. Her cute looks and innocently charming personality made most people give her the benefit of the doubt, and Spinner knew Darmiya didn't have bad intentions, but when it came to Dael, Spinner was protective. To be truthful, she was also protective of herself, of what was stirring between her and Dael even if it'd never amount to anything. She was certain Dael would wise up and recoil at any given moment, but until then, she just couldn't be the one who blew it. When Dael pulled back and slammed on the mask of command, it would be her doing, her decision—not because Spinner had screwed up. She cringed. Who was she kidding? If anyone was a record-holding, certified screw-up when it came to relationships, it was she.

"Spinner?" Darmiya's teeth were clattering now.

"Shit, you're freezing." Spinner bent and picked up one of the fluffy robes they'd brought and wrapped it around her friend. "I didn't mean to yell at you. Well, that's not true. I did mean to yell at the time, but I shouldn't have. I know you're my friend and I could've explained better."

"Oh, you don't have to explain anything." Darmiya still looked utterly miserable, her huge eyes filled with tears and something close to panic flickering over her face.

"Darmiya, calm down. You know me pretty well by now. I blow up, then it blows over, all right?" Concerned now, Spinner rubbed Darmiya's arms. "We learn about each other by these little... skirmishes."

"So you don't hate me?" Darmiya hiccupped.

Pretty sure she'd never seen anything so pitiful, or so cute, in her life, Spinner hugged her spontaneously. "Are you kidding me?" she asked again, but this time with a smile in her voice. "Who in their right mind could ever remain angry at you?"

"Really? You're not just saying that?" Darmiya smiled, her lips still trembling, but her eyes started to regain their usual sparkle. "I'd loathe myself forever if you hated me even for a second."

"Hey, I don't do hate." *Much. Anymore.* Spinner pointed toward the shower area. "How about we hit the shower tubes and get back to our duty stations? I'm due on the bridge, and no matter if I helped save the admiral's life, she can still write me up if I don't do my job properly."

"Oh, she would never! She really cares—oh, there I go again." Darmiya's eyes grew wide. "Just forget I said that. Why are you laughing?"

"You...you..." Spinner managed between paroxysms of laughter. "Only you would say such a thing right after...oh, Creator..." Laughing, she tugged the now-flustered Darmiya with her, and even if her friend had an innate way of stepping in the middle of the cake with both feet, then wiggling her toes on top of that, Spinner felt infinitely better. Inside the shower tube she found herself humming and looking forward to yet another boring shift on the bridge.

CHAPTER EIGHTEEN

"A re you certain?" Dael stood on the bridge, her hands in tight fists at her side. On the main screen, Captain Tylene Vildan of the ship *Rondos* looked grim.

"My chief medical officer has run the tests four times to ascertain the nature of the outbreak." She closed her eyes briefly. "It's the Garazabian plague."

"Creator help us," a voice whispered behind Dael, and she couldn't disagree. The virus responsible for this particular illness could lie dormant in damp places, or inside unsuspecting people, unless they were screened, which the entire crew had been before boarding the ships. This included the Gemosians who had joined the five vessels, which meant the contamination was located somewhere aboard the *Rondos*.

"You know what I have to do, Tylene." Dael pushed her shoulders back and laced her fingers. "Captain Vildan, I hereby place the *Rondos* in quarantine until all evidence of the illness is eradicated and the crew and passengers register as clear of infection."

"I know, sir. I've already deployed sanitation units, and we've assigned extra personnel in the infirmary to help with the infected ones. They're working in hazmat suits as a precaution, but—"

"They could already be infected."

"I apologize that you're going to be a few hands down because of this, Admiral," Vildan said. "I suppose it's better than them bringing the infection back with them to the *Espies Major*."

"Excuse me? I have crewmembers visiting your ship?" Dael took a step closer to the screen. "I will need their names so I can let their families know."

"Certainly. I have a list. Transferring it now." Vildan gestured with her index finger to a crewmember out of view.

"Got it, sir," Ensign Umbahr said. "It contains eight names."

"On screen."

The list filled the smaller screen to the left and Dael quickly scanned it. Blinking, she reread the sixth name. This had to be wrong. Why would Spinner be aboard the *Rondos*? "I have your list." Dael spoke despite tense lips. She read the last three names. Ah, so that was why. She had no doubt transported the Do Voy siblings to the *Rondos* for some reason.

Dael's hands stung and she looked down as she uncurled her fingers. Her blunt nails had managed to make deep, semicircular indentations into her palms.

"Sir?" Captain Vildan gently cleared her throat. "Five of your crewmembers, who all have small children back on *Espies Major*, have been put into protective quarters. They were screened and checked clear. The other three all insisted on volunteering in the infirmary and we placed them in hazmat suits immediately. Their initial screens were clear, so if they can manage to not remove them, and you know as well as I do that some people become completely claustrophobic after a while, they should be fine also."

"You've acted very quickly and astutely, Captain. Keep me informed. I will reduce our speed to half magnetar drive, as you will have other issues to deal with. How long do you estimate before you have a handle on this?"

Captain Vildan pinched the bridge of her nose. She was normally a radiant woman with an immediate, unquestionable authority. Now she looked decisive and ready to tackle the issue at hand, but also tense around the eyes and pale. "You know what the rules stipulate. If we find where the contamination is located quickly, and keep the infected contained while we carry out the screening of the rest of the crew and passengers, we can deal with this in seven to ten days. But it's a big ship."

"I will send any extra supplies you need by unmanned probes." Leaping into action, Dael gave in to the energy reserve inside herself wanting to burst free. "Also, we have to find out what the incubation period is and make sure anyone aboard the other ships who's visited the *Rondos* is quarantined and screened." She nodded briefly at Captain Vildan. "You focus on what you have to do, Tylene. I will take care of everything else. And have my people schedule a video-talk with me when it's convenient."

"Yes, sir." Vildan's expression softened marginally. "Thank you, Dael. You will have updates every hour."

Dael turned to Weniell, who looked stricken. "My office. Ensign Umbahr, you have the bridge."

"Aye, sir." Umbahr moved to the command chair, his face pale but composed.

In her office, Dael motioned for Weniell to sit down in one of her visitors' chairs. She strode over to her computer screen and paged Doc.

"Close the door to your office, Doc. This is confidential." Dael knew it was only a matter of time before people aboard knew something was amiss on the *Rondos*.

"Done." Doc sat down at his desk, his round face somber. Frowning enough to wrinkle half his bald scalp, he rapped his fingertips against the desktop. "So, that bad, huh?"

Dael described the situation to Doc, including the fact that eight *Espies Major* crewmen were aboard the quarantined ship.

He shook his head, which made his heavy cheeks wobble. "It had to be Spinner, right? Wherever that woman decides to go, she either brings trouble with her or finds it waiting."

"I hear you." Dael opened a document on her screen and made sure Doc and Weniell could see it too. "I need you to implement cautionary measures according to regulations. Then I need to you to give me your take on the worst-case scenario."

Tapping his wide, flat nose twice, Doc looked like he'd rather not. "Worst-case scenario? I think you already know, sir."

"I need to hear it from you, for the record."

"We could lose the entire ship." Doc's eyes darkened as he ran his hand over his face. "I'll contact my counterpart on the *Rondos*. I've had some experience with the Garazabian plague and have read some new research results."

"Good. Commander Weniell and I will go through the routines for handling this from our end. What incubation time are we looking at?"

"Twenty-four to thirty-six hours. People who don't come down with it within forty-eight hours and show antibodies are immune. That's about ten percent of the population. Unfortunately, that includes only about one percent of the children under seven and people over eighty." Doc looked apologetically at Dael. "Everyone who's been aboard the *Rondos* during the last four days must be confined to quarters, as well as anyone they've been in close contact with. It's only contagious via direct contact. Not airborne."

"Always something." Dael thought about Nania, trying to mask the twitch of pain shooting through her chest. "You have the quarantined and their families on your plate as well, Doc. If you think of something we can send to the *Rondos* to help them, Commander Weniell will prepare unmanned probes to have on standby."

"I'll keep that in mind."

"All right, we all know what we have to do." Dael took a deep breath. "Dismissed."

The screen flickered into the Oconodian Military Crest, and Weniell stood. "I'll be in my office if you need me, sir. How many have traveled between our ships in the magnetar shuttles, sir? Any idea?"

"I'd say about ten or twenty per day." Dael wished by now that Chief Engineer Korrian Heigel, the genius behind the ships and the inventor of the magnetar propulsion system, hadn't thought of a way to travel between the ships while in the magnetar corridor. Yes, it was handy, until something like this happened. Now, they might lose the *Rondos*. The doc wasn't taking everything into account. Dael shuddered. They could, if everything went to hell, lose all five ships. Another thought hit her. Even if most of the crew survived the outbreak, the impact of losing children and beloved elderly might damage morale beyond recovery.

Decisively, Dael stood. "One thing at a time. Prepare the probes and stay connected to Doc. I will inform the rest of the fleet and make sure the other three ships also implement the same precautions. Any questions?"

"No, sir." Weniell seemed to find new strength. "We'll deal with this like we do everything else. We'll be fine, Admiral."

"Thank you, Tresh." Smiling faintly, Dael appreciated his attempt at positive thinking.

After Weniell left, she allowed herself to think about Spinner for a few moments, but even those secs were enough to make her heart shrink into a hard, painful little lump.

"Admiral Caydoc to Tommus, Hegal, and Mugdon. Emergency 1A2D. Emergency 1A2D. This is not a drill." Pressing her lips together, Dael threw herself into her work. Spinner was a resourceful woman. She could take care of herself and those around her.

❖

"Fuck. Caydoc's going to kill me." Spinner turned to Darmiya and Calagan, trying to get used to the hazmat suit she was wearing. It wasn't as bulky as such suits used to be, and the portable oxygen and computer console wasn't too heavy, yet she felt claustrophobic.

"Why? You were only doing us a favor." Darmiya looked pale and held on to her brother's arm. "How long before we need to top up the oxygen and change the filters in these suits?"

"They last six hours." Spinner rolled her shoulders. "That's not our main concern. So far we're doing fine. Our screening showed we're not infected, so as long as we stay in these things, we're good."

"How the hell do we use the facilities in this suit?" Calagan looked flustered. "I know, I know, intimate question, but I've never been in one before."

"You go through the airlock, remove the suit, wait for the desinfec, use the adjoined bathroom, get back in the airlock, wait for the desinfec again, don a new suit from the recycler. Easy." Spinner crinkled her nose. "Unless you're in a hurry."

"Got it." Calagan still looked uneasy, but who wouldn't when trapped in the middle of a plague outbreak?

"CAG?" Another member of the *Rondos* crew wearing a hazmat suit showed up next to them. "You have a video call in five minutes with your admiral. Follow me."

"With Dael?" Spinner only noticed her slip when the name was over her lips. Luckily the young man didn't seem to notice, but she was sure Darmiya and Calagan did. Still, they were her friends and probably not one bit surprised. "Creator of Oconodos, I'm going to get an earful." Spinner groaned. "I shouldn't have changed places with Gazer."

"We talked you into it." Darmiya glanced at her brother. "Yes, yes. Sorry. *I* talked you into it."

"And I didn't file the change in the computer. Well, at least Gazer's safe with his family." Spinner hoped Dael would see it that way. They'd spent more time together than any of the crew—apart from Helden and possibly Darmiya—realized. Apparently Spinner's breakfast cooking had appealed to the admiral, and she kept inviting Spinner to cook in her quarters most mornings. Now, two months later, they'd reached a comfortable way of making small talk. Mainly ship's business and interests, and never anything deeply personal.

Spinner knew Dael was reserved, but the few times she'd glimpsed the charming, smiling, and even more beautiful woman behind the work persona, the more her own hungry heart craved something more, something deeper. She had no way of knowing if Dael reciprocated at all, but she did know how the occasional, accidental touching of hands and brushing of shoulders felt. Sometimes Spinner would lose her breath so badly she had to fake a coughing spell to buy some time for her voice to come back. Her physical reaction didn't surprise her. The way she *didn't* act on the clandestine, barely there touching was much more confusing. In the past, Spinner hadn't thought twice about acting on an attraction. She wasn't interested in anything lasting, that wasn't her thing, but sex in itself was…fun. Now, she almost felt silly at how carefully, almost shyly, she responded to Dael.

And now they had to endure an evisceration by their admiral, no doubt.

As it turned out, Dael wasn't angry. If anything, she seemed genuinely concerned.

"Don't worry, sir," Darmiya said, her voice gushing. "We're going to make ourselves useful. The infirmary already has more than thirty patients, some of them children, and they need the extra hands."

"As long as it is safe. I need you back here once the quarantine is lifted." Dael looked at Spinner. "I had a grateful message from Gazer's wife. He is also acting CAG in your absence."

"That will be good training for him, sir," Spinner said diplomatically. She trusted Gazer to carry out her job without any snags.

"I know working in the infirmary is commendable, but I also feel that Darmiya and Calagan would be more useful helping the scientists streamline the screening and the testing. That way we can expedite the search for the original contamination and get ourselves out of this situation faster."

"We'll report to the science lab." Darmiya looked longingly at Spinner. "Guess that leaves you to help out in the infirmary. Are you all right doing that?"

"I'll be fine. It makes sense that you guys would do more good using those enormous brains of yours to assist in the science lab. Just don't get out of the suits." She knew she had to emphasize this with Darmiya especially.

"Don't be silly." Darmiya stuck her tongue out before she seemed to remember they were under the scrutiny of the admiral. "Sorry."

"Just be careful. All of you." Dael seemed to hesitate. "Can I have a word with you in private, Commander Seclan?"

Spinner flinched and hoped the suit masked her reaction. "Of course." She turned to her companions. "Off you go. I'll check in on you in a few hours."

Darmiya touched Spinner's arms briefly and Calagan followed suit. "Be safe."

Alone in the small office area, Spinner regarded Dael with trepidation. "Yes, sir?"

"Aniwyn, I can't believe you're over there." Dael's voice sounded oddly strangled. "I just want to ask you to do as your friends asked. Be safe."

"I will. I'll be very careful. I'm sorry—no, I'm lying. I'm not sorry I'm here. I'm relieved Gazer isn't. His family went through enough that first day when his craft malfunctioned."

"So you put me through this instead." Chuckling mirthlessly, Dael shook her head. "You're a difficult person to…to care for."

Spinner's heart constricted so hard she was sure it would never relax and pump her blood again. When it did after all, it actually hurt. "You care?"

"Of course I do." Now Dael looked affronted, which was rather funny when she thought about it. "Would I have breakfast almost every morning with someone I didn't care for? I don't even see my nania that often."

"True." Spinner had to get out of the room before she made a complete fool of herself and said something she couldn't take back and would regret for all eternity. "I—I care too. You know that, right?"

"I didn't think you cooked for me like you do because you were bucking for a promotion, if that's what you think." Dael looked slightly mollified. "This is not the time, or the place, for heart-to-hearts. I merely wanted to ask you to *promise* me to check in every few hours. You are going to be very busy in the infirmary—way too busy—but...anyway?"

"I promise." That was easy. She was going to live for the moments she could see Dael's face before this nightmare was over. "Promise me not to run yourself into the deck completely. Ah, wait. Silly me. Don't promise."

"If I did I'd have to break it. It's my job to drive myself into the deck every now and then."

"All right." Spinner sighed. "I should go. You have a fleet to command."

"I do." Dael raised her hand and seemed to touch the screen. "Be safe."

"You too."

As Dael's face morphed into the military crest, Spinner took another deep breath. She knew it was only in her head that the suit felt so suffocating. Her oxygen level was at ninety percent. She had hours to go before she needed to top off. Straightening, she walked out of the office area and headed for the doors leading to the infirmary. As soon as she saw the many occupied beds, she knew this was going to be hard. So many of the patients were children.

Chapter Nineteen

"She needs to go on life support," Dr. Reys, the *Rondos*'s CMO, a petite woman in her late fifties, barked. Her voice had become increasingly gruff as the number of patients admitted increased.

Spinner nodded and was grateful she didn't have to wear the hazmat suit anymore. After the screening results came back the same way three days in a row—all three times showing antibodies—she unceremoniously removed the suit and kept working without it. Dr. Reys acknowledged that Spinner must've come across the Garazabian plague before and developed immunity.

Now, Spinner pulled up the arc and placed it around the patient's head. The little girl in the bed was pale, with blotchy red and blue bruises covering her cheekbones and chest. Her breathing was labored and even stopped for ten or fifteen secs at a time. She was close to respiratory arrest.

"Intubating." Dr. Reys freed a tube from the arc. "Damn it, she's so rigid already. Help me pull her head back, but be gentle."

Spinner pushed one hand into the curly, blond hair and placed another on the girl's hot forehead. Carefully she tipped the child's head back, feeling the muscles object. This in itself was frightening, as it showed how far the virus had spread. The prognosis wasn't good.

"Good. Exactly so." Dr. Reys pulled out the guiding wire and attached the tube to the little girl's face. She lifted her face to the girl's mother, who stood at the foot of the bed hugging a soft toy. "The ventilator is breathing for Bimi. I'm administering an antiviral cocktail, which should slow the progression of the virus and help her own immune system fight it."

"It all went so fast," Bimi's mother said, tears in her voice. "She was playing with her toys, and…and then she looked up at me, all pale, but with those—are they *bruises*?—on her face." Covering her mouth, the woman sobbed once, a deep, guttural sound of profound anxiety. "Did I get her here too late? Is she going to die because I didn't notice anything until just now?"

"You did nothing wrong," Spinner said. "This is the nature of the beast with the Garazabian plague. It lurks for a while, getting a good foothold, and only then does it make itself known." She placed a gentle hand on the mother's shoulder. "Here. Why don't you sit next to her and hold her hand. Have you been screened yet?"

"Yes, just as soon as we were in the door." The mother sat down on the extendable seat Spinner pulled from underneath the bed.

"Let us know if you need anything and especially if you start feeling poorly. I'll get back to you as soon as we get your results back."

"Thank you." Bimi's mother took her daughter's hand in hers and rubbed it against her wet cheek. "I'm all right."

Dr. Reys and Spinner moved to the office area, where Spinner sat down on the edge of the desk, grabbing a mug of berry-brew. It was cold and slightly bitter, but she didn't care. Downing the rest of it, she pressed a hand to her forehead. "Shit."

"Yes, exactly."

"What are her true chances?" Spinner said, the words scratching at her nerves.

"I doubt Bimi will survive the night. If she has a quiet and uninterrupted sleep and her kidneys don't cease to function, she could end up surprising us. Kids go downhill fast, but those who don't can actually make it."

"That'd be a nice change."

"Sure would." Reys raised her teacup in a quiet salute. "You're a trooper, Spinner, I'll give you that."

"Somehow that doesn't sound entirely like a compliment." Eyeing the stern surgeon, Spinner rinsed out her mug and then drank some water.

"I guess I have the same image of you as many of my peers do. You have a reputation for being insubordinate at times, ready to gamble and party, and...not quite CAG material."

The hurt was about to explode behind Spinner's eyes, and she already detested the threatening tears. *Shit. She found a way to get to me when I'm fatigued out of my mind, didn't she?*

"That's why I'm delighted that you're proving all of us wrong, time after time," Reys said, studying Spinner over the rim of her mug. "And it's also why nobody would dare criticize your performance in front of the admiral." She snorted softly. "They better not try to do so either, the way I hear it."

Spinner swallowed. And swallowed. "So, despite my fun-loving ways, I make a decent soldier, you mean?" She did her best to grin broadly, something that normally came so easily to her. Now, her lips trembled and she wondered if her smile looked as watery as it felt.

"No, that's not what I mean at all. I'd say you're an exemplary soldier." Standing up, Reys placed her cup in the sink. "Don't let anyone tell you differently. Time to get back to work."

Spinner put her mug away as well and followed the surgeon out into the infirmary ward. Nurses, medics, and orderlies moved between the beds in an almost ghostlike fashion. Everybody was wearing soundproof-sole shoes, trying to disturb the patients as little as possible.

Glancing over at Bimi's bed, Spinner frowned. Her mother looked exhausted where she was resting her head next to Bimi's on the pillow, but...something was odd about how still she was. Had she managed to fall asleep in that awkward position?

Spinner tiptoed over to the bed and rounded it. Looking down at Bimi's mother, she flinched. Her lips were dark blue and her complexion colorless. There might have still been hope of life if the mother's eyes hadn't been half open, unblinking, with a milky white film covering the pupils.

"Dr. Reys." Spinner stood and waved the doctor over.

"Her vitals are all right," Reys said, only to frown when Spinner just shook her head. She hurried over and placed her scanner on the mother's left temple. "Damn," she whispered, and for a fleeting moment, Spinner saw the toll it took on this woman to do this job. "She claimed she was fine."

"And we'd screened her. I didn't see any early signs." Spinner closed the mother's eyelids. "This is so bloody unfair."

Reys waved two orderlies over to remove Bimi's mother's body. As they put her on a gurney and covered her with a sheet, Spinner couldn't move. She found herself holding on to Bimi's hand, unwilling to let go. "I want to stay with her. She shouldn't be alone."

"All right. Her maternal grandmother is in isolation with the rest of our uninfected elderly. Once the outbreak is contained, we can reunite them, but in the meantime, she's going to need someone if... when she wakes up."

"No problem." Spinner sat down on the same seat Bimi's mother had used and took the little girl's hand. "How old is she, exactly?"

Checking the chart, Reys shook her head. "Almost seven."

Spinner only nodded and refocused on the pale girl in the bed. Until Bimi's grandmother was allowed to be in the infirmary, she would take the place of the girl's relatives. If Bimi made it, she shouldn't wake up all alone, even if Spinner was a complete stranger. Someone should sit at her side until someone came who loved this little girl.

❖

Dael looked too collected and too normal when Spinner saw her face on the screen. "How's it going?" Spinner asked. "What's the situation back ho—I mean, on the *Espies Major*?" She was taken aback at the word home that nearly crossed her lips. When had the *Espies Major* become home to her? She hadn't even called her apartment in the Oconodian capital home, and she'd had that as her base for six years.

"We've screened the entire crew, found about a third of them are immune, and nobody is newly infected. We've passed the limit of the incubation time, which is a blessing, and I understand from Captain Vildan that the *Rondos* has had no new cases since they blasted the source of the contamination."

"Yes, they located it behind the auto-cookers. It's been dealt with."

"And you? How are you?" Dael's voice softened as she tilted her head. "You look tired."

"I'm hanging in there. It's been...hard." Spinner swallowed against the feeling of imminent tears. "I can't stay long. I have to get back to Bimi. She's doing a little better, and I have to be there when she wakes up."

"Who's Bimi?" Dael asked, resting her chin in her hand.

"She's just a kid. Seven years old. Lost her mom. Everyone else in her family is quarantined. She's all alone and I—I—" Rubbing her face with both palms, Spinner then wiped at her eyes. "I'm sorry. I'm a mess."

"We've lost too many." The mourning in Dael's voice somehow made Spinner feel less foolish and somewhat comforted.

"Eight children, six seniors, and four crewmembers." Spinner bit the inside of her cheek. "Thank the Creator the infection was confined to the *Rondos* alone."

"You took the words out of my mouth." Dael fiddled with something out of view but didn't take her eyes off Spinner. "I've been so worried about you. I mean, the others too, especially your friends in the science lab. Of course."

"Oh, right. Darmiya caught up with me via the comm channel just before I came in here to talk to you. She says, together with some algorithms she and Calagan helped the *Rondos* scientists write, they might be able to shorten the screening for any type of virus, not just this one, by seventy-five percent."

"That's amazing!" Dael straightened in her chair. "That's absolutely fantastic. This will help keep the number of sick down."

"Yes." Spinner knew it was ingenious, but she wasn't quite rejoice in such findings. Not when Bimi was struggling in the infirmary and when Bimi's young mother had lost her life just a day ago.

"As soon as the quarantine is lifted, which will be when the *Rondos* hasn't had any new cases in eight days after the last victim is no longer contagious and all register as free of infection or immune, I want you back here." Dael tapped the screen, making Spinner flinch and refocus on her. "You're almost falling asleep where you sit. When did you get some rest last?"

"Um. I—I think, yesterday? An hour or two?" Spinner squinted at Dael. "And you?"

"I…oh, hell. I should talk. I think two hours on my cot in here last night."

"Not even in your quarters on that lovely couch?" Spinner asked longingly.

"Not even that. How about we make a deal? As soon as you're back and you've been debriefed and checked out by Doc, you should come to my quarters. We'll use the couch, both of us, for an entire day. Just resting. Read, listen to music, whatever you want."

"Whatever I want?" Spinner made her best attempt at her signature naughty grin. "Be careful what you promise, Admiral."

"And you should be ashamed of yourself." Dael's cheeks turned a faint pink, but the smile on her face was softer now, more the real thing.

"See? You may regret such a suggestion before you know it." Spinner chuckled weakly.

"I don't think so." Touching the screen with her fingertips, Dael looked pensively at Spinner. "You know what? I really don't think so."

❖

Her larger-than-life CAG looked like she was actually ill, which didn't make sense as Spinner's immunity had been confirmed and reconfirmed. Dael watched the spinning military crest as if hypnotized, a habit she'd developed during these last four days of video communicating with Spinner. It gave her time to digest what they'd talked about, and this conversation had gone from profound loss, fatigue, and concern to…flirtation? She couldn't find any word more adequate for the last exchange before they disconnected the call. Was Spinner aware of how she looked at her? Dael usually didn't think so. Spinner was an extroverted person who had made really good friends aboard the *Espies Major*.

The nature of being the admiral, the one ultimately in charge, meant not having friends per se. Dael didn't feel lonely because of that. She enjoyed spending time with her nania, and somehow she'd realized that Helden really liked Spinner. It had started with Spinner's daredevil rescue of Gazer on the first day of their journey and grown from there. Helden appreciated directness and guts, and Spinner had all of that and more. Dael rejoiced at the sparkle in Helden's eyes when Spinner's name came up. It also made her wonder what her own expression looked like when she thought of her feisty CAG.

She had asked herself many times what made Spinner return to her quarters nearly every morning to cook breakfast. They had chemistry, that much was obvious, but Dael wasn't sure how much longer she would be able to hide exactly how she felt about Spinner. For weeks, she'd waited for Spinner to grow tired of her boring lifestyle focusing on books and old videos. Dael rarely frequented the different establishments on *Espies Major*, unless it was to boost crew morale, and then it was usually because the ship's counselor carefully pointed it out as a good idea.

And still, just now, Spinner had clearly flirted with her. Perhaps this was how she was with everyone, but if so, Dael hadn't witnessed it. She'd thought Darmiya's initial crush on Spinner would lead to something, as the young Gemosian woman was very beautiful and as exuberant as Spinner could be. When this didn't happen, the two women and Calagan had instead formed an easygoing and close-knit friendship.

Perhaps Dael wasn't the only one who responded internally to accidental touches and lingering glances? Shaking her head now at this fruitless train of thought, Dael stood and walked onto the bridge. The *Espies Major* was returning to normal routines, and once the *Rondos* lifted the quarantine, they would be at full magnetar drive again.

Then Spinner would be back and she might just get some answers to all these questions and thoughts. Dael wondered if she would be brave enough to handle that.

CHAPTER TWENTY

Bimi slowly opened her eyes. Looking up, she smiled drowsily. "Nania." Holding out a weak little hand, she looked at Spinner. "Mama?"

"Mama's not here right now, sweet thing." Spinner tucked the soft toy in next to Bimi and glanced at the older woman across the bed. "But your nania is. Look. She's been so worried about you."

"Nania," Bimi whispered, her worry-frown vanishing. "Nania."

"I'm right here, treasure. I'm right here next to you, and I'm not leaving."

"When will Mama come?" Bimi turned her head into her nania's shoulder.

"Shh. Just rest, little treasure. We'll talk about that later. Just you go back to sleep." Tears streamed down the grandmother's cheeks as she clung to the little girl who was the only thing she had left of her daughter.

Spinner's stomach trembled and she tried to tell herself that Bimi at least had her grandmother. She wouldn't be all alone and abandoned, doomed to live with a parent that became an abusive stranger. *Her situation is different than Pherry's and mine.*

"I don't know how I'll be able to tell her," the grandmother, Spinner couldn't remember her name, said. So many names and faces over the last two weeks.

"You just tell her the truth in the kindest way possible. Reassure her that she has you. If it helps, tell her that she has a very, very good friend in the *Espies Major*'s CAG." Smiling tremulously, Spinner patted the older woman's hand and stood. "I'm due back on my vessel now. Please keep me updated on how Bimi's doing. Anything you need, anything at all, you just page me. If you can't reach me for some reason, leave a message for me on the bridge."

"You've been wonderful. I hope we'll get to see you soon, Commander. The effort you put in on the *Rondos* will never be forgotten." Bimi's grandmother kissed Bimi's hand. "And this little girl will be fortunate to have a friend like you. I'll make sure she knows."

"Thank you. I have to go now." Before she lost her self-restraint and burst into tears, Spinner hurried out the infirmary door. She'd already said good-bye to Dr. Reys, and now she half-ran to the closest lift. It took her swiftly to the assault craft bay where the magnetar shuttles sat waiting. Darmiya and Calagan were already on board.

"Oh, it's going to be great to get home," Darmiya said. "I've missed having my own quarters, working at my own desk. You know. Still we did help, didn't we?"

"You came up with stuff that will help keep outbreaks like this to a minimum." Spinner nodded appreciatively at her. "Dr. Reys says if this happens, or something similar, she'll be able to run the screenings and general testing in one tenth of the time it usually takes. I'll say you've earned your keep many times over."

"Anything we can do to help is only a small price to pay for what you and your people did for Gemosis," Calagan said solemnly. He pulled his sister in for a hug. "And she says 'we,' but the truth is, Darmiya came up with the concept, and then we worked together from there."

"You're smarter than you look," Spinner said, teasing Darmiya to lighten the mood. "Pity it doesn't translate to spin jack for you. You simply have no spin-jack face."

"Thank God." Darmiya grimaced. "How would that look?"

Snorting, Spinner maneuvered the controls, making the magnetar shuttle hover. "*Espies Major* CAG to *Rondos*. Ready to embark."

"You have confirmed go-ahead, CAG. Have a safe run back to *Espies Major*."

"Thanks." Spinner moved the shuttle toward the tight-fitting airlock. Inside, she had only a few centimeters of wiggle room, but that was all she needed. Once the inner door was locked in place, the outer would open and suck them into space, well within the magnetar strip. It was a clever way to travel between the ships in the convoy but not entirely harmless. If your shuttle had a technical or mechanical malfunction and started swaying, you could be crushed against the hull of the closest ship or the magnetar strip walls.

The launch went smoothly, and Spinner made sure the computer was set on reaching the *Espies Major*'s aft assault-craft bay. The hardest part of the entire flight was guiding the cylinder-shaped shuttle into the airlock. You only got one attempt.

"How about you, Spinner?" Darmiya asked. "You must be so relieved to be back on our own ship. You had the hardest job on the *Rondos* of us three, anyway."

"It was all right." Hedging, Spinner closed her eyes hard for a moment. She could have swiveled her chair but was glad she kept it facing the screens. She wasn't keen on Darmiya's perceptive eyes examining her. Not only was her friend a genius, but she was also a damn mind reader as well. "But, yes, it'll be good to get back to normal." She huffed inside her mind. Normal. Whatever would qualify as normal after this? She'd seen so much during her years in the service and had considered herself jaded, but these last two weeks had been life-altering. No doubt Doc, and perhaps even Dael, would suggest she go see the counselor. Another person to poke around in her past, diagnose her feelings, and chastise her for bottling them up. She already knew these things, so why would she repeat it to someone? A waste of time.

"I heard rumors that they're throwing us a party," Calagan said, not sounding very pleased. "I hope it's not tonight. I don't know about you, but I'm exhausted. Haven't slept much."

"Me either. I've worried too much. About everything." Darmiya sounded unusually muted, which made Spinner swivel her chair.

"We'll be fine. I trust the admiral would know we're not in the mood to celebrate anything tonight. Perhaps in a few days we can be persuaded to have some brandy and dance on the spin-jack tables. What do you think, Darmiya?"

"Yes, possibly." A pale smile flickered briefly across Darmiya's features. "Even if I'm a lousy card player."

"Yes, you are." Speaking gently, Spinner took Darmiya's hand. "But you know what? You're a terrific friend." She was relieved when Darmiya lit up.

An alert pinged, making them all jump.

"What's that?" Calagan looked at the screens. "Something wrong?"

"Nah, we're just a tad off course." Spinner grabbed the lever and adjusted the shuttle's trajectory. "The controls are slow. This might be a bit of a bumpy docking procedure. Deploying security harnesses." Pressing the sensor, Spinner heard Darmiya give a yelp in the back as the extra harness wrapped tightly around her. Spinner's own harness was also enforced, and she needed the support as the shuttle began a slow spin, which wasn't a good sign.

"Hold on!" Tearing at the controls and hammering in new commands, Spinner tried to will the shuttle to accede to her wishes. The sleek vessel, shaped like an expensive, silver-clad cigar, bucked under her hands, and Spinner saw the transparent sparkles that indicated the magnetar strip wall had come closer. Furious now, she slammed her feet against the floor pedals, something they rarely used these days, but she found them a great help when all else failed. She was damn well going to see Dael again and have her quiet evening on the couch as she'd been promised.

The airlock hatch was open, brightly lit, beckoning her. "CAG to *Espies Major*. We're coming in hot. Prepare for emergency docking."

"Bridge to CAG. We know. Everything's in place. Safe docking, Commander."

Somewhere in the back of her head, Spinner recognized Umbahr's voice. She focused on not slamming into the magnetar pods; it would destroy the shuttle and cripple the *Espies Major*.

"Oh, please, oh, please, oh, please," Darmiya whispered frantically behind Spinner.

"Just hold on, just a bit longer, just a little bit." Praying in her own way, Spinner saw the stern of the shuttle enter the airlock and knew they were coming in way too fast. Having a sense of doing yet another repeat of the landing she'd taken Gazer on at the beginning of their journey, Spinner saw the far wall of the airlock chute approach. This was going to be painful.

The shuttle slammed into the bulkhead, tossing Spinner against her harness. She'd have some serious bruises, but the landing wasn't as hard as she'd feared.

"Ow." Calagan moaned. "Thanks for flying with Spinner Air Service."

"Funny." Spinner swiveled and unbuckled her belt. "You two all right?"

"We're fine. Rattled, but fine." Darmiya stood and nearly tripped as the shuttle door opened and two medics poked their heads in.

"We're okay." Spinner repeated Darmiya's sentiment. "No need for any more doctors or nurses."

"So very unappreciated," one of the medics muttered, but still grinned broadly at Spinner. "Welcome back, Commander. Glad to see that textbook landing didn't cause you too much damage."

"Ha-ha. Someone's been taking humor classes." Spinner snorted. "I guess we need to swing by the infirmary so Doc can verify the screenings done on the *Rondos*."

"Yes, that was my next act. Guiding you to the fast-lift. That way you don't pass any of our crew until Doc sees you."

"All right, all right." Muttering, Spinner slipped out of the hatch and followed the medic to the small elevator that barely held the three of them. The medic remained outside, operating the controls that sent them straight up to the infirmary. Spinner was relieved when the door opened and they could step outside.

And there stood Dael.

Spinner stared, knowing full well how hungry her eyes were as they roamed Dael's form. She stood there, arms at her side, feet slightly apart, so incredibly correct in her impeccable uniform, and she'd never looked more beautiful.

"It's good to see you," Dael said, her voice steady and sounding entirely normal. Only the fact that her eyes sparkled with delight made the words something more than what they would have implied otherwise.

"Likewise." Spinner managed only one word, which was of course rather pitiful, but it seemed to please Dael.

"Darmiya. Calagan. You've returned in one piece despite Spinner's attempt to concuss you." Dael nodded amicably at them.

"I know Doc wants to get the screening and tests over and done with, and, thanks to you two, it will take only a few minutes."

Spinner could've written up her friends for the Emerald Order medal for those last words. Minutes. Brilliant.

The doc looked quite emotional to see them, which in his case meant he wasn't frowning and didn't huff when Spinner refused to lie down to have the testing done. As expected, Spinner tested immune and the siblings uninfected.

"Swing by Commander Weniell for the debriefing, Commander Seclan," Dael said. She was standing closer now that the last medical issue was taken care of. "Then I want you to report to my quarters." She stopped talking, her earlobes turning a faint pink. "If you are up for it tonight. I realize you might be—"

"I'm up for it." Any more up for it and she'd kiss Dael right there in the infirmary, which wasn't a good plan. Perhaps something of what went through her head showed on her face, because Dael took half a step backward.

"Good. See you then." Dael nodded briefly at Spinner, Darmiya, and Calagan. "Welcome back."

Spinner just stood there, watching Dael leave when Darmiya elbowed her upper arm. "Reel your tongue back in, will you?" She giggled and easily avoided Spinner's faint attempt at retaliation. "Go get debriefed. Calagan and I'll go say hello to our colleagues, and then I for one intend to shower and then go to bed for two days straight."

"Sounds good." Spinner was only half listening. Waving to them, she went over to one of the main lifts that would take her to Weniell's office. Her mind wasn't on the debriefing but on the woman she'd dreamed of every time she'd closed her eyes while aboard the *Rondos*. The way Dael had looked at her with terror-filled delight in her eyes was confusing, at best. Dael clearly wasn't any more certain about what might be going on between them than Spinner had been.

Before the plague, she hadn't acknowledged fully just how much she cared about Dael. Sure, she could never deny her attraction, but to evolve from there was intimidating. And if Spinner felt like that, Dael must feel twice as vulnerable. She was the admiral, the ultimate power in this nomadic existence of theirs. Every single decision, or action, was her responsibility. She was their leader or, in a sense, their queen. Most likely, that meant she could never be Spinner's.

❖

Dael stood in her office over by her desk. She wasn't sure how long she'd been rooted in place, clutching her computer tablet. Not until it actually cut into her hand did she take a deep breath and sit down. She forced herself to reread its content, each word piercing her heart like arrows on fire. It was her burden of command, an expression she normally loathed, that she received the messages from Oconodos in encrypted form to be read in private. She was trained in which information to pass on, and which not to. Oh, how she would've wanted to let the crew keep going without knowing this! It just wasn't possible. She would have to withhold any personal messages for the crewmembers sent from families and friends on their homeworld for this to remain classified. That was simply not doable.

Making sure she looked impeccable, with her hair in her usual austere bun, she paged Weniell and asked him to join her in the conference room. Next, she had Ensign Umbahr contact the people listed in a category called Advance Summit. This meant Umbahr would have the bridge and they wouldn't be disturbed unless an emergency occurred.

"Good afternoon, Admiral. I just saw Spinner and she looked pretty good—" Weniell stopped midsentence and sat down after she wordlessly motioned for him to do so at the table. In front of them, the large view screen began to flicker and show video of the other captains and their first officers. When all of them were accounted for, Dael opened the audio channel.

"Good afternoon. This is a briefing I hoped never to perform. Two days ago, riots erupted in the Oconodian capital. The police were present but clearly had underestimated the number of the crowds. Four hours later, what was left of the crowd dispersed."

"Sir? What do you mean, what was left of the crowd?" Captain Vildan asked, her lips thin.

"They had approximately 18,000 fatalities. The number is expected to rise."

The other captains and their first officers all stared at her with different levels of horror on their faces.

"Creator of Oconodos, what happened?" It was the first officer of the *Mugdon*.

"The Oconodian authorities estimate that somewhere around 50,000 are wounded." Dael had to keep going and not take too long looking at her captains. They were professional and seasoned military officers, but they also had people left behind whom they missed and who could be among the hurt or killed. "The situation is confused and the timeline sketchy, but the information I have suggests that approximately 250,000 people had gathered to demonstrate against some of the laws constricting the changers. Apparently, the less reactionary faction of our government had voted against automatic incarceration from birth for the changers. This made many people take to the streets, and a call went out via the computer-lines to gather at the Oconodian Mother's Square. Soon, the streets were filled with enraged people, scared people, and that's when some of the changers decided to mount a counter demonstration. Some of the original protesters were armed but had no real chance against the changers, who used their specific abilities to outmaneuver them. Our leaders managed to add some film clips and footage of the incident."

"Have you watched it?" Tommus' captain asked.

"I have. I'm transmitting it now." Dael really didn't want to see it again but still stayed where she was, viewing it with her subordinates.

The first clip showed part of a vast crowd yelling less than politically correct terms regarding the changers. They waved posters, fists, and occasionally tools and thick branches as they rallied against what they all feared.

"Put the fucking mutants on a frozen island!" one woman close to the cameraman screamed. "Keep us safe, that's your job!"

Suddenly something hit from above and the crowd went quiet all at once, which made Dael shiver even though she'd seen this before. Soon, something so fast it was only a blur on the screen flew over the heads of the people. People screamed, and Dael saw several grope at their faces and necks and then frantically start to wipe themselves on their sleeves.

"What the hell?" Weniell murmured.

Another blur and the whole scene erupted into flames. The cameraman clearly stumbled backward quickly enough to keep filming, but the camera movements made it hard to see anything but glimpses of the mayhem unfolding in front of him.

"This is…insanity." Captain Gossamay had lost most of his color. "They're…was that kerosene, that first flyby?"

"That or some other flammable substance." Weniell's hands balled into tight fists. "And the second flyby was the flame…"

"Did someone else see what I saw?" Captain Vildan frowned and pressed something on her end, making the video replay from the first flyby. She pressed again, stopping the image.

Dael hadn't noticed it the first time around, and now she just stared. "Oh, no," she whispered.

"It's a person. A winged person!" Gossamay roared. "It's one of the damn mutants. They can fly."

"One of them can, at least," Dael said. "Sit down, Captain Gossamay. And no name-calling in my presence. Yes, the changers suffer from mutations, but we do *not* refer to them as mutants. This is not a comic-book story to entertain and thrill. We just watched hundreds, maybe thousands of people being burned by one or two disturbed individuals. You can watch the rest of the transmission at your own discretion, but we need to focus on how to tell our crew and the civilians. We will have grief, worry, and perhaps even upheaval among the civilians and need to be ready."

"I suggest a meeting with our respective ships' counselors," Captain Olli of the *Hegal* said, her voice matter-of-fact but her dark eyes glimmering dangerously. "There are protocols even for things like this. Give the crew and civilians controlled means and places to work through their pain and confusion. Have them send audio and written messages to the loved ones they are worried about. Inactivity is our worst enemy right now. Crewmembers off duty will be encouraged to sign up for extra shifts as aides to the counselors. That should be voluntary, though."

Dael gave inner thanks to Captain Olli for her clear thinking. She'd already considered a similar course of action, as it was stipulated in the protocol, but it was better when suggestions came from her captains. Especially now. The crew needed to see that they had five trustworthy, competent leaders. It was vital.

"Very good. Form teams consisting of senior crewmembers, counselors, medical personnel, and anyone else among the civilians you think can be useful. Brief them. Once that's done, I'll make a full five-ship announcement on the screens with all your teams in place to answer questions. You have one hour. Any questions?" Dael could see they had many questions and yet none. She knew just how they felt. "Very well. Report back in an hour. Dismissed." Dael closed the screen and turned to Weniell. "Let's split the task between us. You bring in the crewmembers we need. I will go through the civilian passenger manifest and see who I can approach."

"Yes, sir." Weniell stood. "This is going to be hard."

"Yes, it is." Dael regarded her usually conceited first officer and saw something else, something she hadn't readily noticed about him before. Perhaps it took something like this for him to let down his guard? He seemed more genuine. "Come on, Tresh." She touched his arm briefly as she passed him. "We have work to do."

CHAPTER TWENTY-ONE

Aniwyn Seclan
Commander and CAG
Day 207
Advance mission
Personal log

I must've been staring at the computer screen for half an hour and just blanked out. The last twenty-four some hours have been so tumultuous, and with that I mean damn insane, that I feel completely gutted. I'd just come home from the Rondos *and was so ready to relax and just spend some downtime with Dael. Both of us needed to heal after the breakout. We really did. And now this.*

I saw the video transmissions and agreed with the decision not to make them public. Nobody should have to see them. Nobody should've had to live through those scenes. I don't think I'll ever get the images out of my head completely. Certainly not out of my heart.

I felt guilty for being grateful that Pherry and his family live too far from the center of Oconodos to have been there. I mean, the risk is minimal. Still, I won't even start to feel right until I hear from him. Why didn't I persuade them to come with me? Why did I think it was safer to wait for the big ships?

Now, this isn't doing anyone any good. I need to stay focused and be of help and service where I can. If Dael can be so strong, so can I, right? I've never been as proud of another person as when I witnessed her addressing the five ships. First, she and Weniell gathered all of us belonging to the senior crew and gave us the bottom line of what had just happened back home. She let Weniell speak and actually sat next to me at the conference table, looking so collected and calm. I didn't realize how affected she really was until she took my hand under the table and clung to it. That was when I felt those fine, invisible tremors reverberating from her. I did my best to absorb them and squeezed her hand back. At the same time, my head was actually hurting from the topic of the briefing, and having been through so much on the Rondos, I thought I might lose it. And I didn't want that, not in front of everybody and certainly not when Dael needed me.

After the briefing, Dael asked me to accompany her to the small broadcasting studio. I nearly forgot to let go of her hand before we stood, but something tells me she wouldn't have cared at that point.

As she addressed the crew and passengers, her voice was steady, and those amazing eyes of hers were clear as water. She spoke with empathy and radiated reassurance, but out of the viewers' sight, her hands were clenched in such tight fists, her knuckles were chalk white. Perhaps I was the only one who knows her well enough to spot the tiny, tiny muscle spasm at the left side of her jaw.

Afterward, we each had our duty shift, but before she left the broadcasting room, she turned to me. We were the only ones left and she brushed her lips against my cheek. "Later tonight, when you're off duty and things have mellowed, would you come to my quarters after all?" she asked, sounding noncommittal, as if a rejection wouldn't really matter. I knew this was the exact opposite of the truth. Her eyes now burned with this silver glow, and she seemed to hold her breath.

"Absolutely." I wanted her to know there was no doubt in my mind—or my heart.

Dael gave me the code for her door lock, made me repeat it twice, and then left with a mere nod.

I went to the assault-craft bay, wanting to be with my pilots as their commanding officer and offer what support I could. All over the ship, as I passed through the corridors, I heard agitated and upset whispers. Some people were crying, others demanding more information, more answers. The pilots were all quite subdued. Most of them sat with their family and friends, which increased my crowd times four. I didn't have to say much; it seems the most important part was that I was present. One of the counselors stopped by after an hour to offer his services. As I guessed, most of the pilots weren't interested, but I also knew that, with time, when they realized they might not be coping as well as they thought, several of them would take him up on it. Another unknown factor is, of course, if they know any of the dead or injured back on Oconodos. After two hours, we seemed to be all talked out for the moment and began to leave. I stayed until everyone else was gone and then made my way to Dael's quarters.

And here I sit now, computer tablet in hand, on the couch in Dael's quarters, wondering what state she'll be in when she gets here. No matter what, I know she'll need someone. I might be conceited and selfish, but I want that someone to be me.

End recording

The door to Dael's quarters opened and Spinner stood immediately.

"Really, Spinner. As you were." Dael smiled wryly as she stepped inside, tossing her jacket on a chair. "If there ever was a time for that brandy, it's now." She walked over to the row of cabinets and closets and pulled out a large bottle. Turning around, she snorted as she met Spinner's gaze. "You looked shocked. Didn't you think I knew about the moonlighting?"

"Um. I suppose it's your job to know everything that goes on." Spinner wanted to hug Dael so badly, but her expression wasn't exactly inviting.

"You suppose correctly." Dael stopped on her way to the kitchenette. "You've been cooking?"

"Yes. Have you eaten anything? If not, I fixed a vegetable casserole. Only a couple of the ingredients are fresh. The rest is freeze-dried stuff that was compressed enough for me to have to venture a guess. Tastes all right, though."

Looking deflated, Dael put down the bottle and slumped at the kitchenette counter. "I haven't eaten. Have you, or will you join me?"

"I waited for you. Of course I'll join you. I'm not going anywhere." Spinner made sure her voice projected her determination. "You need someone—no, *me*—here."

At first it seemed like Dael took Spinner's last words as a challenge. Her back straightened and she raised her chin. Her hands gripped the countertop hard enough to make her grimace and look down at them in surprise. With a deep sigh she slumped against the work surface again. "Yes. Yes, I do."

"Why don't you kick off your boots and take a seat at the table while I get us some plates?" Spinner moved quickly into the kitchenette.

Dael took off her boots and placed them neatly next to her desk. She sat down and merely stared at the screens showing the shimmering magnetar-strip wall and the stars beyond it.

"Want something to drink? Or are you happy with the brandy?" Spinner asked.

"I'm having second thoughts. It's a really bad idea to drink alcohol as a remedy for something."

"You don't have to tell me that." Spinner regretted the words as soon as they passed her lips.

A new spark lit Dael's eyes and she turned her attention fully on her. "Oh? You've experienced this?"

"You know I don't mind partying with all it entails, including the brandy and whatnot. I do have a strict, self-imposed limit. Even after all this time, I'm sensitive to alcohol. It doesn't take much to make me drunk." Spinner hoped her long-winded explanation would make Dael think she'd got her answer.

"So who used it as a remedy, then?" Clearly Dael wasn't easily distracted.

Spinner sighed. All right. This was about trusting and sharing. She might as well go first. She took two plates from the heater and placed them on the table, which she'd already set with utensils, napkins, and mugs. Placing a pitcher of water in the center, she sat down at a right angle from Dael. "My father."

"Aniwyn, I'm sorry." Dael rubbed the back of her neck. "It's none of my business."

"It doesn't matter. Really." Spinner motioned toward Dael's plate. "Try to eat some." She took a bite and chewed. It tasted fine, but she wasn't hungry. Only the knowledge that she needed the nutrition and that Dael did too kept her going. She managed half her portion before she put down her utensils. Sipping her water, she leaned back. "My father didn't take my mother's absence very well. He drank most days. Just a little at first. Then that wasn't enough, so he added a few chemicals to the mix to enhance the experience." Shrugging, Spinner did her best to try for flippant. "That had some interesting, albeit painful, effects."

"Sounds like it would make a man volatile," Dael said carefully.

"Yes."

"Did he beat you, Aniwyn?" Dael pushed her half-eaten portion to the side, resting her elbows on the table.

"He mainly targeted my younger brother, Pherry, but when I was present, I put myself in the middle. So, yes, he hit me. He never meant to, I'm fairly sure, but my brother, who was only nine years old when our mother left, was the scapegoat for anything that went wrong in our father's life. We kept up appearances until I was old enough to leave. I took Pherry with me and that was the only time I threatened my father. I said if he didn't give me Pherry, I'd testify against him. That worked. He was a general in the military with more medals and awards than any of his peers. He preferred to lose his son rather than lose face in front of them."

"I'm so sorry." Dael's eyes were dark, whether from sympathy or anger, Spinner couldn't tell.

"I shouldn't have brought this up now. Today. Compared to what's happened, it's nothing." Spinner stood and cleared off the table, not sure why she was suddenly so rigid, so stiff that it actually hurt.

"Days like today bring up all sorts of emotions and memories."

"And I was waiting here to be a sounding-board and help you feel better. That sure backfired." Spinner stowed the plates in the cleaner and closed the lid. A faint hum proved it had started the washing process instantly. "You still want me to hang around or…" Only now did she notice she was twisting the end of her left sleeve until she'd constricted the blood flow to her hand.

"Yes. I do. I know it's not what we planned, but if we could just sit on the couch for a bit, that'd be perfect." Dael stood and passed Spinner on the way to the couch.

Not sure how it happened, as her arms moved so fast and, it seemed, of their own volition, Spinner pulled her into a fierce embrace. Dael gasped, almost stumbled, but then clung to Spinner, her arms around her waist. Spinner held on to Dael with one hand around her tank-top shoulder strap. When Dael sank into the hug, Spinner shifted her grip and wrapped her arms around Dael's neck.

"I hurt. I never thought I'd hurt this badly," Dael murmured. "It's as if I carry the pain of each and every one of my crew and passengers. I can't breathe. I can't."

"Yes, you can. Just let it go." Spinner felt back in control of her own emotions by putting Dael's wellbeing first. "You have all the help of your senior staff, the counselors, everybody. Yes, we look to you for guidance, but we're also your support, your shoulders to lean on, if you will. And you have me—in whatever capacity you need me. I'm here." She was walking on loose sand now, offering more than she'd ever offered anyone, apart from Pherry and his family. Perhaps even more.

❖

"Oh, Aniwyn." Dael pushed her face into Spinner's neck. The soft fragrance of soap and something sweet and fruity pulled her farther in, and she shamelessly clung to Spinner's waist.

"Hey, let's sit down. Didn't mean to ambush you." Spinner tugged her along to the couch where Dael let go enough to sit down. Spinner followed suit and pulled a blanket over both their legs. The warmth was such bliss, but it was the shared comfort that made it possible to finally draw deep breaths. Dael knew she hadn't taken one full breath since the news hit. When she closed her eyes, she saw the images of burning people, of structures falling on crowds, crushing them, and other demonstrators holding their heads in desperate grips as they screamed for seemingly no apparent reason.

"I've always defended the changers," Spinner murmured, and began unfastening Dael's hair, pulling one hair-tie out after another until her long hair lay in thick tresses around her shoulders. "I've maintained my opinion that they never could choose," Spinner continued, "that they were born with this dormant genetic makeup triggered by the Creator knows what. Most of them are harmless people that the so-called normal population harass."

"And now we've seen the ones who are hostile and use their new powers with evil intent. They might have convinced themselves that they had to do it this way to bring their cause to the forefront. Such fools…If anything, this makes everyone hate and fear them even more."

"Yes, I know. I knew of several changers who had to leave the service because of DNA screenings. I objected to the screenings." Spinner pulled Dael against her shoulder.

"Lights at ambiance level." Dael drew her feet up under her. The intimate closeness was making her heart hammer in a much more pleasant way than it had during this hellacious day. "I did too. At least twenty percent of the ones with the dormant changer genes never notice any new and supernatural abilities. Though I admit, I thought the rumors of the ones who could fly were hoaxes. I've seen amazing things among the changers—psychic abilities, telekinetic gifts, camouflagers, fire-starters, impenetrable skin, etc. Never anyone flying, though. "

"Me either." Spinner started rubbing Dael's bare arm under the blanket. "I'm torn about the next report—impatient to know more, to hear from family and friends, but also afraid what it might disclose."

"You probably share those mixed emotions with just about everyone here. I stopped by Nania's quarters on the way here. That's why I was later than I intended. She's handling it well, but of course, she's stunned like the rest of us." Dael tipped her head against the backrest. "I was concerned since she's old and her heart isn't as strong as it used to be."

"You can usually tell how well she's doing if you pay attention to her gallows humor."

"True. Wait. How do you know?" Dael turned her head, looking at Spinner, who was literally squirming.

"I visit with her sometimes. At her request, but the truth is, I really like her. I should've told you, but Helden didn't want me to. Not sure why."

"Oh, I can guess," Dael muttered. "Don't worry. I'm not angry and I don't mind. In fact, if Helden enjoys your company and you're all right with it, I don't see why you couldn't visit with her. If anything, I may be a little bit envious."

"I realize she's your nania—"

"That she gets so much of your time." Dael felt less weighed down every time she dared tell Spinner something true on a personal level. Admitting something close to jealousy like this was huge.

Spinner hummed something inaudible and bent Dael over the backrest, so very gently. Dael could only look up into Spinner's dark eyes, now gleaming with something other than tears or pain. In fact, the way Dael scanned her was close to predatory.

It was inevitable. Spinner slowly lowered her head and pressed her lips to Dael's. Softly, she kept them there, not deepening the kiss, but repeating it over and over in small, gentle caresses. Dael knew this was a complication she could ill afford, but the kiss was like no other she'd received. That was just it; Spinner's kisses were like gifts.

Trembling now, Dael pushed her hands into Spinner's curly hair. Soft like a baby's, it twirled itself around her fingers, pulling her in even more.

"Oh, Dael…Dael…" Spinner moaned against Dael's lips. "I've wanted this for so long." She let her lips travel along Dael's jawline toward her neck.

Dael in turn massaged and scratched Spinner's scalp gently. "So have I. But it's not right. I mean, it's not fair on…oh!"

Spinner used her tongue to caress the indentation at the base of Dael's neck. The fire inside Dael erupted, and suddenly images of burning people interfered, flickering across the inside of her eyelids. Moaning, she pushed at Spinner.

"Aniwyn. We have to stop. I…can't. I can't." She was shaking and trying to breathe evenly.

Spinner pulled back, her eyes huge. "Am I hurting you?"

"No. No! I just can't do this. The intimacy. You know, between us." Dael sat up and made sure their legs didn't touch. "It's—I can't be involved like that. With a subordinate. I'm sorry…Aniwyn?"

"Because I'm a subordinate? I've been under your command since day one. We all are."

"Yes, or course, but—" Dael knew now she was in pain after all. "I feel what you feel. If things were different, I would've pursued this…you much sooner." Standing up, Dael tugged at her fingers, trying to explain.

"So, despite knowing how good we could be together, how well we fit, and the way we feel…or at least I do…" Spinner pushed her hair out of her face. "Or you might not feel like I do at all?" To hear her sound so confused and lost tore at Dael, beat at her chest until it was hard to breathe.

"Oh, don't sound so forlorn. You're killing me with those big, dark eyes." Flinging her hands in the air, Dael tried to corral her rampaging emotions. "I don't want to lose you." Panic started to simmer under the surface, which she clung to in an effort to maintain her equilibrium.

"Let me see if I understand. You don't want to lose me, but you don't want me like this. Like a lover." Spinner looked like she was really trying to understand, but it was equally clear that she didn't.

"I've been very selfish," Dael said quietly. "I've allowed myself to enjoy this closeness, this flirtation, if you will, hoping nobody would get hurt. Least of all you. I could see how you looked at me, how you reacted physically to our proximity. I thought it would pass, that you'd move on. You have quite the reputation for being…"

"Frivolous?" Spinner filled in the word with a noncommittal voice. "Or perhaps even promiscuous?"

"No! No." Dael sat back down next to Spinner. "I'd never think of you as either of those. You know I value your friendship and respect." She swallowed against the increasing dryness in her throat. "This other part of it, the sexual tension, I…I was taken aback and couldn't resist you…your beauty and your innate sensuality."

"I wish you hadn't strung me along, then. You made me hope for more." Spinner spoke thickly, her eyes glossy. "Because I want more, much more. I guess that's not what people in general would guess when they're considering my image as a cavalier spin-jack gambling, brandy-drinking, and most definitely shallow kind of woman." Bitterness crept into her voice. "Who in their right mind would set out to have a meaningful, deep relationship with someone like me? The fact that my former lovers never bothered to stick around long enough to find out who I really am also speaks for my lack of taste in women. Then there was you, in command. You took my breath away. Can you imagine how stunned I was when we danced and then you kissed my cheek? After that, I lost my heart to you, bit by bit."

"Spinner." Dael had misjudged this woman and the depths of her feelings, her sincerity. "I can't do this today. I can't have this discussion. I'm sorry."

"You're sorry?" Spinner looked at her, the pain clearly visible. "You don't have to be sorry for the way you feel. It is what it is. I should've known better." She began to get up. "I'll just—oh!"

Dael panicked at the thought of them parting with all the hurt still simmering, so she wrapped her arms around Spinner's neck and hugged her. "I'm sorry. Don't go like this."

"Dael?" Spinner sounded more dazed than upset.

"We have to figure this out, and we will, but not today. That doesn't mean I want you to go. Please stay. Please, Aniwyn?"

Spinner pulled back some and cupped Dael's cheeks, caressing her temples with her thumbs. Humming, she kissed Dael's forehead. "Hush," she said in a low murmur. "Don't panic."

"Don't go." Dael knew she was becoming unraveled, and not only because the situation with her and Spinner but all of the horrific events that had occurred without time to process in between. "Damn it." Her voice hitched and she began to tremble.

Spinner's lips softened even more as they covered Dael's mouth again. She melted into the kiss before she realized she was reciprocating again. Her synapses fired off a distinct sizzle in her brain. Spinner made the kisses even impossibility lighter, barely noticeable on the lips, but very much so in the rest of Dael's body. They went from arousing to hypnotic without Dael realizing it, and then, she finally relaxed as they lowered themselves into a reclining position. Exhausted, she fell asleep on her couch with Spinner for the second time.

When she woke up a few hours later, she was firmly tucked in with the blanket, her boots on the floor next to the couch, but Spinner was gone.

Chapter Twenty-two

Spinner opened her eyes and groaned at what clearly was a mistake. "Ow. Ow-ow-ow." She stood on wobbly legs and tried to remember what woke her up.

Her door chime rang, reminding her in yet another painful way.

"Hold on." She gazed down at her rumbled uniform. Sleeping with her clothes on wasn't smart at all. A glance at the mirror in the small closet area confirmed that she looked like she felt. Gray-toned skin, dark circles, and bloodshot eyes.

"Spinner, are you all right?" a bright voice asked from the other side of the door. Darmiya.

Groaning again, and regretting even that as it hurt her head, Spinner opened the door. Darmiya brushed past her and pivoted so quickly, Spinner could feel the draft from her movement.

"Are you trying to kill yourself?" Darmiya spoke with as much anger as someone so vivacious could muster.

"What are you talking about? And while we're on the subject of talking, please keep it down a bit. I have a headache."

"No wonder! You played cards all night, and it was a miracle you won anything as you never let go of that bottle of brandy the whole time." Darmiya glared at her, but she was clearly concerned.

"How would you possibly know?" Spinner moved to the bathroom and began to undress. A quick visit to the shower-tube together with some herbal tea would help.

"Because Calagan was one of the players. He came home and said you were acting so out of character that he was worried. He even talked about going to the admiral—"

"No." Spinner poked her head out, half undressed. "That's not necessary. I'm fine. I just need to kick back and relax in my own way when I'm off duty."

Darmiya wasn't buying it. Her eyes singed Spinner's as she took a step closer. "Didn't you once tell me that as CAG, much like the admiral and Doc, you're never off duty? Your pilots might need you at any given time. Or did I dream up that whole conversation?"

Cornered now, and hating it, Spinner pulled back into the bathroom. "You know what I mean. Don't I have the right to some rest and relaxation?"

"Of course you do." Darmiya's voice softened marginally. "But when your means of relaxation is hurting you, and potentially endangering those you command aboard the ship, you need to question yourself."

"I'm not endangering anything or anyone!" Spinner stepped into the shower-tube and put the setting on extra hot. The recycled water hit her shoulders with such force, it hurt. The pain felt good, as it was cleansing her, and she just stood there, letting the spray do the punishing.

As she rolled a towel around herself, Spinner listened for sounds from the living area of her quarters, half hoping Darmiya had left.

"I'm still here if you're wondering," Darmiya said, as if reading her mind. "I've made tea and breakfast. I hope you like cereal."

"Thank you. It's fine." Spinner dressed in a light-gray leisure suit. She wasn't on duty until late afternoon. She'd have time to recycle her uniform before then.

In the living area, Darmiya had set the table and even added three small flowers to a water-filled mug. Had she had them when storming through the door? Spinner couldn't remember. She sat down and greedily gulped in half a mug of tea. She poured more from the kettle and kept drinking.

"You realize that's yet another effect of too much brandy." Darmiya sounded so sad, Spinner flinched and stared at her.

"Drinking tea?"

"No. Gulping two mugs down in less than twenty secs. Restoring symptoms of dehydration and regulating the blood glucose and level of saline. Typical for a hangover. This will help too. She pushed some cereal and a protein bar toward Spinner.

"You seem to have read up on this." Spinner peeled the wrapping off the protein bar and bit off a piece.

"I did, actually. I also talked, hypothetically speaking, to Doc."

"What?" Spinner dropped the protein bar. "You told Doc? Don't you realize he will write me up and that way you might as well have sent a memo to Dael?"

"Listen to me. I spoke to Doc about a hypothetical person, and even if he guessed it was you—and he might—he can't write you up. I'm not stupid." Darmiya spoke softly now. "Aniwyn, please."

Suddenly swallowing against tears, which she hated and simply refused to let run down her cheeks, Spinner picked up the bar and finished it. "Just give it a rest, Dar."

"Didn't you once tell me your father was a drunk, and a mean drunk at that?" Darmiya asked softly.

The question, put forward in such an innocent voice, hit Spinner right between the eyes. She was about to turn into her father. The woman she cared about more than anything didn't feel the way she did...rejected her, really, and so she turned to gambling and drinking... just like her father had done after her mother left. How could she have gone on like this for weeks and not realized?

"Yes, I did," she answered, her voice so husky it was barely carrying.

"You're mainly hurting yourself, but if you ever took the time to look at the admiral, you'd see how she's suffering too." Darmiya rounded the table and put her arm around Spinner. "It's none of my business what goes on between you, but it is my business when my friend is skidding down the wrong path."

Spinner was so close at snapping at Darmiya for bringing up Dael she had to pinch the skin between her thumb and index finger to stop herself. *A mean drunk.* "I'll stop. I'm not just saying that. I see what you're saying and I will stop. Not the spin jack," Spinner added with a wry grin, "but the brandy. I promise." She meant it. No way she was turning into the man who'd hurt her brother so badly. No fucking way.

"Good." Darmiya tugged at one of Spinner's curly tresses. "I think you have a lot to figure out, and doing it in a haze of brandy fumes is making it harder than it has to be."

"Yeah."

Darmiya stayed as Spinner finished her breakfast, chattering in her usual harmless way, but Spinner knew Darmiya was making sure her words had sunk in.

Spinner regarded her friend with new eyes. She couldn't think of any other person that she'd met who would do what Darmiya had dared to. Confronting someone in Spinner's condition and frame of mind took guts. The elfin-looking young woman, her black curls flowing down her back, looked fragile and certainly acted like an airhead some of the time, but she was the best friend Spinner had ever had.

"What do you say," Spinner said, "feel like going swimming?" It had been a long time since they'd done anything together.

"Yes!" Clapping her hands, Darmiya bounced off the chair. "I'd love that."

"All right. Let's go then." Spinner grabbed her bag containing her gear. As she stood, she noticed her headache was dissipating. Perhaps the mere hope that her world was righting itself made her feel physically better?

"I bet I can beat you this time," Darmiya said, her eyes glittering.

"You know what? I think you can too." Spinner smiled wistfully as Darmiya giggled.

Before they left her quarters, Spinner casually grabbed the last bottle of brandy she owned and poured it in the recycler. The look in Darmiya's eyes made the gesture worth it.

CHAPTER TWENTY-THREE

Spinner placed the freighter in high orbit, locked the console on auto, and turned around. Behind her, Lieutenant Schpay, Darmiya, and the team of geologists and security looked expectantly at her.

"I'm going to land soon, but I want to make sure we don't end up being chased by homicidal rats this time. Darmiya and Lieutenant Schpay will perform high-definition scans while I perform low flybys, one sector after another. Once we've covered nine squares of the grid, I'll allow a team of two geologists, four security officers, and Darmiya to enter the one in the center of the nine squares. By doing so, we're reasonably sure the surroundings sectors are safe and provide a buffer. We'll do the same at a section farther north and then repeat this undertaking three more times. We have twenty other freighters carrying out the same procedure, and when we're done, we'll hopefully have enough for the admiral to go by when she makes her decision."

"Oh, this is so exciting!" Darmiya literally bounced in her seat, held in place only by the harness. "My first mission and such an important one."

Spinner smiled. "After 250 some days on this mission, I'm happy about the chance to go planetside no matter what." The image of Dael entered her mind unbidden, but she refused to let her heartache disturb such a good and different kind of day. Being stuck in a rut for two months did very little to heal a bruised heart. Decisively, she pushed away the memory of how Dael had felt in her arms that night after the horrible news from Oconodos. All in all, a ghastly day.

"What are you going to do?" Darmiya asked. "I mean, while we're working?"

"Oh, let me see," Spinner said, tapping her chin with her index finger. "I suppose I could go shopping, or hook up with some fun-loving chick, or—"

"Oh, please." Darmiya covered her forehead. "So funny. Or not."

Chuckling, since Darmiya was such a rewarding person to tease, Spinner shook her head. "All right, all right. I'm going to do runs between the two teams, back and forth, in case you need assistance. That way you'll never have to remain without backup for more than four, five minutes at a time. Keep in constant contact. All right?"

"Yes, sir," the crew echoed, except Darmiya, who made an affirmative gesture by placing her thumb against her little finger and raising the three middle fingers to the ceiling. Learning Oconodian popular gestures was one of her hobbies. Spinner teased her often that she'd be able to stop talking at all very soon.

Soon her teams were deployed, and she received constant reports from the others around this beautiful planet. The eight assault craft that had joined them as part of the security detail made continuous visits with all the team leaders.

The planet held three large continents stretching across the equator. At the far end of the poles, ice thicker than their instruments could judge created two smaller continents of sorts, both rich with wildlife that seemed to have adapted to such a cold environment. The various scenery consisted of grass-plains, woods, jungles, and mountains, which reminded Spinner of Oconodos. The oceans appeared to be full of wildlife as well, and they had to make sure no sentient beings lived in the deep either.

It was boring as hell to run back and forth between the two groups she was directly responsible for, but no way were they going through any disasters as with the horrible rodents they'd encountered last time. This was the first potentially viable world they'd come across since then, and Spinner was carefully optimistic.

"Darmiya to Spinner."

Spinner slapped the sensor to respond. "Spinner here. What's wrong?" She'd already turned the freighter toward where she'd let Darmiya off.

"Nothing's wrong," Darmiya said, laughing. "I just want to you know that I found what registers as edible mushrooms. I've examined them with my biologically enhanced scanner, and they are in fact tremendously nutritious. Isn't that great?"

Spinner chuckled. Who could ever stay annoyed at such exuberance and joy? "It sure is. I'm swinging by you in a few minutes."

"I'll be waving."

"You're in a wooded area, silly. I won't see you."

"If you use the new feature on your scanner Calagan and I came up with, you will." Darmiya snickered.

"Oh, you're so clever. All right. Wave away." Spinner pulled the lever to fly lower over the forest.

The dangerous thing about not having anything more cerebral to occupy her time was that her mind tended to drift toward Dael. She fought the tendency but gave up, as this seemed to be what her heart wanted to dwell on right now. She missed their closeness and the breakfasts they used to share. In fact, she'd never struggled with such loneliness before. After the disastrous evening when they kissed and Spinner had mistakenly thought her feelings were reciprocated, she'd withdrawn. Dael had made a few attempts to approach her, but Spinner had never felt this raw and exposed. She reacted by being polite and correct toward Dael and by throwing herself into her old habits. At this point, she'd cleaned out most of her pilots while playing spin jack and used a lot of her winnings to buy brandy. That could've ruined her if Darmiya hadn't stepped in with her wide-eyed but so very effective approach.

Spinner hadn't thanked Darmiya yet for being the voice of reason, and she couldn't imagine anyone else having nearly the same success. She hadn't touched any brandy the last twenty-some days. She didn't miss it. The clarity of her mind made the heartache over Dael harder to deal with, yes, but all the brandy in the universe couldn't erase how she felt anyway.

Eight hours later, the last of the freighters had finalized their surveillance and sample-collecting and returned to meet the others. As they pushed into half magnetar, Spinner tensed. She'd been able to relax while flying over the planet, having some distance from the *Espies Major* and what waited when they returned, but now her shoulders pushed up and started to ache in a familiar way. How long would it be before she could exist around Dael without this gut reaction?

The rendezvous point was four hours away at half-magnetar speed, which was the normal traveling speed for freighters, even if they were capable of going faster. Spinner set the freighter on auto and moved back to have something to eat with the others. This helped take her mind off things, as the scientists were very optimistic about the planet they'd just visited.

"No damn squirrels," one of the geologists said. "But clean water, prime soil for growing crops, and enough flat surfaces not to have to do a lot of restructuring. I even found gold."

"I like the no-squirrel part the best," Darmiya said. "Those little beasts were definitely a deal breaker."

"I take it you never had pet rats as a child?" Spinner deadpanned.

Darmiya paled. "Pet *rats?*" she said, her voice a mere squeak. "Did you?"

"As a matter of fact, I had several types of them. I even competed with them." Spinner smiled, as this was one of her happiest childhood memories.

"Doing what? Eating cheese the fastest?" Calagan chuckled as she munched on a sandwich.

"Ha-ha. Obstacle courses, actually. My rats won a lot. I ran illegal betting among my friends."

"You were a gambler already then." Darmiya crinkled her nose fondly. "Why am I not surprised?"

"It paid for my other interest when I got older," Spinner said. "Flying lessons."

"So, your career started with rats. That should go on your curriculum vitae." Calagan laughed and the others followed suit once they saw their CAG didn't object to their mirth.

"*Espies Major* to CAG. *Espies Major* to CAG." A stern voice interrupted the laughter, and Spinner jumped up and took her seat at the helm.

"CAG here. We're only an hour away, *Espies Major*."

"We're under attack. Have weapons ready at your return." Ensign Umbahr's voice was strained. "I'm sending you tactical updates. Is Lieutenant Schpay on your freighter?"

"He is."

"The admiral wants you to work with him on the safest way to approach the battle."

"Wait. Where's the admiral?" Spinner had to ask.

"Right here, but busy."

"Got it." The console pinged. "I have the tactical data."

"Good, we are taking heavy…and cannot…longer…" Static replaced Umbahr's fragmented words.

"CAG to *Espies Major*. CAG to *Espies Major*." No reply. "CAG to any Advance team ship. CAG to any Advance team ship." Spinner punched another sensor. "CAG to all freighters and assault craft. The convoy is under attack. Engage maximum magnetar drive. They need our help, and we should be there in less than forty-five minutes if we step on it."

Still no answer. Glancing behind her, she knew she didn't have to repeat anything as they had all heard her orders. Lieutenant Schpay placed his computer tablet against the console and downloaded the data. "We have work to do," he said darkly.

Spinner nodded. "Yes, we do." Nodding to one of the crew-members to take over the helm, she moved to a table in the far corner. "We have forty-five minutes to plan. Then we join the fight, or what's left of it."

❖

The *Espies Major* bucked and turned under Dael's feet. Stumbling, she had to throw herself into her command chair, where the emergency harness immediately strapped her in.

"They're coming about, two large vessels accompanied by twenty-four smaller assault-type craft." Weniell had taken Lieutenant Schpay's console in the tactical officer's absence.

"Time to circle the wagons." Dael pressed a sensor on her armrest. "Admiral Caydoc to all Advance ships. Defensive pattern zero. I repeat: defensive pattern zero. Acknowledge."

The other four ships confirmed receiving the order, and soon they were in a star-shaped formation, able to fire in all directions. All assault craft were already deployed and circling them, firing back at the attackers.

"Trying this again," Dael muttered. "Admiral Caydoc of the *Espies Major* to unknown vessel. Why are you firing? We're not your enemy. I repeat: we are not your enemy. Stop firing on us or we will be the ones to end this. Your firepower is great, but we're stronger in number, and if you've scanned us, you can tell we have enough to match you."

The attackers kept firing without responding. After another ten minutes of constant bombardment, during which Dael alternated between giving tactical orders and trying to establish audio or video with them, a scratchy voice came in over the communication array.

"You are trespassers in the Alachleve sector. This is considered an act of assault."

Frowning, Dael thought quickly. "We did not know this was a bordered part of space. We have no indication of any buoy markers or—"

"You are trespassers. Stand down your weapons, call back your fighters, and prepare to be boarded."

"I cannot allow you to board our vessels. We're just passing through and don't mean any harm. Call back your attack and we will be out of this sector within minutes."

The gruff voice now sounded lethal. "You have made the wrong decision and will regret it." The Alachleve representative gave a low growl and cut communications.

"Caydoc to all assault craft, prepare for renewed attacks." Dael turned to a junior ensign. "Run to Fleet Admiral Caydoc's quarters and assist in getting her here—fast."

"Aye, sir." The young woman left without wasting any time.

"Here they come, Admiral," Weniell said.

"Assault craft. Diamond formation. Return fire." Dael wanted to stand, to pace back and forth on the bridge as was her habit. It helped clear her mind and made her think better. Instead, the unrelenting harness held her prisoner in her chair and she just had to work around that restriction.

"Any sign of the CAG and her teams?" She refused to let the thought of Spinner and the 170-some crewmembers who had gone on yet another planet survey distract her for more than a couple of moments.

"Their ETA is two hours. Depending on what they found on the planet, it could differ by half an hour, more or less." Umbahr spoke through gritted teeth as his hands flew across the console before him.

"We need to stand our ground until we can leave without being followed. As soon as the survey team is within range, we have to warn them so they don't run into this unprepared."

"We could use the reinforcement," Weniell said.

"As I said, not unprepared." Dael let her gaze fly between the screens. Everywhere she saw, different size vessels were engaged in combat, explosions reverberating around them. Her people were already carrying out the diamond-pattern assault on the attackers. She just had to be patient and follow their progress, while thinking of contingency plans for whatever outcome the crew's efforts would have.

They would know soon enough.

CHAPTER TWENTY-FOUR

"Coming out of half magnetar. Stay alert, people!" Spinner, piloting the first of twenty freighters, pushed the two sensors down to march-speed two. The space around them wobbled for a few moments, and then it took her only another two secs to realize they were too late.

Pieces of technology and parts of damaged or destroyed ships whirled toward them, and Spinner tugged at the levers, barely dodging them.

"CAG to survey freighters. Watch out for debris. Stay in my wake for now and maintain radio silence. Acknowledge." She barely heard the voices responding from the other ships. Instead she tried to decipher what she saw. In the periphery, assault craft fired on alien-looking ships, and farther away, behind dust particles and wreckage, she could barely make out the larger outlines of the Advance-team vessels. Something cold ran through her veins, as she counted only four of them.

"Holy hell," she whispered, and placed the freighter on a semicircle trajectory around the battlefield. "Where's the fifth ship?" She hardly dared look too closely at the pieces of wreckage floating in space. If she saw anything that resembled the hull of the *Espies Major* or the other ships, she would lose her composure. "Dael, what the hell happened?" Spinner whispered. "Please, be safe."

A huge explosion, followed by more fragments and dust, hurtled toward them as Spinner's freighter neared where Advance assault craft in formation moved in on one of the alien ships. Spinner could tell the assault craft were slowly driving the attackers away, not giving them time to regroup or counterattack.

"You've trained them well, CAG," Calagan said from behind. He slid into the co-pilot's seat and the harness hugged him instantly. "One of ours is missing. Did they manage to go to magnetar drive?"

"I doubt it," Spinner said, her jaw hurting as she spoke. "Dael would place her ships in a circular star formation to give them the widest range to fire from. And she would only do so if diplomacy failed. She's definitely not the trigger-happy kind."

"Nor does she hesitate when firing is required," Calagan said, and nodded. "Schpay is running scans in the back. He sent me up here to let you know."

Schpay knew better than to yell across the bridge of the freighter in a tense situation like this.

"Good. From what I can make out, the assault craft have managed to send most of the smaller alien vessels packing. The ones who aren't in miniscule pieces."

"Can you make out which ship is the *Espies Major*?" Calagan squinted at the screens.

"Not yet. I tried to magnify, but all I got were blurry images due to the space dust. We have to wait until we get closer. I think I'll dare to use the comm system now." Pressing the sensor, she cleared her voice before speaking. "CAG to *Espies Major*. CAG to *Espies Major*."

"Caydoc to CAG. Spinner, we just picked you up on sensors. Move in behind the *Tommus*, coordinates 5-9-9-3-00. They will have the freighter bay open for half your survey team. The rest of you, round the *Tommus* on the starboard side and enter the *Espies Major*'s bay. You have to be quick. We're ready to go to magnetar drive now that the assault craft have plowed a route for us. The window could close any minute." Dael's voice was mechanical, as if the admiral was running on pure professionalism, which was probably the truth.

"Aye, sir," Spinner said, and corrected her course toward the given coordinates. She let the rest of her team know, deciding also that the first ten freighters behind her would use the *Tommus*'s freighter bay, and the rest would follow her to the *Espies Major*.

As the last of the freighters entered the *Tommus*, Spinner took point and guided the others on the starboard side toward their goal. The sight when the *Espies Major* came into view made Darmiya moan behind them. "Oh, Spinner."

"I see it." Spinner registered the scorch marks, the broken hull around deck fourteen, and the gaping hole where one of the few promenade decks with large view ports had been located. "She's taken such a beating."

"But she's still operational," Calagan said. "Spinner—watch out!"

Three small alien assault-craft type vessels appeared from underneath the *Tommus* and headed toward them.

"Weapons ready, Schpay!" She maneuvered the freighter to give him the best angle.

"Firing." Schpay kept up the barrage of fire until several of the other freighters made it into the bay. Another freighter covered them from a ninety-degree angle, firing nonstop.

"CAG to freighter 19. If we're both going to make it onto the *Espies Major*, we need to hit them where it hurts."

"Which means getting in closer," the bright female voice of the pilot of the freighter said calmly.

"Exactly." Spinner let her hands caress the controls, moving the freighter forward. "Keep your stern toward them. Give them less of a target."

"Aye, sir."

"Aim for their weapons' array. Shot for shot, make them count."

"Every single one, sir." Freighter 19 moved parallel to Spinner's vessel, never stopping the firing.

"Keep an eye on the third one in the back," Spinner said to Calagan. "If it moves forward at all, let me know. I'm running low on ammunition, but there's always the last resort."

"Ramming them," Darmiya murmured from behind.

Spinner smiled joylessly. Darmiya never ceased to amaze her. "Exactly. We can't risk them firing on the mother ships." She turned her head quickly toward Schpay. "Target their weapons' array and take them out."

"Aye, sir."

Just as she turned her attention forward again, there was a blinding light and a shockwave as a vessel exploded somewhere on their port side. Spinner shielded her eyes as she tried to make out the outline of Freighter 19. She couldn't see it.

❖

"Move in two klicks to our port side." Helden clung to the armrest of her automatic chair. "Roll the ship, belly toward them, and raise the stern two degrees."

Dael was over at tactical, as Weniell was lying unconscious in the impromptu triage area down the corridor. Bringing Helden in had been a gamble that paid off. The older woman simply took over as Dael stepped over the injured and kept firing as she alerted the medics.

"Laying down cover fire to assist the last freighters." Dael aimed for the smaller alien vessels, taking out the one in the back. The explosion was enormous, which proved these three carried the same missiles as the ones that had taken out one of her mother ships.

"*Espies Major* to CAG," Helden barked. "We're covering you. Get inside now. We've got to get out of here."

"CAG to Caydoc. I hear you."

"Can you detect them?" Helden asked Umbahr, who had his head almost entirely covered by bandages. "Are they inside?"

"Freighter 19 is inside. They've sustained heavy damage."

"And Freighter 1?"

"Not yet."

Dael cursed under her breath and kept firing, taking out the second small craft. "The last enemy assault craft is firing up something I can't judge the magnitude of. I can't get a weapons lock."

"Freighter 1 is on board. All remaining assault craft are accounted for." Umbahr leaned heavily at his console.

Helden tapped a sensor with her good hand. "Caydoc to Advance fleet—go to magnetar drive to previously set coordinates. Now. Acknowledge."

"*Tommus* to magnetar drive."

"*Hegal* to magnetar drive."

"*Rondos* to magnetar drive."

Dael's heart was like an achingly cold void as no voice reported from the *Mugdon*.

Helden spoke curtly. *"Espies Major* to magnetar drive."

The ensign at the helm slapped her hand on the console, and then everything became quiet as they left the hostile, lethal part of space behind them. Dael nodded to one of the junior ensigns to take over tactical and made her way over to her nania. "Are you all right?"

"I'm fine, dear." Helden looked pale but composed. "And before you say anything, it was an amazing accomplishment for you not to lose more people, or ships, than you did. The Alachleves are a particularly hostile and, when it comes to weaponry, well-equipped people. I don't think we'll ever know why they fired first and never bothered to ask any questions."

"I lost the *Mugdon*."

"We all lost it. Those aboard were taken from us, and we owe them to do our damndest to find the new Oconodos. So, I'm going to retire. I am a bit tired, I admit. When you've finished the no-doubt endless debriefings, you can stop by. If you're too tired, I'll see you tomorrow. My door is always open for you, Dael. You know that."

"I do." Kissing Helden's cheek, she turned to retake her command chair, when a frail hand on her arm stopped her.

"And go make sure Spinner is all right at the first opportunity. That woman holds your happiness. You know that too." Helden patted Dael's arm and then maneuvered her chair toward the corridor.

Dael's mind reeled for a short moment before she slammed down her command mask once again. She would talk to Spinner eventually. Right now, she needed to know just how bad things were. Sitting down in her chair, aching all over, she gazed around the bridge with calmness. "Report."

❖

Spinner ran through the corridors, Darmiya and Calagan right behind her. Now that they were safely on board and the ship had gone to magnetar drive, all she could think of was making sure Dael was all right. She realized Dael would be insanely busy during the upcoming hours and in no mood to talk to her about anything personal, but she needed to *see* her.

"We're going to head for the science lab and see what damage has been done," Calagan gasped behind her. "Say hi to the admiral."

"Later." Spinner rounded the corner and found the elevator inoperable. Not hesitating, she grabbed the ladder mounted on the bulkhead next to it and began climbing the twelve decks to the bridge area.

Out of breath, she finally reached the mayhem that was the corridor outside the bridge. She could hardly believe her eyes when she saw Doc leading physicians, nurses, medics, and volunteers in the crowded corridor.

"Good to see you, CAG," the doctor bellowed from the other end. "You better enter the bridge via the conference room over there. We need the space here for a while."

"I can tell. Do you need me to help?" She thought she should ask, as the number of wounded looked staggering.

"No, we have it under control now. I think the admiral is expecting you on the bridge. You better get there. Fast."

Confused at his choice of words, Spinner pushed the broken door open to the conference room. Even in there, wounded were everywhere, but these seemed to have been tended to. They leaned against the bulkhead as they sat against the walls, and a few were lying on thin mattresses on the table. Carefully making her way among the crewmembers, Spinner stopped a few times to check on some of her pilots before she entered the bridge.

The impressive bridge of the *Espies Major* had looked better, but everything seemed functional. Dael stood in the center, her hair in disarray and flowing down her back, her uniform torn and actually scorched. Umbahr looked like he had a winter hat made of bandages, and Weniell wasn't even there.

"CAG!" Umbahr lit up. "Good to see you in one piece, sir."

"Thank you, Ensign. You're setting a new trend for headwear, I can tell." Spinner stepped closer to Dael, who slowly turned around. "CAG reporting for duty, sir."

"Ani—Spinner. You're back." Dael boasted a large bruise on her left cheekbone. "Good job returning all the freighters."

"They're great pilots, sir."

"They do you proud." Dael walked carefully over to the command chair and was about to sit down when Weniell entered the bridge on crutches but looking all right.

"Your turn, sir," he said, and waved one crutch toward the door. "I ran into Doc in the corridor. He says if you don't get that cheek looked at, he's going to pull medical rank."

"For the love of—"

"He means it this time, sir. Never heard him more serious." Weniell looked somberly at his next in command. "I'll take the next shift."

"What about your leg?" Dael glared at him.

"I have a broken ankle. I wasn't the one who flew headlong into the helm console."

Spinner took another look at Dael and, seeing she was exhausted and not entirely steady, she stepped up next to her. "I have to endure the usual post-mission hoopla at the infirmary anyway. Why don't we go down and get it over with?" She was certain Dael would reject her. After all, Spinner had avoided any personal interaction with Dael for weeks.

"All right." Dael nodded briskly at Weniell. "You have the bridge, Commander. I expect you to forward all reports to my tablet."

"Of course, sir." Weniell sat down and placed the crutches on the floor next to the command chair. "Take your time," he mouthed to Spinner as Dael began to walk away.

Spinner raised her three middle fingers to the ceiling, out of sight of Dael, as she turned and followed suit, letting Weniell know she had the situation under control.

The corridors were still full of people, some wounded, some caring for the wounded. Dael kept stopping to check on her crewmembers, but Spinner stealthily nudged her to keep walking. "What are the first reports saying?" she asked, hoping Dael would focus on her tablet and not how many crewmembers and civilians had been hurt.

"We lost the *Mugdon*. Twenty-five hundred people. Crewmembers. Civilians."

And children. Spinner had realized the *Mugdon* was lost but had nurtured an unrealistic hope it might have gotten away somehow. "How did it happen?" She knew Dael wanted to tell her by the almost relieved look on her face.

"They had us surrounded, but we held them off. Your assault-craft pilots were doing a great job, and we managed to maintain the star formation. All the training paid off and it looked like they were running low on ammunition. Then, smaller craft appeared, which at first seemed less threatening." Dael stopped and turned into an empty part of a dead-end corridor. In there, the lights were on minimum, which was a blessing after the harsh light in the corridor. "When they opened fire, I knew it was going to cost us. They didn't even bother with the assault craft or the freighters. They were aiming for the mother ships, and despite how good our shields are, their shells penetrated them easily."

"I saw a large hole in the bulkhead near the promenade." Spinner leaned against the wall, effectively shielding Dael from anyone looking in their direction.

"Yes, that was one of their shells. They kept firing them and eventually hit the *Mugdon* just beneath the propulsion system where the magnetar coils are located."

"Damn."

"Yes." Dael drew a deep breath and pressed her back against the wall. "Captain Gossamay pulled away, knowing what was going to happen. He managed to send off freighters full of civilians, mainly children and key personnel that were near the freighter bay. He knew if the *Mugdon* exploded while we were in star formation, she'd take us all out."

"He saved the Advance team. Oconodos." Spinner whispered the words as Dael moved closer. "I may not have liked him personally, but he was a good captain. With guts."

"Yes. He was." Dael raised her gaze. "While he was saving us, we managed to take out the smaller ships, and it didn't seem they'd sent any more, until you drew them out."

"You risked a lot by waiting for us."

"I lost the *Mugdon*, but I wasn't going to sacrifice you or your team." Dael sounded raw, as if every word hurt her throat. "It wasn't an option."

"And we made it. We'll be long gone before the Alachleves have time to regroup."

"Yes. Yes, we will." Dael closed her eyes briefly. "I regret that all the hard work you performed on the planet today was for nothing."

"The planet? Oh, yeah." Spinner hadn't even thought of the lush planet she'd just surveyed. "Too close to the Alachleve sector, I'd imagine."

"I could never risk bringing our people here when a volatile race is only hours away." Dael raised her arm and slammed her fist backward, into the bulkhead. "Damn it to hell!" She then pushed past Spinner, her lips tense. "Let's go to the infirmary."

"Right behind you." Spinner remained focused on Dael's increasingly unsteady steps. She hoped the elevator would function now, as she doubted Dael would be able to climb down the ladders.

Dael stood in the center of the infirmary, looking at all the occupied beds. "I shouldn't take up any of the physicians' time. I have a black eye, so what?" She glared at Spinner, who wasn't moving.

"Do you want Doc to take you off duty and have that on your permanent record?" Spinner raised a deliberate eyebrow.

"Of course not." Dael hissed the words out of sheer frustration.

One of the medics approached, saw who the patient was, and didn't hesitate. "Dr. Jobal!"

"What?" A lean young man turned his head from what he was doing. "Ah. Admiral. Take a seat over there," he said, pointing toward two empty chairs by the far wall. "I'll be with you as soon as I've set this shoulder."

Dael walked over to the chairs and sat down without a word. The only thing good about being away from the action in the infirmary was the silence. A glass safety wall separated the niche from the rest of the main room.

Spinner sat down next to Dael, leaning back with a deep sigh. "Is it a sign of weakness if I admit that I'm exhausted?" She made a face and opened the collar of her uniform.

"Not at all. I've been perkier myself." Dael smiled faintly at Spinner's funny face.

"I think these chairs recline." Spinner glanced to her left. "Yup. They do. Just pull that lever thing."

"It's tempting, but how would it look if the crew spots the admiral snoozing in the infirmary at this point?"

"They'd think 'finally, the admiral is resting a bit. Maybe I can do that too.'" Spinner looked intently at Dael. "How about setting an example in that direction as well? We're safe, and the uninjured are tending to the wounded. Weniell is collecting the data you require, and you have nothing to do but wait for Dr. Jobal. Who knows when you'll be able to put your feet up once everything catches up?"

"It's dangerous when you start to make sense," Dael muttered, and pulled the lever. This lowered the backrest and raised her legs, making her whole body melt into the chair. "Oh, sweet Creator."

"Glad you think I occasionally do make sense." Spinner sounded cheerful, but something else, something strained, colored her tone.

"I was joking." Dael turned her head, examining Spinner's beautiful profile. "You realize that, don't you?"

"Yes. Yes, of course."

Concerned now, Dael turned farther on her side to be able to see Spinner better. "When we've dealt with the fallout of this, I mean, the practical end of it, we should talk. Don't you think?"

Spinner slowly turned her head and met Dael's gaze. "I'm not sure I can handle another 'yes, but just like friends,' Dael," she whispered. "I've done my best to *deal* with that over the last few weeks."

"I know. Once you stopped being the brandy moonlighter's best customer, you handled that better than I did. Helden is complaining that I've become a horrible dinner guest and says it's my own fault."

"How so?"

"Because I let you go." Dael had no idea where her courage to be truthful came from.

Spinner in turn seemed at a loss for words. She merely stared at Dael, her lower lip sucked in between her teeth.

"Now, let's scan this cheekbone, sir, so you can finally get out of here." Dr. Jobal stepped into the niche, scanner in hand. "Sorry, I didn't mean to startle you," he added when Spinner jumped. "I guess I need to place you in the full-body scan, CAG."

"Don't worry. I know where it is." Spinner stood and ventured over to one of the booths at the other side of the room. She stepped inside and was immersed in a faint, green light.

Dael barely registered Dr. Jobal's ministrations as he dealt with her facial injury.

"Another mild concussion, Admiral. No fracture. I'm going to use the synaptic stimulator and also clear up the bad bruising for you before you go." He placed two metal plates on other side of Dael's temples, kept in place by a silicon strip. After that he used a capillary-infuser over her face, which took care of a lot of the pain.

"Thank you, Doctor. Am I good to go?"

"Just sit ten minutes longer with the synaptic stimulator. I'll inform Doc that you were most cooperative," the young physician said. "He did warn me of the opposite."

Dael had to smile. "He would know." She sat eight minutes more before she lost her patience and had a nurse remove the stimulator. Standing up slowly to make sure she was steadier on her feet, she walked over to the full-body scanner where Spinner was still confined. "I'm going back to my ready room. Once I've received a good overview of the situation on all ships, I plan to retire to my quarters. Dare I be presumptuous enough to ask you to join me?"

Spinner opened her eyes and squinted through the misty green light. "I guess it depends. I don't want it to end like last time."

Dael couldn't fault Spinner for being blunt, even if it hurt like taking a rifle blast point-blank to the chest. "It won't. Let's both agree to that?"

Spinner tilted her head. "All right. I'll be there."

Relieved, Dael smiled carefully. "You still remember the code to my quarters if I'm running late?"

"I do."

"See you later then." Amazed how much lighter her steps felt than before, Dael walked back through the corridors toward the bridge. She stopped many times to check on crewmembers and civilians she came across. All of them looked like her presence, and her interest, meant a lot to them. They took her hand and thanked her for keeping so many of them safe, if a bit banged up. Before Dael actually reached her ready room, she had to stop to dry her tears. She'd never been this moved or felt such a strong sense of belonging before. Now she also had hope that she could resolve this awkwardness between Spinner and herself. She needed Spinner. It was as simple as that. To deny the feelings erupting inside her as soon as she saw, or thought of, the amazing, infuriating, one-of-a-kind woman that was Spinner was foolish.

Entering the bridge, Dael only shook her head at Weniell. "You still have the bridge, Commander. I'll be in my ready room, reviewing the reports. Tomorrow, we'll gather all the department heads and have the other mother ships do the same, and thus gain a complete perspective of what we have to deal with. For now, only use the most necessary crewmembers for the normal duty roster. The rest will no doubt have things to tend to with loved ones and in their quarters."

"We're on the same page, sir. I have the orders prepared." Weniell nodded from the command chair.

"Thank you, Thresh," Dael said quietly. "Carry on."

In her blissfully quiet ready room, the décor and furniture sat reasonably untouched. Only her shelf of memorabilia had fallen over and would need repair. She bent and picked up her collectables, placing them on her desk. Her computer tablets filled the rest of the space, and twelve of them were blinking an insistent yellow, showing they held reports for her to read. She sat down at her desk, grabbed the first one, and pressed the sensor. Time to get back to work.

CHAPTER TWENTY-FIVE

Helden gazed up at Spinner, her face serious. "You cannot let her off the hook this time," she said. "If you leave her alone too long, she'll regroup, convince herself that staying just friends with you is her duty, that her personal happiness is secondary, if even that. Giving her space is a mistake. Go to her. You're an expert spin-jack player. Be prepared to go for broke when you convince her that the two of you are meant to be."

"Meant to be?" Spinner gaped. "I never would've pegged you for the romantic type, Helden."

"Ha. Shows how much you know. I will have you know, my husband and I shared a long and passionate marriage. Unfortunately, it spawned a son who wasn't equally interested in marital bliss. He left his family home alone most of the time. His wife, Remery, was lovely, but not very strong. She was a curator at a gallery and preferred to surround herself with art and other objects rather than raise her daughter, which I did after my husband passed away. Dael usually traveled with me wherever I was ordered to go. When she decided to follow in my footsteps, her mother had the gall to be insulted that Dael chose not to take over the gallery after her. Instead, Dael became one of the youngest admirals in Oconodian history and ultimately the one chosen to save our people."

"And you think I'm the right person for this formidable person." Spinner wanted to hear how Helden justified this crazy idea.

"You're not only right. You're perfect." Helden pushed the joystick and moved closer. "She needs you, and she's been utterly miserable since you had that falling out. Dael hasn't told me any details, she would never let me in that much, but judging from both your reactions, it was bad."

"It was…" Spinner sighed. "I won't betray her trust by blabbing about it, but yes, it was bad. You say she needs me—and I can see that. I can. That doesn't mean she loves me. And that's what I want. That's what I *need*."

"Oh, Aniwyn, she does. I shouldn't be the one to tell you this, but I can see I have to. She loves you, even if I sometimes wonder if she's confessed that to herself."

Spinner pressed a hand below her sternum, trying to keep the jitters under control. "I'm prepared to approach her again, risk my heart, if you will, but as you knew my mother, you also know why this is so hard for me."

"Yes, I do understand. The way Pamas left you and your brother was selfish, even if she did it to save herself."

"She saved herself from my father's violence, but my brother paid the price. He just switched to another punching bag after she left."

"Perhaps she never thought he'd turn to his children in the manner he'd hurt her?" Helden shook her head, looking sad. "I feel responsible. I helped her, but in my defense, we planned for her to take her children with her."

"You helped her?" Spinner's mouth grew instantly dry, and she grabbed the tea mug and drank. "She just disappeared and didn't even leave a note. For years, I thought he'd killed her."

"She told me she'd arranged for a new identity for the three of you. That was clearly not true, or perhaps it was and her plans didn't work out the way she intended. I don't know, and I'm so sorry you and your brother were left alone to deal with your father's—"

"Yes." Spinner took Helden's weak hand between hers. "Now listen." She wet her lips. "I don't blame you. At least you tried to do something. Not many people do even that. And I don't know if you heard, but I had reassuring news via the buoy messaging service. My brother and his family are doing well, and they've promised to stay away from any of the protests on Oconodos. They're ready to leave as soon as the Exodus plan is set in motion."

"That is great news. I know several who lost friends and family in the attack against the protesters." Helden regarded her carefully. "So, about Dael, go find her and convince her that the two of you deserve to be happy. All right?"

"How can I refuse an order from a fleet admiral?" Spinner crinkled her nose. "I'll try. I promise. If…if I fail, I just want you to know, I'm not sure I have it in me to try a third time. Your granddaughter has the power to shred my heart. Careful as I am, I'd never have let it go this far with someone else. Dael…is Dael. She's the one."

"I understand." Helden placed her good hand on top of Spinner's. "You've reached her inner being, something I've never seen happen. I think you're equally guarded when it comes to your emotions. If you dare to share your feelings with her, that will strengthen your relationship, in whatever form you want it to be."

"All right." Spinner let go of Helden and stood. "I heard you were amazing on the bridge, by the way. Guess it never goes away, does it?"

"What doesn't go away?" Helden looked puzzled.

"The commanding persona. The identity that you and Dael slip into like you're wearing a second skin." Spinner smiled. "It's quite something to see."

"You don't realize you do the same?" Helden smiled up at Spinner. "Going from the extroverted party-girl who loves to gamble to the CAG in the blink of an eye?" She chuckled. "I'd say that's an even more amazing transformation."

"Perhaps." Spinner checked the time on Helden's wall-mounted clock. "Better run. See you tomorrow."

"I'm not going anywhere." Helden waved as Spinner pressed the door sensor and left.

❖

Dael stepped inside her quarters, tired, but jittery. To her surprise, the rooms were dark, with no sign of anyone having been there. Slumping against the closed door, she drew a trembling breath. Clearly Spinner had changed her mind. Who could blame her?

"Lights on ambiance," Dael said, her voice tired.

The light came on and then she saw Spinner sitting in her recliner. She stood, dressed in black trousers and a sleeveless white shirt, looking stunning. Moving with sure strides, Spinner wrapped her arms around Dael. Spinner's soft lips pressed against her throat. Inhaling deeply, Dael recognized Spinner's scent, so familiar. "Aniwyn," Dael whispered, and held on tighter.

"Don't think. Don't talk," Spinner said in a raspy tone. "I want you so much. I have, for the longest time, and I need you...I do." She tugged at the fastening of Dael's jacket, opened it and pushed it off her shoulders, and let it land on the floor. Despite sounding so passionate and greedy, Spinner handled her gently, as if making sure this was all right.

Dael could hardly breathe. Arching into Spinner's touch, she tried to communicate how much she needed her in return. Her nipples hardened, and the sweet ache between her legs spoke for itself.

"You're so stunning. So beautiful," Spinner whispered against her skin. "Let me. Please, let me." She wormed her hands in under Dael's tank top, slipped them around her back, and held her closer.

"Aniwyn." Dael moaned and drove her fingers into Spinner's hair. The soft, wild curls filled her palms, tickled her, and sent shivers up her arms. "Kiss me?" She wanted Spinner to know how much she needed her kisses, how she'd dreamed of them so many times.

"Mmm..." Spinner murmured her way up to Dael's lips. She hovered there, just for a moment, their breaths mingling, but it was enough to make Dael whimper impatiently.

"Come here," Dael whispered, and tugged lightly at Spinner's curls, pulling her in. Parting her lips just a little, she nibbled at Spinner's lower lip, teasing it.

Spinner in turn groaned against Dael's mouth before she slipped her tongue inside to caress the inside of her lips. Dael responded in kind, matching each caress with one of her own.

Letting go for a moment, Dael guided Spinner back to the recliner. She pushed slightly at Spinner's shoulder. "Just sit." Efficiently, Dael removed her boots and then climbed into the chair, which was wide enough for them if she half-sat on Spinner's lap. Gazing at Spinner this closely, she saw several buttons had come undone, and her mouth watered at the sight of the soft, full breasts and the lean muscles playing under the copper-brown skin.

"Hello there," Spinner whispered, and ran her hand up and down Dael's arm. As she reached the shoulder, she let her finger travel in under the shoulder strap of Dael's tank top, following the fabric down to her collarbone. "You feel so good, so smooth."

Dael slowly unbuttoned the rest of the buttons of Spinner's shirt. "You feel amazing." She spread her fingers wide as she caressed Spinner's chest, trying to cover as much skin as possible. "Like silk."

Spinner smiled. "Would you undo your hair for me?"

Knowing her voice wouldn't carry, Dael only nodded and pulled the hair-ties from the thick bun at the nape of her neck. Her hair billowed out around her, and Spinner's eyes grew even darker.

"So beautiful." Shifting, Spinner lowered her head and caught Dael's lips again. Her tongue flicked against Dael's, over and over until Dael cried out, arching to increase the sensation.

"Don't stop. Aniwyn…"

"Never."

Dael gasped for air, pulling back enough to look into Spinner's eyes. "I'm yours, Ani. I'll do my best to make you believe me."

Spinner ran a gentle fingertip down Dael's neck in between her breasts, tugging at the neckline of her tank top. Not taking her eyes from Dael's, as if constantly checking for permission, she slid her finger farther down, across Dael's stomach, where she ran it along the waistline of Dael's uniform trousers.

"May I?" Spinner studied Dale through her curls that kept falling before her eyes.

"Yes," Dael whispered, and began to tremble again.

Spinner unclasped the trousers and slowly pushed her hand inside. "Tell me if I do something…something you don't like, or want."

"Please, touch me, Ani." Not even hesitating, Dael spread her legs, wanting to feel Spinner even closer.

❖

Spinner moaned from sheer bliss as Dael made room for her hand. Dael was so wet, and Spinner knew she was too. Returning to Dael's mouth, she tugged gently at her lower lip with her teeth and then deepened the kiss again. She simply couldn't get enough of the sensation of Dael's skin or the sound of her voice as she gasped Spinner's name. Dael's hair surrounded them like a beautiful blond river.

"I need more," Dael whispered huskily. "I need you…more."

"Anything you want, Dael. Just tell me."

"I need to feel you inside." She pushed long tresses of hair from her face and looked up at Spinner with glowing eyes. "To be yours."

Spinner's heart picked up speed, making it nearly impossible to breathe. "Mine."

"Yes." Dael raised her hips, her breathing coming in short gushes.

Spinner slid her fingers into Dael's briefs, reveling in the satin-smooth skin. She carefully parted the slick, engorged folds between Dael's thighs and slid two fingers inside.

"Oh, yes." Dael groaned. "So…hot."

Spinner moved her hand, pressing her fingers deeper and curling them as she pulled back again. Moving as much as Dael's clothes would let her, she trembled from the heat surrounding her. Dael clung to her, fingers in her hair, one leg hooked over Spinner's.

"You're so wet." Spinner grunted, out of breath.

"Because…of you. All you." Dael was trembling violently now.

"And about to come?" Spinner slipped a third finger inside, which made Dael howl.

"Yes!"

"Now?" Smiling tremulously, Spinner didn't even blink, not wanting to miss a thing.

"Ah! Ah! Yes!" Dael's hips elevated high above the recliner as her body tightened around Spinner's fingers. Convulsing over and over, she whimpered until she was a listless bundle in Spinner's arms. Spinner couldn't remember ever witnessing such a sensuous and sexy display as she gazed at the dazed woman before her. Her heart thundered and she wanted to remain like this forever. Still, she slowly pulled her fingers out and wrapped her arms around Dael. She shifted until she had Dael firmly on her lap. Dael sat curled up under Spinner's chin, her hands tightly fisted around Spinner's shirt.

"That…that was so good." Dael freed one hand and cupped Spinner's cheek as she kissed her neck. "So good."

"Yes, it was." Spinner kissed the top of Dael's head. "I hope I'll get to do it again. Whenever you want me to."

Dael smiled. "Sounds fine to me." She kissed Spinner's neck again and trailed her collarbone with the tip of her tongue. Then she suddenly shifted, making Spinner sit on the recliner while she herself knelt on the floor. She pulled Spinner toward her, balancing her hips on the edge of the seat, and moved farther in between her legs.

❖

"Dael?" Spinner ran her fingers through Dael's hair.

Kissing Spinner's hand and up her arm as far as she could reach, she then repeated the caresses on her other arm.

Spinner hummed. "Feels great, but—"

"—but what, love?" Dael tilted her head and watched Spinner carefully. "I just want to reciprocate, to make you feel like I just did… may I?"

"If you want to, yes…please." Spinner sat up straight and unbuttoned her shirt and pulled it off. She wore nothing underneath, and Dael's mouth watered at the sight of the dark-maroon, hard nipples.

Spinner cupped Dael's neck and scratched her scalp with one hand and offered her left breast to her with the other one. Dael didn't need to be asked twice. She leaned in slowly, took the nipple between her teeth, and sucked in long, languid movements. The taste and texture of the puckered nipple made her moan against it, which, to her delight, sent shivers through Spinner.

She worked her way over to the other nipple, gave it the same treatment, and then back again to the first one. Eventually, she could tell they were becoming oversensitized. Gazing up at Spinner, she noticed that Spinner was squirming, even rocking, on the seat, clearly seeking relief.

"Can we take your trousers off?" Dael asked quietly.

"Trousers. Sure. Yes." Spinner stood, and Dael quickly pulled off the black pants and then nudged Spinner to sit down again, still at the very edge of the recliner. She spread Spinner's legs wider and caressed her slowly, first with her fingertips along her damp, hot sex, and then, as she couldn't resist, she bent forward and placed her mouth on the fabric, right over the area where Spinner's clitoris was located.

"Ah!" Spinner jerked and clung to the armrests. "Dael!"

Dael pressed her tongue against the engorged labia, felt them separate beneath the thin fabric of the briefs. Next time there would be no fabric between them whatsoever, but now, this was how she wanted to do it. The scent of her lover, together with the moaning, the not-so-quiet "Don't stop, don't stop" urging her on, made Dael's own level of arousal climb again.

"Dael, you're…you're going to…" Spinner began to tremble violently, arching, and Dael held on to her slender hips, keeping her in place so as not to lose track of the pulsating clitoris. Wanting to share the moment with Spinner, Dael let go with one hand and shoved it between her own legs. It only took a few strokes, and she moaned Spinner's name over and over before she locked her mouth firmly against her.

"Oh, Dael, Dael…" Spinner slumped sideways and Dael had to hold on to her so she didn't fall off the chair. She took a blanket from the armrest of the couch next to them and climbed up on the recliner and wrapped an arm around Spinner, helping her sit comfortably. Draping the blanket over their sweat-soaked bodies, she held Spinner close. Gradually their breathing slowed and Dael's heart rate became normal.

"Celestial Lords, you're awesome. I feel completely drained." Spinner sounded astonished.

Dael chuckled and tucked the blanket in tighter around Spinner with tender hands. "It's you who are amazing. You seem to have figured out how to handle me."

"I'm not so sure about that, or that you need 'handling' at all, but if by that you mean I understand you better, that may be true. Thanks to Helden, to some extent."

"Helden?"

"Oh, don't worry." Spinner grinned. "She didn't give away any family secrets but merely encouraged me to not give up on you."

"Good for Nania." Dael placed her head on Spinner's shoulder. "And good for you. You're braver than I am. I've never been so afraid of losing you like I was today. With so much unexplained."

"And unexplored." Spinner pressed her lips against the top of Dael's head. "We have so much to talk about."

"I know. It's just…"

"That we're exhausted as hell."

Dael could once again tell just how in tune they were. Spinner easily finished her sentence correctly. "Yes."

"So why don't we sleep and then talk about things tomorrow?" Spinner suggested. "I mean, the way you made love to me and allowed me to touch you, I'd say we're well underway, don't you think?" Spinner bent over Dael, and the faint, barely there hint of uncertainty made Dael ache inside.

"I totally agree." Cupping Spinner's cheeks, she tugged her down for a soft kiss. "As long as you realize that after this, after you came to me like this, I—I don't think that I could ever let you go."

Spinner melted into the hug. "Dael, surely you know that I love you. I have for a long time." She was shaking and Dael held her very close. Reaching behind her head, she fumbled for a second blanket and managed to drape it over them.

"Aniwyn, I love you too. I've never felt this way about anyone else." Dael couldn't even remember being close to this consumed by someone else.

"So, the reason you fought me was…?" Spinner rested her head in her hand, her free hand caressing Dael under the covers.

Realizing Spinner still needed some reassuring before she could fully relax and rest, Dael reached for the roaming hand and pulled it up to her lips. "Fear. Apprehension. Self-doubt. More to do with me than with you, even if you were far from what 'type' of person I used to envision myself falling in love with. I gave up on falling in love, let alone meeting my type. And then there were you. You leveled my defenses one by one, just by being you."

"So when you pulled back from me?" Tucking Dael back onto her shoulder, Spinner seemed to relax some more.

"I thought it was the right thing to do. I know different now. You've never known me to lie, have you, Ani?"

"No." Another kiss landed on her head. "I believe you. Besides, perhaps you weren't ready. I should've realized that."

"You were just as vulnerable and afraid as I was, I think."

"Yes." Spinner literally purred as she settled down into the recliner farther. "But we're together now."

Dael held Spinner closer and then melted against her, unable to keep her eyes open. "Thank the Creator," she murmured.

"Illumination zero," Spinner said, and the room went dark again.

Dael listened to their respective breathing, so soothing and hypnotic. Without a doubt, this time Spinner would be there when she woke up.

EPILOGUE

Dael Caydoc
Admiral
Day 411
Advance mission
Admiral's log

On our fifth day in orbit around the fourth planet in this solar system, my crew and I are becoming increasingly optimistic regarding its basis for sustaining the life of the Oconodian people. It consists of forty percent landmass and sixty percent ocean. We have found ruins that our archeologists have dated to be more than five thousand years old. The wildlife is diverse, with some carnivores that we need to learn more about, but with a healthy balance between them and the herbivores.

The eight continents consist of grass-plains, jungles, forests, mountains, and deserts. This is similar to Oconodos, and I believe it will help our people to feel at home. Our ships' counselors agree.

Reports filed by our geologists assure me that the planet is seismically stable and no more prone to earthquakes or volcanic eruptions than Oconodos. I am transmitting all our findings to the Oconodian authorities and will await their judgment. If they want, we will keep looking, but I cannot help but send a prayer to the Creator that this will be the new home for our people. If so, I will lead the initial mapping and stake the claims for the new capital, something that will be a tremendous honor.

The crew has gone through a difficult mourning period after losing the Mugdon and its entire crew and passengers, as well as the crewmembers that were killed on the rest of the mother ships. Now, a hundred days later, the death toll since we left Oconodos is 2,680 souls. Their sacrifice will never be forgotten.

Whether this is our new home or not, our prolonged stay has been a welcome shore leave for the passengers and the crew that is off duty. The long beaches around the equator have provided the opportunity for recreation, which has infused new energy in the people I have come to think of as family.

Until we can officially name this world and call it home, I, and the crew and passengers with me, await the verdict of our government on Oconodos.

End recording.

❖

Aniwyn Seclan
Commander and CAG
Day 411
Advance mission
Personal log

This beach has got to be the most beautiful one in the universe. The color of the sand goes from white to gold, and the sky is so blue, it nearly hurts my eyes. Still, despite being surrounded by such wondrous scenery, the most beautiful thing I see is Dael. She sits right next to me in a beach recliner, reading, and this has got to be the most relaxed I've ever seen her. Her hair is down, all the way to her waist, and she's wearing a sun hat and sunglasses, which make her resemble a rich socialite rather than the boss of all things around here.

Darmiya and Calagan have two temporary habitats set up not far from ours. They have been in contact with their government and are awaiting the same decision we are. They worry about the living conditions of their displaced people; apparently the refugee camps are swamped and the Gemosians aren't faring well.

I swear, if the Oconodian government doesn't approve of this planet, I'll start an uproar. Yeah, yeah, I'm kidding, but this just feels right. There is enough "wrong" with the place for it to be right. The desert that takes up most of the southernmost continent, for instance. The polar ice caps, where nothing grows, where the ice is so thick, the entire part of the ocean is frozen all the way down to the bottom. Too cold for anyone to stay there. These imperfections make me think this world could feel like home.

Then I look up at Dael and I know, no matter if we have to travel with our convoy for yet another 400 days, I'm already home. As long as she loves me, I will have a home. For some unfathomable reason, I know she would never leave me. Not because I'm conceited enough to think I'm such a wonderful catch, but because she makes it clear to me every day how she feels. I'm blessed by the Creator and I don't deserve it, but I accept it and will do my best to be worthy of her love for the rest of my life.

End recording.

Transmission from the Presidential Palace, Oconodos
Received time index D412-H14-M45
Advance mission via buoy 129
Eyes only: Admiral Dael Caydoc

Admiral Caydoc,

You have outdone yourself in leading these vessels to our new home. We regret the loss of the *Mugdon*, but Captain Gossamay and his crew and passengers will be kept in revered memory.

A decision has been made based on the information and data sent by your teams. I trust you will experience the same positive expectation in taking the Exodus plan into its next phase. My cabinet and I are convinced that this planet, temporarily named P-105, is a good choice for our people.

According to our plan we now require your official proof of acceptance of this message and confirmation that the preparations for our arrival have commenced.

The capital is still under martial law, with checkpoints at all major intersections. The knowledge that your team has found a planet well equipped to sustain our people will give hope to our people and hopefully stop the rioting. If not, we plan to begin moving our citizens to the Exodus ships prematurely. We will keep you informed regarding our progress.

Go with the Creator, Admiral Caydoc, until our next exchange of buoy messages.

Mila Tylio
President of Oconodos

__End of transmission__

About the Author

Gun Brooke resides in the countryside in Sweden with her very patient family. A retired neonatal intensive care nurse, she now writes full time, only rarely taking a break to create web sites for herself or others and to do computer graphics. Gun writes both romances and sci-fi.

Web site   http://www.gbrooke-fiction.com
Facebook   http://www.facebook.com/gunbach
Twitter   http://twitter.com/redheadgrrl1960
Tumblr   http://gunbrooke.tumblr.com/
Live Journal   http://redheadgrrl1960.livejournal.com/

Books Available from Bold Strokes Books

Venus in Love by Tina Michele. Morgan Blake can't afford any distractions and Ainsley Dencourt can't afford to lose control—but the beauty of life and art usually lies in the unpredictable strokes of the artist's brush. (978-1-62639-220-5)

Rules of Revenge by AJ Quinn. When a lethal operative on a collision course with her past agrees to help a CIA analyst on a critical assignment, the encounter proves explosive in ways neither woman anticipated. (978-1-62639-221-2)

The Romance Vote by Ali Vali. Chili Alexander is a sought-after campaign consultant who isn't prepared when her boss's daughter, Samantha Pellegrin, comes to work at the firm and shakes up Chili's life from the first day. (978-1-62639-222-9)

Advance: Exodus Book One by Gun Brooke. Admiral Dael Caydoc's mission to find a new homeworld for the Oconodian people is hazardous, but working with the infuriating Commander Aniwyn "Spinner" Seclan endangers her heart and soul. (978-1-62639-224-3)

UnCatholic Conduct by Stevie Mikayne. Jil Kidd goes undercover to investigate fraud at St. Marguerite's Catholic School, but life gets complicated when her student is killed—and she begins to fall for her prime target. (978-1-62639-304-2)

Season's Meetings by Amy Dunne. Catherine Birch reluctantly ventures on the festive road trip from hell with beautiful stranger Holly Daniels only to discover the road to true love has its own obstacles to maneuver. (978-1-62639-227-4)

Myth and Magic: Queer Fairy Tales edited by Radclyffe and Stacia Seaman. Myth, magic, and monsters—the stuff of childhood dreams (or nightmares) and adult fantasies. (978-1-62639-225-0)

Nine Nights on the Windy Tree by Martha Miller. Recovering drug addict, Bertha Brannon, is an attorney who is trying to stay clean when a murder sends her back to the bad end of town. (978-1-62639-179-6)

Driving Lessons by Annameekee Hesik. Dive into Abbey Brooks's sophomore year as she attempts to figure out the amazing, but sometimes complicated, life of a you-know-who girl at Gila High School. (978-1-62639-228-1)

Asher's Shot by Elizabeth Wheeler. Asher Price's candid photographs capture the truth, but when his success requires exposing an enemy, Asher discovers his only shot at happiness involves revealing secrets of his own. (978-1-62639-229-8)

Courtship by Carsen Taite. Love and justice—a lethal mix or a perfect match? (978-1-62639-210-6)

Against Doctor's Orders by Radclyffe. Corporate financier Presley Worth wants to shut down Argyle Community Hospital, but Dr. Harper Rivers will fight her every step of the way, if she can also fight their growing attraction. (978-1-62639-211-3)

A Spark of Heavenly Fire by Kathleen Knowles. Kerry and Beth are building their life together, but unexpected circumstances could destroy their happiness. (978-1-62639-212-0)

Never Too Late by Julie Blair. When Dr. Jamie Hammond is forced to hire a new office manager, she's shocked to come face to face with Carla Grant and memories from her past. (978-1-62639-213-7)

Widow by Martha Miller. Judge Bertha Brannon must solve the murder of her lover, a policewoman she thought she'd grow old with. As more bodies pile up, the murderer starts coming for her. (978-1-62639-214-4)

Twisted Echoes by Sheri Lewis Wohl. What's a woman to do when she realizes the voices in her head are real? (978-1-62639-215-1)

Criminal Gold by Ann Aptaker. Through a dangerous night in New York in 1949, Cantor Gold, dapper dyke-about-town, smuggler of fine art, is forced by a crime lord to be his instrument of vengeance. (978-1-62639-216-8)

The Melody of Light by M.L. Rice. After surviving abuse and loss, will Riley Gordon be able to navigate her first year of college and accept true love and family? (978-1-62639-219-9)

Because of You by Julie Cannon. What would you do for the woman you were forced to leave behind? (978-1-62639-199-4)

The Job by Jove Belle. Sera always dreamed that she would one day reunite with Tor. She just didn't think it would involve terrorists, firearms, and hostages. (978-1-62639-200-7)

Making Time by C.J. Harte. Two women going in different directions meet after fifteen years and struggle to reconnect in spite of the past that separated them. (978-1-62639-201-4)

Once The Clouds Have Gone by KE Payne. Overwhelmed by the dark clouds of her past, Tag Grainger is lost until the intriguing and spirited Freddie Metcalfe unexpectedly forces her to reevaluate her life. (978-1-62639-202-1)

The Acquittal by Anne Laughlin. Chicago private investigator Josie Harper searches for the real killer of a woman whose lover has been acquitted of the crime. (978-1-62639-203-8)

An American Queer: The Amazon Trail by Lee Lynch. Lee Lynch's heartening and heart-rending history of gay life from the turbulence of the late 1900s to the triumphs of the early 2000s are recorded in this selection of her columns. (978-1-62639-204-5)

Stick McLaughlin: The Prohibition Years by CF Frizzell. Corruption in 1918 cost Stick her lover, her freedom, and her identity, but a very special flapper and the family bond of her own gang could help win them back—even if it means outwitting the Boston Mob. (978-1-62639-205-2)

Edge of Awareness by C.A. Popovich. When Maria, a woman in the middle of her third divorce, meets Dana, an out lesbian, awareness of her feelings brings up reservations about the teachings of her church. (978-1-62639-188-8)

Taken by Storm by Kim Baldwin. Lives depend on two women when a train derails high in the remote Alps, but an unforgiving mountain, avalanches, crevasses, and other perils stand between them and safety. (978-1-62639-189-5)

The Common Thread by Jaime Maddox. Dr. Nicole Coussart's life is falling apart, but fortunately, DEA Attorney Rae Rhodes is there to pick up the pieces and help Nic put them back together. (978-1-62639-190-1)

Jolt by Kris Bryant. Mystery writer Bethany Lange wasn't prepared for the twisting emotions that left her breathless the moment she laid eyes on folk singer sensation Ali Hart. (978-1-62639-191-8)

Searching For Forever by Emily Smith. Dr. Natalie Jenner's life has always been about saving others, until young paramedic Charlie Thompson comes along and shows her maybe she's the one who needs saving. (978-1-62639-186-4)

A Queer Sort of Justice: Prison Tales Across Time by Rebecca S. Buck. When liberty is only a memory, and all seems lost, what freedoms and hopes can be found within us? (978-1-62639-195-6E)

Blue Water Dreams by Dena Hankins. Lania Marchiol keeps her wary sailor's gaze trained on the horizon until Oly Rassmussen, a wickedly handsome trans man, sends her trusty compass spinning off course. (978-1-62639-192-5)

Rest Home Runaways by Clifford Henderson. Baby boomer Morgan Ronzio's troubled marriage is the least of her worries when she gets the call that her addled, eighty-six-year-old, half-blind dad has escaped the rest home. (978-1-62639-169-7)

Charm City by Mason Dixon. Raq Overstreet's loyalty to her drug kingpin boss is put to the test when she begins to fall for Bathsheba Morris, the undercover cop assigned to bring him down. (978-1-62639-198-7)

Let the Lover Be by Sheree Greer. Kiana Lewis, a functional alcoholic on the verge of destruction, finally faces the demons of her past while finding love and earning redemption in New Orleans. (978-1-62639-077-5)

Blindsided by Karis Walsh. Blindsided by love, guide dog trainer Lenae McIntyre and media personality Cara Bradley learn to trust what they see with their hearts. (978-1-62639-078-2)

About Face by VK Powell. Forensic artist Macy Sheridan and Detective Leigh Monroe work on a case that has troubled them both for years, but they're hampered by the past and their unlikely yet undeniable attraction. (978-1-62639-079-9)

Blackstone by Shea Godfrey. For Darry and Jessa, their chance at a life of freedom is stolen by the arrival of war and an ancient prophecy that just might destroy their love. (978-1-62639-080-5)

Out of This World by Maggie Morton. Iris decided to cross an ocean to get over her ex. But instead, she ends up traveling much farther, all the way to another world. Once there, only a mysterious, sexy, and magical woman can help her return home. (978-1-62639-083-6)

Kiss The Girl by Melissa Brayden. Sleeping with the enemy has never been so complicated. Brooklyn Campbell and Jessica Lennox face off in love and advertising in fast-paced New York City. (978-1-62639-071-3)

Taking Fire: A First Responders Novel by Radclyffe. Hunted by extremists and under siege by nature's most virulent weapons, Navy medic Max de Milles and Red Cross worker Rachel Winslow join forces to survive and discover something far more lasting. (978-1-62639-072-0)

First Tango in Paris by Shelley Thrasher. When French law student Eva Laroche meets American call girl Brigitte Green in 1970s Paris, they have no idea how their pasts and futures will intersect. (978-1-62639-073-7)

The War Within by Yolanda Wallace. Army nurse Meredith Moser went to Vietnam in 1967 looking to help those in need; she didn't expect to meet the love of her life along the way. (978-1-62639-074-4)

Escapades by MJ Williamz. Two women, afraid to love again, must overcome their fears to find the happiness that awaits them. (978-1-62639-182-6)

Desire at Dawn by Fiona Zedde. For Kylie, love had always come armed with sharp teeth and claws. But with the human, Olivia, she bares her vampire heart for the very first time, sharing passion, lust, and a tenderness she'd never dared dream of before. (978-1-62639-064-5)